The Darkness of Death

A JOHNNY ONE EYE NOVEL

The Darkness of Death

A JOHNNY ONE EYE NOVEL

David Stuart Davies

ROBERT HALE · LONDON

© David Stuart Davies 2010
First published in Great Britain 2010

ISBN 978-0-7090-8868-4

Robert Hale Limited
Clerkenwell House
Clerkenwell Green
London EC1R 0HT

www.halebooks.com

2 4 6 8 10 9 7 5 3 1

Typeset in 10.75/14pt Sabon
Printed in Great Britain by the MPG Books Group,
Bodmin and King's Lynn

To Katie
the bubbles in my champagne
the froth on my coffee
the chewing gum on my bedpost overnight
the love of my life

London. Midnight. November 1943. A clear blue sky canopies the darkened sleeping metropolis. A few stars sprinkle the heavens and occasionally an errant spotlight scans the skies in search of alien aircraft.

But it is a quiet night.

The Thames rolls its leaden way through the city and, down by the Embankment, just beyond Westminster Bridge, the area is deserted until a large motor car, its hooded headlights carving a faint track along the road, squeals to a halt. The driver gets out and casually surveys the scene. It pleases him. There is no one in sight. No patrolling copper, no ARP Warden, no drunk wandering home, or no sex-starved couple taking advantage of one of the benches by the parapet. No one around to see him.

The driver opens the boot of the car, still keeping an eye out for intruders on the scene. Slowly he heaves a weighty object from the interior. It flops heavily on to the road. The driver closes the boot and, with practised nonchalance, drags the object towards the parapet.

And leaves it there.

Mission accomplished, he hurries back to the car, a broad smirk on his face, and in a matter of seconds he has driven off into the shadows of night as though he never existed.

It is quite some time before anyone else appears along this stretch of the river. Shortly before 1 a.m. Police Constable Barraclough arrives dragging his weary feet on his nightly patrol. He is bored and fed up and longing for his bed. To his mind, quiet nights are the worst. He longs for a bit of action, something to liven up his lonely shift. In due course he notices the large shape huddled by the parapet. Mildly interested, he approaches it and very quickly determines that it is a body.

Another drunk, no doubt.

He bends down and shakes the chap's shoulders. 'Come on, matey. You can't kip here,' he says. 'You'll catch your death. Get yourself home and sleep it off.'

There is no response. He shakes the man again, this time hard enough for his body to flop over on to his back and his pale face to stare up sightlessly at Constable Barraclough. He shines his torch on the man to get a better look. He is smartly dressed, white-haired and well nourished. Not the usual sort of drunk that the policeman encounters on his nightly perambulations. But what is really unusual about his appearance, something that causes Barraclough a great deal of consternation, is the amount of congealed blood around the man's neck and splattered down the front of his coat. Then the astute constable observes the reason for this. This man is not drunk: he is dead. He has had his throat cut.

O N E

Leo Bernstein left behind the fug of smoke and the cacophony of the gaming room and made his way by the back stairs to his office. He felt weary, depressed and old. His body seemed to creak in unison with the old wooden stairs. Even the two brandies he'd consumed at the bar had done nothing to lift his spirits or dull the pain. In these last few days he had really felt his age. There was no longer a spring in his step or a fierce twinkle in his eyes. He was conscious of his overweight body with all its accumulated minor aches and pains and the tired, haggard face that glowered back at him from the shaving mirror. It was as though the cushion of enthusiasm and delight had been extracted from his soul.

And he knew why.

Apart from the dim rays of moonlight that slanted through the Venetian blinds, his office was in darkness and he decided to leave it that way. With care he made his way to his desk and lowered himself down in to the large leather chair. He sighed and reached out in the gloom for his silver cigar box, scooping up one of the fat Havanas. As he did so, a match flared in the darkness and hovered near his face.

'Allow me,' said a voice, a rich, velvety, female voice.

'What the....' he cried in surprise, reaching out swiftly and switching on the desk lamp.

The room materialized around him in shadowy relief. Standing by the desk was a woman holding the proffered match. She was tall and slim but her face was beyond the pool of light cast by the lamp.

'Who the hell are you?'

The girl held the dying match to her face just long enough for him to see her features clearly before she blew it out.

'Gina!' he cried.

'Yes, Gina.'

'My God, you nearly gave me a heart attack.'

'I'm sorry, Uncle Leo. I guess I've got used to doing things in secret for so long, they become a habit to me and I forget the effect that this might have on other people.'

Without a word, Leo rose from his chair and moved around the desk to face the girl.

'Is it really you?'

She grinned and nodded. 'In the flesh.'

'Oh, Gina,' he said, embracing her and kissing her lightly on the cheek. She responded by hugging him tightly. They stood like that for over a minute, each one not saying a word.

At last Leo broke free and switched on the lights. 'Let me look at you properly. It is ages since I last saw you. You had pigtails then,' he said, standing back to gaze at the girl. She was in her late twenties, very pretty with boyish, narrow features, dark lustrous hair and two astonishingly vibrant grey eyes.

'Will I do?' she said mischievously.

Leo smiled. 'You are beautiful, my dear.'

She returned the smile but said nothing.

'Why are you here?' he asked. He could not keep the concern out of his voice.

'Isn't it obvious?'

'You're not planning on going to the funeral?'

'Of course. As soon as I got your letter I flew here immediately. How could I not? But don't worry, I will not be part of the official party. I don't want to upset any apple carts just yet, but I do intend to be present when they bury my father.'

At the mention of Gina's father, his brother, Leo felt a wave of despair crash down upon him and his shoulders slumped once more. 'I am so very sorry.'

Gina perched on the arm of a chair and lit a cigarette. 'I need to know the details. Your letter was sketchy.'

'The details are sketchy, I'm afraid.'

'He was murdered, wasn't he?'

Leo nodded. 'We assume so.'

'Assume.' Gina spat the word out in disgust.

'Well, yes, Michael was killed but whether this was a result of a robbery that went wrong or whether he was targeted ... I don't know.'

'Please don't give me that hogwash, Uncle Leo. My father was found on the Embankment with his throat cut. This wasn't the result of a bungled robbery. You know more. Who is in the frame?'

Leo hesitated for a moment, but realized that to prevaricate would be foolish and wrong. The girl had a right to know. 'We think it was Paulo Ricotti.'

'Who the hell's he?'

Leo afforded himself a sour grin. 'He fancies himself as one of the new big shots around town. A bully boy and a gangster. Your dad and he were involved in a big deal for some illegal booze. But it was a deal that was going wrong. Paulo wanted more than his fair share.' Leo shrugged. 'You know your father: he wasn't going to allow that. I told him, warned him, let the boy have his head on this deal. Don't rock the boat. But he wouldn't be told. He knew that Paulo's a ruthless, volatile bastard, but when Michael smelled a big profit, he went for it despite the risks.'

'But he was always careful.'

'Up to a point. Less so of late. Old age, I suppose, made him less astute. Anyway, I stayed clear of the business. To be honest, your father and I had not been seeing eye to eye all that much recently. I wanted to back pedal a bit on the illegal side of things now that the war is in full swing. It seemed a bit unfair to cheat on your own country ... the club does all right. We have a healthy turnover without the need ...'

'You wanted to go legit?' Gina made no attempt to keep the surprise and disdain out of her voice.

Leo shrugged his shoulders. 'In a way. I'm getting a bit long in the tooth for the other stuff now.'

'You're only two years older than my dad.'

'I guess I sucked on a different teat.'

'So you reckon this Ricotti got rid of Dad because of him being a bit of a threat to his profits.'

That's what Leo thought, but he hadn't really admitted the fact to himself, let alone verbalized it. He shifted awkwardly and then nodded. 'I suppose so,' he said quietly.

'There's no other likely candidate?'

'No.'

'So it's Paulo Riccotti.' Gina's pretty face had turned sour and her lips creased into a snarl.

'The police thought so, too – but the swine had a watertight alibi. There's not a speck of dirt on him. He is a clever son of a bitch.'

'So, what are you going to do about it?'

'Do?' Leo swung round and faced the girl again, his eyes moist.

'You're not going to let him get away with it, are you? This Ricotti. He killed your brother – my father.'

'What can we do? We're in a strait-jacket here. If anything happens to him, the police will be down on us like a ton of bricks.'

'So you get yourselves a bleedin' watertight alibi as well.'

'It's not that easy.' Leo mumbled the words, embarrassed at their weakness.

'What about "the boys"? Have they got no backbone? Are they bloody milksops? Don't they want to revenge their uncle's death?'

'We're not killers, Gina. We run a small family business that steps over the legal boundary from time to time but we've never been involved in violence … murder.'

'Apart from the early days,' she sneered.

'The early days were a long time ago.'

'I can't believe I'm hearing this,' Gina snapped, her eyes flashing with anger. 'You are a bunch of bloody cowards. Well, I can tell you, I'm not going to stand by while some jumped-up little creep gets way with murdering my father. I'll sort the bastard out myself. It's my call anyway, I suppose. Don't you worry, Uncle Leo, I'll make sure that you and my lily-livered cousins don't get any blood on your delicate hands.'

'For God's sake, Gina, don't do anything rash. We can sort it out in time.'

'I'm going to sort it out now. But, as I say, don't fret, it will be my affair. However, I can tell you this, Uncle Leo. I'm back. I'm back for good and, as the eldest, I shall be taking over my father's share of the business – that's fifty-five per cent which gives me the controlling interest. I think it is time that Vic and Anthony found out that they've got a cousin, don't you? A cousin who, you can assure them, is a tough, hard-hearted bitch. A chip off the old block.'

T W O

The funeral party was small. Less than ten in attendance and two of those were policemen. They looked conspicuous like official twins in their identical belted raincoats and brown trilbys, standing somewhat apart from the real mourners. No doubt they were there not just to pay their respects to a murder victim, thought Gina, but to keep an eye out for any suspicious character who might turn up – the murderer for instance, gloating over his triumph. How naïve, she thought, but that's the bleedin' police for you.

One thing was for sure: they hadn't clocked her standing some twenty feet off in the shrubbery watching the proceedings. She scanned the faces of the others gathered around the graveside. There was Uncle Leo of course, his haggard face eloquently displaying his pain and anguish, and his two sons, her cousins Vic and Anthony. She'd never met them and had only seen photographs, but she was able to identify which was which. Her dad had told her quite a lot about them. He confessed to her that he didn't think much of his brother's offspring. 'They haven't got that Bernstein spark,' he'd said, cradling her face. 'Not like you, angel.' She smiled at the memory.

Vic was tall and dark and quite handsome in a gaunt kind of way. He held himself in a stiff awkward manner and his face was a taut bland mask. She had no idea what he was feeling or thinking. Occasionally he would look off into the distance as though his thoughts were miles away – but what thoughts they were she could not begin to fathom. Anthony was shorter and plumper with large bulging eyes set within a flabby, flushed-red face. He seemed to be acting out the role of diligent mourner, trying to look suitably sad and distressed, but Gina observed that he kept shifting from one foot to the other and twisting his hat around in his fingers as though he were bored. There were two grey-haired men in their seventies whom Gina assumed were friends of her father. And there was a middle-aged woman she had never seen before. Her deferential behaviour suggested that she was a secretary or some kind of employee. It was, thought Gina, with a sharp pang of sadness, a small number indeed to mark the passing of a man's life.

An image of her father flashed into her mind. It wasn't the man she had last seen some six months ago, the overweight ageing fellow who had developed a stiff gait and rheumy eyes. It was the young Michael with the spring in his step and the irresistible smile that constantly lit up his face: the man who had been a regular visitor to her at the convent in Ireland. He always bore gifts and flowers and crushed her with firm loving embraces. He had always wanted a better life for her – a life away from shady deals and crime, but to her he always carried an aura of glamour with him that Gina wanted for herself. Her father was, in many ways, her hero. She saw nothing wrong in what he did. Just as his charming exterior masked a ruthless iron will, she fostered the same qualities in herself. Pretty as she was as a child, a prettiness that developed into beauty as she matured, she made herself immune to sentiment. Self-contained, determined and ferociously ambitious, Gina Bernstein was very much her father's daughter.

When the coffin had been lowered into the grave, Leo cast a handful of earth on to it and intoned a few words. His voice was hoarse and hesitant and Gina could not make out what he said but she could tell that he was close to tears. Hesitantly Vic put his arm around his father for support while the priest concluded the ceremony.

It was all over in ten minutes. A man's life erased in such a short time. Sixty-odd years of living now encased in a wooden box stowed in the damp ground to rot. An overwhelming sense of grief threatened her, but Gina fought it off. She was not going to cry. It was not in her nature. She was not going to mourn until her father's death had been revenged.

When the funeral party had departed, Gina emerged from the shrubbery and stood by the open grave. She dropped a single red rose down on to the earth-strewn lid of the coffin.

'Goodbye, Pops,' she said quietly.

Her eyes were dry but clearly mirrored the pain and the determination she felt. As she gazed down at the grave, the breeze blew the stray wisps of her dark hair which had escaped her hat down across her forehead but she ignored them, her attention never wavering. She had come to make a promise and a promise she would make. As she stood alone with the early morning mist shifting gently around her tall, slim silhouette, the over-riding passion that filled her heart and mind was anger. It gave her strength and shielded her from the fierce autumn chill and, more importantly, the real pain of loss. She was her father's daughter. There was no doubt about that and she drew comfort and determination from all that this implied. As she made her silent promise to the man she had loved and worshipped now lying in the wooden box before her, strangely she found herself smiling. Not a broad, bright smile, but one that was gentle but also cruel. The edges of her red lips curled slightly and her eyes brightened for a moment. She had given her word. Now it was time to act.

Paulo Ricotti gazed at himself in the mirror of the gentleman's lavatory at the Chameleon Club and grinned back at himself. He was pleased with what he saw. He thought himself handsome. Rudolph Valentino reincarnated: the slim, sallow features with the aquiline nose and brooding brown eyes, the black hair slicked back with a patent sheen and, above all, the sardonic aura of vain Latin arrogance which not only informed his features but all his gestures and body movements also.

However, what Paulo Ricotti did not possess was the alluring Italian accent to match his appearance. Born within the sound of Bow Bells of Italian immigrant parents, he spoke with a soft and slightly grating Cockney brogue.

Paulo adjusted his bow tie, ensuring each wing balanced exactly with the other, and touched the carnation in the lapel tucked neatly in the buttonhole of his dinner jacket before brushing imaginary specks of dust from the sleeves. He must appear immaculate before entering the arena. Tonight he felt lucky and he wanted nothing to mar his chances. Besides he had his own standards and he was intent on maintaining them.

Moments later he emerged from the lavatories and made his way to the main bar. It was quite early in the evening, not yet quite nine o'clock, but the Chameleon Club was already busy. There was a gentle hum of conversation as the wealthy customers, immune from the main deprivations of the war, chatted amiably in this cocoon of selfishness, clinking glasses, cigar and cigarette smoke and the gentle seductive rattle of the roulette wheel.

Paulo managed to find himself a stool by the bar and ordered his favourite cocktail, a sidecar. While he waited for the drink to be mixed, he drew a cigarette from a silver case and lit it with smooth deliberation. After lighting it he allowed the smoke to drift before his eyes causing him to squint. To him this was a pleasant sensation and he felt good when it happened.

When his cocktail arrived, he took a gentle sip allowing the alcohol to trickle slowly down his throat, savouring the taste and the gentle burning sensation it carried with it, and then turned around on the stool to survey the room. There were several women who caught his eye, flashy bright-eyed creatures with enticing cleavages and arresting curves, but they all seemed to be with someone. He hadn't the patience this evening to try and seduce a girl away from her man – although he knew he could do it if he wanted. But it was so tedious dealing with hurt or outraged boyfriends or husbands afterwards. It took the edge off the conquest.

'Can you light me?'

The woman's voice was just louder than a whisper and close to his ear. Paulo turned to find the owner standing very near to him, so near he could smell her perfume. She was a looker all right: tall, very slender, in possession of a boy's body, with long blonde hair and grey expressionless eyes. Her mouth, however, turned up at the corners in a wry fashion suggesting humour and warmth. She held up a Dunhill before her.

Without a word, Paulo slipped the lighter from his pocket and lit the girl's cigarette. She blew the smoke to one side and then gently ran her fingernails across the back of Paulo's hand as he retracted the lighter.

It seemed that he didn't have to go hunting tonight. Apparently *he* was the one who was being stalked.

'Can I get you a drink?' he asked, pocketing his lighter.

'Champagne,' she said, with an amused nod of the head.

'Expensive lady.' He looked serious for a moment and then flashed her a broad smile.

'I'm only interested in the best,' she said, with no trace of humour.

He beckoned to the waiter and ordered a bottle of champagne, 'I'll join you,' he said, helping her on to the stool next to his.

'Thank you, Paulo.'

'You know my name.'

'Of course. You don't think this was a chance encounter, do you?'

He shrugged his well-cut shoulders. 'You tell me.' He was more intrigued than amused now. Little surprises, however entertaining, did not please him. He spent his life in an attempt not to be surprised.

'I'm a very particular lady and when it comes to the company of men friends, I like to pick my own.' She blew out a stream of smoke which momentarily obscured her face and then she stubbed out the half-smoked cigarette in the glass ashtray on the bar top. Her lipstick had left a bright, blood-red blemish around the tip.

'And you're picking me.'

'Let's say I'm giving you an audition.'

Paulo laughed out loud. 'Well, you're an original, lady, I'll give you that. What's your name?'

'Mary. Named after Mary Pickford, you know, the film star.'

Paulo nodded. He knew. He was a great fan of the movies.

At this point the champagne arrived. The waiter made a performance of opening the bottle – well at £2 a time the price demanded a suitable fuss. Black-market booze wasn't cheap. And the ostentatious cork popping ceremony was insisted upon by the manager of the club, who at this moment was watching it with hooded eyes from his usual vantage point near the gaming table. He hoped the theatrical display would encourage other punters to indulge themselves.

Paulo raised his glass, the bubbles still dancing and shimmering in the subdued lighting. 'Here's to Mary.'

'And here's to us,' Mary responded with a slight pout of the lips.

They drank, each eyeing the other over the rim of their glasses.

'OK, Miss Mary,' Paulo said at last. 'What do you want?'

'Want? What does any girl want? A good time?'

'And you think I can give you one.'

'I am sure of it. I've done my research.'

This girl was certainly full of surprises. 'And what have you found out?'

Mary took another sip of champagne before replying. 'Paulo Ricotti, aged thirty-three. Owner of several clubs in London – not this one at the moment, but maybe it's next on your list. Now head of the Ricotti business after your father died of a heart attack last year. I know the police are interested in some of your activities but you manage to keep your nose clean. You have expensive tastes and can show a young lady a good time. How will that do?'

The smile had faded from Paulo's lips. 'And who are you? What are you after?'

'I told you. I'm Mary. Mary Sutherland. And I'm after a good time. That's all.'

'You speak the spiel like a copper.'

Mary laughed. 'What, with my record?'

'What record?'

'I like nice things. Nice things cost money. So I make sure I have the money in order that I can have nice things. I'm not too particular how I get it.'

Paulo narrowed his eyes. 'You're a thief.'

'That's rather a harsh term. I don't like to think of it in those terms, but what's a middle-class girl got to do if she wants nice things, go to nice places like the Chameleon and meet nice fellows like Paulo Ricotti?' She leaned forward and her hand slid across the bar top and touched his. 'You see, I like you. I like you a lot.' She lowered her lids as she spoke and stroked his hand, her finger cold and sensuous against his skin. Despite himself Paulo felt a tingle of electricity run through his body. The girl was intriguing, enigmatic, and something of a challenge and he liked challenges, even if he didn't really trust her.

Suddenly she pulled her hand away and lifted her champagne glass. 'So, Paulo, where are we going to eat tonight?' she asked brightly.

Despite or maybe because of his reservations, Paulo Ricotti took Mary Sutherland out to dine that evening. He knew she was a hot and dangerous package, but he reckoned he had enough savvy and guile to handle her. No bit of skirt had got the better of him yet. Over dinner she had been charming and witty, no longer the enigmatic siren she had presented herself as at the Chameleon. Following the meal they had visited a music club and danced. He found her slender boyish body remarkably erotic and held her tighter and tighter as the night wore on. She seemed not to object. To Paulo's surprise he'd had a thoroughly good evening. She was a bright girl who had the ability to listen and to amuse him. And she was, as he had first observed, a looker. There was certainly something so alluring about her lithe figure and those grey seductive eyes of hers. One thing was clear to him: he intended that she should spend the night at his place. He certainly wanted to bed the girl. Whether she would last beyond breakfast was another matter, but dawn was a long way off at present.

It was nearing one in the morning when they returned to his car. 'I insist you come back to my flat for a final night cap,' he said.

She responded without hesitation. 'Of course,' she said.

He grinned. She obviously wanted the liaison too.

Some twenty minutes later, his car pulled up outside a block of flats in Kensington. 'Here we are,' he said, his voice a little weary with alcohol. 'I have the penthouse.'

'Sorry, but I'm afraid this is as far as I go,' said the girl, her voice suddenly cold and hard.

Paulo frowned and turned to her. What game was she playing? In the dim lighting provided by the glow of the dashboard, he could see that she now had dark hair. The blonde locks had disappeared. His brow creased with consternation.

'I wore a wig, Paulo,' the girl said in answer to his unspoken query.

'Who the hell are you? What is this?' His body stiffened with apprehension and to his surprise he realized that he was beginning to feel uneasy. It wasn't an emotion he was familiar with and it unnerved and unsettled him. He shook his head in an attempt to alleviate the effects of alcohol and tiredness on his brain.

It didn't work.

'I am the angel of death, Paulo, here to settle a score. That's who I am.'

Before he knew what was happening, the girl had produced a pistol from her handbag and thrust it hard against his forehead.

Now he was scared. His stomach churned and for a brief moment he thought he was going to be sick. This was like a scene from a bad dream. Reality had faded into the shadows and he was adrift in a nightmare landscape.

'The name is Gina,' the girl was saying. 'Gina Bernstein. Daughter of Michael Bernstein. You recognize the name. He was the man you murdered. My father. I'm here to avenge his death.'

Paulo opened his mouth to speak but no words escaped.

Gina smiled. 'Time to say goodnight and goodbye, Paulo. Sweet dreams.'

Without another word, she pulled the trigger. There was a loud bang, a strong smell of cordite and Paulo Ricotti's head recoiled backwards in a sudden violent fashion. A ragged poppy-shaped wound materialized in the centre of his forehead from which two thin streams of blood dribbled down his face on to his jacket. He remained frozen, held like a waxwork dummy, eyes wide with shock, mouth slightly agape, and then slowly he slumped forward over the wheel, totally surrendering himself to the darkness of death.

The girl sat some time, the gun held limply in her hands, staring at the dead man, his handsome face ghoulishly illuminated by the dashboard, the staring eyes now unseeing static brown orbs. She wore a mask of indifference, no emotions were registered on her smooth features until, at last, secreting the gun in her handbag, she reached for the door handle, and then she allowed herself a brief smile.

As she began to walk away from the car, she suddenly found herself crying. The tension, anger and determination had now dissolved. She had been true to herself and to her father. Now she could grieve. Now she could cry her heart out.

T H R E E

'Do you believe in ghosts, Mr Hawke?'

I gazed in some surprise at the wiry little man who had posed this question. He was Brian Garner, an intense-looking fellow with challenging eyes, wiry of build with fine, wispy, sandy-coloured hair which was thinning and turning grey making him look, I should guess, somewhat older than he was, which I put around forty years of age. He sat in my office, his hands on his lap, exuding an air of mothballs and peppermints, making this enquiry about ghosts with all seriousness.

Brian Garner was a potential client, a rare commodity in the fading weeks of 1943, and so I didn't want to frighten him away with a blunt and brusque reply. I could have said, 'No, I don't believe in ghosts. I have enough trouble with the living without letting my imagination allow me to contemplate the ridiculous notion that dead people are walking about interfering with our lives. It's mumbo jumbo. Fairground chicanery. Claptrap.'

But I didn't.

Instead, I replied politely, 'Not really. Why do you ask?'

'Because I've seen one.'

My heart sank. It looked like I'd caught a nutter in my net.

I shuffled some papers on my desk. 'I am a private detective, Mr Garner. I deal with real people and real incidents. This isn't Halloween Investigations. Perhaps you would be better consulting a clairvoyant or a medium....'

Or a psychiatrist.

'No, no. You don't understand,' he protested, wriggling in his chair.

My heart sank further. Oh, no, he was going to explain!

'Let me explain …'

I knew it!

'My wife died two years ago in a car accident. And yesterday I saw her.'

I did not respond to this statement simply because I didn't know what to say. I thought it safer to remain mum and wait for more information. Garner took my silence as his prompt to provide it.

'I was on the platform at South Kensington underground station yesterday morning when I saw this woman on the opposite plat-form. At first she had her back to me, but I'd recognize that shape and turn of the head anywhere. When you've been married to someone you get used to all their tics and movements and such. Eventually she turned round and … well, I can tell you, Mr Hawke, my blood ran cold. It was Beryl all right. No doubt about it. Beryl, my wife. Instinctively, I called out to her across the tracks. And when she saw me, her jaw dropped open. She looked terrified as though … well, as though *she'd* seen a ghost. And then she panicked. She ran. She took to her heels, rushed from the platform and disappeared down the stairs into one of the passageways. I raced down the steps from my side hoping I'd catch her but … there was no sign of her. She'd just disappeared.'

Well, I thought, that's what ghosts do. It's part of their nature.

I tried to reason with him. 'Mr Garner, it couldn't actually be your wife if she is dead. Isn't it more likely that it was just someone who looked like her and when you shouted at her you frightened the poor soul and she ran away?'

Brian Garner's features tightened and his eyes bulged with fierce earnestness as he leaned forward in his chair. 'Mr Hawke, there is no doubt about it. That woman *was* Beryl, my wife.'

There was something powerfully convincing about this threadbare little man's conviction. He really believed that he had seen his dead wife. Maybe he was deluded, but I no longer thought he was a crank. My instinct told me that the situation had possibilities. Could it be that I really had a case after all? I decided to find out more.

'You'd better tell me about the circumstances of your wife's death.'

'As I said she died in a car accident. Things hadn't been going well between us for about a year and she had taken it into her head to leave me. She said that she'd found someone else who was "more sympathetic to her needs". Those were her exact words: "sympathetic to her needs".'

'What did she mean by that?'

He gripped the arms of the chair, his face suddenly suffused with anger. 'God knows. I certainly don't.'

'Who was this "someone"?'

Garner shook his head. 'I don't know. Even now I haven't a clue. I thought it was perhaps someone she'd met at work, but apart from her boss all her work colleagues were women. She worked in a ladies hairdressers in Camden.'

'What about her boss?'

Garner curled his lip. 'Harold Crabtree is not the kind of bloke who's interested in women if you get my drift.'

I gave a nod of understanding; I got his drift.

'After she'd left me, I did all I could to find out who this mystery bloke was but I drew a blank. It seemed as though he'd disappeared off the face of the earth.'

'Or maybe he didn't exist in the first place.'

Garner's surprised expression told me that he hadn't contemplated that particular scenario.

'Tell me exactly what happened,' I said, lighting up a cigarette. I was interested now and I wanted to get the full picture.

'Well, I came home from work one day – I run a little electrical shop in Harper Street, just off Russell Square – to find two cases in the hallway and Beryl waiting for me in her best fur coat. "I'm leaving you," she says. "The marriage is over." Just like that. Well, I can tell you it was all a shock to me, Mr Hawke. I knew things hadn't been particularly harmonious with us for a while. We kept having rows, all about something and nothing, but nothing that serious. You know how it is.'

I didn't, but I gave him another nod of understanding.

'But I'd never reckoned on this. That she would leave me. Then she tells me that she's found someone new to love and care for her, someone who was "more sympathetic to her needs".'

Old Garner was certainly fond of that phrase. It had engraved itself on his heart. I gazed at my tenacious little client and wondered in what way he had not been 'sympathetic to her needs'. I decided to broach this subject as delicately as I could.

'Be honest with me now, Mr Garner, what would you say was at the cause of the disharmony in your marriage?'

His eyes flickered with irritation. 'You'll have to ask Beryl,' he snapped. 'I don't know. Her leaving me came right out of the blue.'

He was lying but I thought it best not to press the matter now. That could come later. I gestured that he should continue his story.

'I tried to reason with her, but she was adamant. She was going to leave me and never come back. I asked where the hell she was going, but she wouldn't tell me. She said she was taking the car and that I'd never see her again. I tried to stop her but she was a strong woman and I'm not a violent person, Mr Hawke. I couldn't really attack my wife. So she grabbed her cases and … drove off, out of my life. Then, about four hours later I got the news. The police came to tell me there'd been a crash. The car had gone off the road on a narrow bend near Blackheath and hit a tree.'

Here he paused, his eyes focused on the wall beyond my head where, no doubt he was witnessing pictures of the event projected from the imagined images in his mind.

'Apparently,' he continued some moments later, his voice strained with emotion, 'the petrol tank exploded on impact and the vehicle went up in flames. Beryl hadn't a chance. She … she was burnt to death. It was terrible, Mr Hawke. All that was left of my poor wife was a blackened shell.'

He turned his head away while he rooted in his pocket for a handkerchief to wipe away the tears. I remained silent. I couldn't help his grief; that was his own burden.

'We identified the body by her jewellery and the suitcases in the boot which survived the worst of the flames.'

'There was no one else in the car?'

'No.'

There was a possible scenario forming here. I wasn't sure if it had occurred to Mr Garner, but at the present time I was not about to alert him to it.

'This other person … her lover never came forward?'

Garner shook his head with some vehemence. 'I wish to God he had. There are so many unanswered questions. Like, what happened to the money.'

'The money?'

'Unknown to me at the time, Beryl had drawn everything out of our joint account, over a thousand pounds, the day before the accident. No doubt it was to be used to set up the little love nest with her fancy man.'

The case was intriguing and had possibilities. I was slowly being drawn in.

'So in fact you don't really believe you saw a ghost. You believe you saw your wife – living and breathing.'

Garner nodded. 'I do. It was her all right and she looked as guilty as hell. I want you to find her. I want my money back.'

'Finding her will not be easy. We have no clues as to where she is or what she is doing now.' I paused and raised a questioning eyebrow. 'Or do we?' Maybe old Brian was keeping something back from me.

'None that I can think of, except she was on South Kensington tube station at eight-thirty yesterday morning.'

I lowered my eyebrow in disappointment. That piece of information was about as useful as a chocolate teapot.

'Do you have a picture of your wife?'

'I do.' Garner fished a shiny snap from his wallet and passed it over to me. The woman staring back at me from the grainy photograph seemed fairly nondescript. She had fair curly hair with a snub nose and wide fleshy lips. She was dressed in a tight jumper and a pencil skirt. She wasn't smiling.

'That was taken about six months before … before the accident.'

'And when you saw her yesterday, she looked much the same as she does here?'

'A little thinner maybe, but yes.'

'Did she have any distinguishing features … a mole, a scar something like that?'

'No. She wore glasses to read. She was quite vain about them. She didn't like to wear them in public.'

'What about family?'

'Her mother's still alive, but they didn't really get on. She had a brother but he was killed at Dunkirk.'

'Friends?'

'No special one as far as I know.'

The situation looked hopeless. This jigsaw had so many pieces missing that it wasn't clear what the overall picture was.

I sighed and spread my hands on the desk. 'I'll be frank with you, Mr Garner, I reckon I've as much chance of finding your wife as you have of nabbing a black cat in the black out ... but I'm prepared to try, if you're prepared to hire me.'

'Oh, I am. I am.'

When Brian Garner had gone, I sat quietly at my desk nursing a cigarette, watching the grey tendrils drift aimlessly to the ceiling. I had taken down as much detail as my client could give me about his 'ghostly' wife – date of birth, where she worked and so on in the hope that something would provide me with a lead, something that would point me in the direction of the truth. As I turned this information over in my mind while I watched the patterns of the drifting smoke, I did not feel particularly inspired.

However, beggars can't be choosers and while I was not exactly a beggar, work had been thin on the ground of late. As a one-eyed private detective trying to scrape a living in the damaged capital, I was feeling the pinch. So here I was – about to chase a ghost. However one thing did excite me about the case, something that had been the deciding factor in me taking it on. If Beryl Garner were alive and kicking and living a completely new life, as hubby Brian believed, whose body was it in the burnt-out car? Who had died in her place?

FOUR

Detective Inspector David Llewellyn peered into the interior of the car and gazed stoically at the corpse of Paulo Ricotti. The blood around the savage wound to his forehead had dried now and formed a dark blackcurrant-coloured crust with spidery tendrils down his face. The sightless eyes continued to stare down at the dashboard still registering his final moments of shock. It was, thought Llewellyn, like a tableau from the chamber of horrors at Madame Tussaud's wax museum: gruesome and strangely unreal.

'Well, there can be no doubt regarding the cause of death.' The remark, barely more than a whisper, was addressed to himself, but Sergeant Stuart Sunderland, who was standing close behind him and also gazing at the dead man, took it as a prompt for one of his dour ironies. 'Some kind of violent headache I should say,' he observed.

'Well, it looks rather like a tit for tat job.'

'You mean the Bernsteins.'

Llewellyn pulled back. He'd seen enough. Viewing dead bodies first thing in the morning on an empty stomach was not one of his favourite pastimes. 'Yes,' he said, before taking in a gulp of fresh air. 'All the evidence pointed to Ricotti for Michael Bernstein's murder a few weeks ago but, as you know, there was no proof. It wouldn't be surprising if the Bernstein boys decided to take the law into their own hands. A return match if you like.'

Sunderland frowned. 'They're wrong 'uns, but I would have thought murder was a bit out of their league.'

'You could be right. Certainly I think old man Leo is past putting a bullet in someone's brain, even if it is to revenge his beloved brother, but the two young ones … who knows. I would have said they lacked the guts to go that far, but in family matters there are no boundaries.'

'Well, we'd better round them up and have one of our chats.'

David grinned. 'Always the diplomat, eh, Sunderland.'

'I try, sir.'

'However, on this occasion I think I'll leave the Bernstein boys alone for a few days. Let 'em stew. If they are responsible for this' – he gestured to the corpse – 'they will expect us to come pounding on their door. If we don't, that might confuse them a bit, make them nervous, careless even and make it easier for us to eventually prise the truth out of them. If they are involved, that is. In the meantime, let's get our friend here back to the Yard and see if the path boys can dig out the bullet. That might give us something to work on – but I doubt it.'

David Llewellyn slammed the car door shut and breathed deeply, expelling the stench of death from his lungs.

Twenty-four hours later, nine o'clock on a winter morning and the dawn was still struggling to make its presence felt. The year had just slipped into December and dark shadows of night lingered in the streets while a patina of frost decorated the pavements and roofs. Pedestrians wrapped up like mummies against the cold exhaled steam as they hurried by. Vic Bernstein was striding purposefully towards the Bamboo House, the Bernsteins' night-club on Bedford Street in Covent Garden when a voice called out to him. He turned and saw his brother some steps behind.

'What's it all about?' Anthony asked, without ceremony.

Vic gave a shrug of the shoulders. 'Search me. Some sort of family conference, that's all I was told. The old man rang me late last night, told me to be at the club by nine-thirty. Said it was urgent.'

Anthony nodded. 'I got the same message. I think I've got an idea what's up. Look, let's grab a cuppa before we meet him. I've got something to show you.'

The brothers repaired to a little café around the corner from the Bamboo House. Once seated at a corner table and having given their order to the girl on duty, Anthony pulled out a newspaper. 'You seen the *Mail* today?'

Vic shook his head. 'I've seen nothing this morning. I only surfaced about an hour ago.'

'Then I think you'd better have a gander at this.'

Anthony folded the newspaper over and passed it to Vic, his finger indicating a small item on page four headlined MURDER IN KENSINGTON.

Vic read it carefully and then emitted a low whistle. 'So, someone has done in our friend Ricotti. It couldn't have happened to a nicer chap. Whoever bumped him off certainly did us a favour.'

Anthony leaned over the table and grabbed Vic's sleeve. 'It wasn't you, was it?' he said in a hoarse whisper.

Vic smiled. 'Of course not. I'm not that stupid. And I presume it wasn't you.'

At this point the girl returned with their mugs of tea and they sat back in their chairs and said nothing until she was gone.

'You don't think Dad had anything to do with it, then?' said Anthony.

'Are you joking? Not at all. You know as well as I that the old feller's lost his nerve. He'd think twice before swatting a fly. The fire has gone out of his belly. It's time he gave up and let us take over. Now Michael's gone there's no firm hand on the tiller. I'm itching to get my hands on things.'

'I don't want to push him. He'll go in his own good time.'

'Maybe, but his time does not suit mine.'

Anthony did not reply; he didn't want this conversation again. He was not as eager or desperate to take over the Bernstein business as his brother. Vic was in a different league to him. He had brains and ambition while Anthony was quite happy to play second fiddle – for the time being at least. Responsibility was not one of his strengths. He liked girls and gambling – business got in the way of these pursuits. His eyes drifted back to the newspaper report. 'Who, then? Who killed Paulo Ricotti?'

Vic pursed his lips. 'Don't know. But, as I say, whoever it was did us a favour. In one sense a least.'

'What do you mean "in one sense"?'

'Well, the police are bound to think one of the Bernsteins did it and be on our tails. Still we can cope with that, I reckon. Especially as in this case we are innocent.'

Anthony tugged at his tie. 'I can get guys to vouch for me – whatever time the bastard was done in.'

Vic grinned at his brother. It wasn't a warm grin, but one imbued with icy mockery. 'I'm sure you can.'

'You, too, eh?' said Anthony, missing the sarcastic tone in Vic's voice.

'Indeed … "whatever time the bastard was done in".' He chuckled at his own conceit and then suddenly rose from his chair. 'Well, as we didn't kill the bastard, we really have nothing to worry about.' He smacked the newspaper with his gloves. 'Anyway, no doubt that's what the old man wants to see us about. Come on then, let's see what he has to say.' Vic rose swiftly, snatched up his hat, slipped on his gloves and headed for the door. Anthony grabbed his mug of tea and took a final gulp before racing after his brother.

The Bernsteins' club, the hub of their little empire, was lively and crowded at night, but at nine-thirty in the morning it was a dank, dismal and rather depressing place, reeking of stale alcohol, sweat and cigarette ash. Old Barney, the cleaner-cum-caretaker, let the brothers in and they made their way up the back stairs to Leo's office. They entered without bothering to knock and discovered their father in conversation with a young woman who was sitting casually in an armchair before his desk. She was wearing a smart dark suit with a white blouse with ruffles at the neck. At first glance Vic observed that she was pretty, self-assured and appeared somewhat aloof. She was slim with shiny black hair and feline grey eyes. She glanced casually in the brothers' direction as they entered, but she did not register any emotion.

'Take a seat, boys,' said Leo uneasily.

They did so without a word. Anthony was desperate to ask his father who this bit of skirt was but uncharacteristically he held his tongue.

Leo sat forward in his chair and rubbed his hands together nervously. 'Victor, Anthony, I want to introduce you to Gina.' He paused nervously before adding, 'She is your cousin.'

'Cousin?' Anthony shook his head in confusion. 'This is news to me that we had a cousin.'

'Gina was your Uncle Michael's daughter.'

'But he didn't have a daughter,' said Vic.

'I reckon I'm proof that he did,' said the girl, her voice quiet but steely. 'Yes, I'm the daughter. The one you never knew about.'

'She is telling the truth. I can vouch for that,' said Leo. 'Michael always wanted a boy. A young man who would one day succeed him as head of the family business. But it was not to be.'

'Yeah, yeah,' said Anthony. 'We know Aunt Sophie had a little boy who was born dead and she died shortly after....'

Leo nodded. 'Yes, that's how it was. But around the same time, when Aunt Sophie was very ill, Michael had an affair with a young actress and she gave birth to a baby girl ... a daughter Michael treasured above all things.'

'Are you serious?' asked Vic, his features darkening with consternation.

'I know this will be a bit of a shock for you two—'

'Shock!' cried Anthony. 'That's a bleedin' understatement. Are you telling us that this ... this girl here is our cousin. Uncle Michael's—'

'Bastard?' said Gina coolly. 'If you want to put it like that. Yes, I am Michael Bernstein's daughter. I was the secret child. No tough young fellow to follow in my father's footsteps – just a girl. So I was hidden away from the world. Protected from what my father regarded as his violent way of life. He wanted me well away from any potential enemies, too. I was his sweet innocent little girl, his lady, and I was treated as such. Only Uncle Leo knew of my existence.'

'Is all this really true?' Vic asked his father. His voice was low and cool, but there was a note of anger there.

Leo nodded in assent. 'I was only doing what my brother wished. He made me swear.'

'So where the hell has she been all this time?' growled Anthony.

'*She* will tell you,' said Gina. 'Shortly after my birth I was taken to Ireland. I was brought up by nuns—'

'Christ almighty!' exclaimed Anthony, his eyes bulging with disbelief.

'My father wanted me to be a good girl.' She almost smiled. 'He visited me regularly and made sure I was happy. When I left the convent – unscathed by the holier than thou attitude and the Catholic drivel they tried to instil into me – my father set me up in a small flat in Dublin and provided me with a comfortable income but would not hear of me coming back to London. He said he didn't want me to be near the business. He didn't want me to be contaminated by it and the people involved in it.'

'Charming!' observed Anthony.

'But he was wrong. I wanted to be contaminated … I am a Bernstein after all. I am part of the family, part of the business.'

'That is a matter of opinion,' said Vic.

'Yeah,' said Anthony. 'I reckon Uncle Michael was right. This isn't a business for women.'

'Well, it's certainly not a business for lily-livered men.'

Anthony half rose from his chair in indignation. 'What's that supposed to mean?'

Gina Bernstein's relaxed features suddenly changed. Her jaw tightened, her nostrils flared and her eyes blazed with anger. 'I'll spell it out for you, shall I? It means that you're a bunch of bleedin' cowards. That's what it means. Some jumped-up eyetie bastard kills my father, your uncle, and you do nothing about it. Nothing. You just hide like frightened rabbits in your warren. Paulo Ricotti murdered the head of the family, your own flesh and blood, and you do *nothing*!' Her voice was fierce and shrill and the last word echoed around the room like a curse.

The three men remained silent. Each, in his own way, was acknowledging the truth of Gina's assertion, no matter how begrudgingly.

'It was left to me to avenge my father's death.'

'You! You mean it was you …' said Anthony, his eyes wide with disbelief.

'Yes, it was me; I put a bullet in that Italian bastard's head.'

Vic brought his hands together in a slow hand clap. 'Bravo. Give the girly a coconut.'

Gina did not rise to the bait. 'That remark just about sums you up, Vic. Sarcasm in place of guts.'

'Why, you—' Vic took a step in her direction and raised his hand.

'Sit down, Vic,' Leo ordered. 'We're not here to argue. Gina is family.'

'And you wouldn't hit a woman, would you, Vic?' Gina said softly.

'What the hell does she want – coming back here after all these years?' asked Anthony.

'I'll answer that, Uncle Leo,' said Gina. 'As the daughter of Michael Bernstein, I have come to take charge of the business.'

'The hell you have,' snapped Anthony, casting a glance at Vic for confirmation of this assertation.

'It is her right,' Leo said wearily.

'What do you mean, it's her right? How can she turn up here out of the fuckin' blue and think she can just take over? She knows nothing of the business. She's just a scrap of a girl with a big mouth.'

Gina gave a wry smile. 'Yes, you're right there, Anthony, I do have a big mouth. I've found it helps when you want things done. Unbeknownst to Dad, I ran my own little operation in Dublin and did very nicely out of it, thank you. Apart from the big mouth, I've also got a sharp brain and a strong stomach. At present the Bernstein family business is stagnant – it's going nowhere. I intend to change all that.'

'She deserves our support. It is her right as Michael's daughter,' said Leo. 'You boys must toe the line.'

'The hell I will,' barked Anthony. 'No young tart is going to tell me what to do.' He rushed from the room, slamming the door hard as he left.

'He'll come round,' said Leo. 'He's always been a hot head.'

'And what about you, Vic?' asked Gina turning to him.

With slow deliberation, he took a pack of cigarettes out of his coat pocket, extracted one and lit it. 'What have you in mind?' he said quietly, blowing the smoke over his shoulder.

FIVE

More often than not I found myself heading to Benny's café in the morning for breakfast. It was a combination of laziness – an inability to fend for myself at that time of day – and a desire to mix with humanity after a night alone in the dark. It was good to have a natter with the old chap over a plate of warm grub and he rarely charged me the full whack. The cocoon-like warmth of the café with the steam and smell of bacon fat and the hot sweet tea helped me face up to the rigours of another day. Benny's was like a second home to me. On Fridays whenever possible, I took along Peter after school for an end of week treat. In fact, routines were rapidly becoming part of my life and I had to admit that I found the experience rather comfortable. In my thirty rather disturbed years I was more settled now than I ever had been before. Business wasn't great but I survived at least – and I had a girlfriend, Max, who, to my continued surprise and delight, lavished affection and kisses upon me, commodities that had been missing most of my life. Certainly affection was an alien concept in the various orphanages where I spent my formative years. I had been shunted from one soulless establishment to another without experiencing the warmth and security of family life that most kids enjoy and take for granted. Now I seemed to have constructed one from a set of disparate individuals. Benny was like a wise, caring and sometimes cantankerous father; I had my lovely Max who seemed to care for me despite my penury and damaged features; and Peter, who had been part of my life for three years now, was like a son, or perhaps a younger brother. Peter lived with two spinster ladies Martha and Edith

Horner who, while doting on him, were not sentimental enough not to keep him on the straight and narrow or over-indulge him. Already Peter had a way with the female sex, but Martha and Edith had proved immune to his more extreme blandishments. So far, at least. Not that they had a hard task. He was a good lad and was desperate to follow in my footsteps and become an 'ace detective' – his words, not mine. It was all very cosy. Although occasionally a voice somewhere in my head questioned whether it really was all just a little *too* cosy and suggested that there was a danger that it could become claustrophobic or, worse still, something I came to rely on and that one day it would be taken from me. I tried as hard as I could to silence that disturbing little voice, but it would pipe up when I least expected it. But then I was one of the many who faced this fear. War had removed all certainties; home, family, friends and freedom were all at risk now.

On arriving at the café, Benny greeted me with a cheery wave and a beaming smile. 'Take a seat, Johnny, I'll be with you shortly,' he whispered, as he swept past me into the kitchen. Slipping off my overcoat, I did as I was told. The café was very busy, as it usually was in the morning. There was a fine cross section of Londoners all tucking into Benny's cheap but comforting breakfast fare: there were pinstriped office workers, shop girls, highly painted and carefully coiffured, a few servicemen and a couple of weary-looking ARP wardens grabbing a bite to eat before heading home to the comfort of warm beds. Since the outbreak of war there was very little good food to be had anywhere. The stuff on offer both at home and in cafés was all diluted, improvised and imitation versions of the meals we had before rationing had been instigated. Gravy was made with powder, eggs also and vegetables replaced meat and, where meat was available, it was usually the less appetizing sections of the beast like skirt, flank or leg. Of course, you could get old-fashioned grub if you had contacts or knew where to go for a black market feast, but Benny wouldn't have any truck with that business and so he did the best he could with what was legally on offer. In general he made a good stab at it, although I always steered clear of his watery custard tarts, which tasted of nothing but upset the stomach within minutes of consumption.

Benny moaned about business regularly but he and I knew he had a little goldmine here.

'What's new with you, Johnny boy?' Benny asked, as he delivered my tea and bacon sandwich. (A genuine bacon sandwich with little slivers of chopped bacon supplemented by layers of fried tomatoes.)

'Same old. Same old.' I rarely discussed my cases with Benny – not out of a matter of privacy but, in truth, it often bored me to regurgitate my problems and concerns regarding work. Similarly, the old guy was not really interested in my professional activities, unless there was a particularly lurid episode that I'd been involved in and then he was eager to hear all the details. But in the main Benny was more concerned about my love life.

'You proposed to her yet?' he said, slipping into the seat opposite me.

I shook my head, my mouth full of food. 'I've only known the girl for a few months,' I said at length. 'What can I offer her? Certainly not a home and comfort.'

'You love her, don't you?'

'I think so.'

Benny rolled his eyes in exasperation.

'Such prevarication. I've seen you two together. A match made upstairs, I tell you.'

'You're an old romantic.'

'And you're a young one. You don't think I can tell? We recognize the breed, my boy. Look at me. Only yesterday I was courting my wife. There I was, a straight-backed, dark-haired boy with a youthful gleam in his eye. Today I am looking seventy in the face. A widower with no one to warm my sheets at night. Life is short, Johnny. And it's got even shorter since Herr Hitler came on the scene. You've got to grab happiness while you can. You never know what's around the next corner.'

I grinned gently. 'Here endeth today's lesson.'

'You know, you know, Johnny Hawke, that I speak the truth. Don't waste time. As I said: you never know what's around the next corner.' With that he hurried away to greet two new customers.

Little did I know then that I would come to remember that

conversation with a cruel vividness in the weeks ahead. 'You never know what's around the next corner.'

Chez Harolde was part of a row of shops on Camden High Street trapped between a tobacconist and a hardware store. The painted sign aimed at sophistication but missed by a mile. It boasted the legend: 'Chez Harolde – Hairdressing Salon to Ladies of Choice'. It looked, as did the shop frontage, a little faded and time-worn. Beneath in smaller lettering were the words: 'Prop: Harold Crabtree'. How disappointing to discover that Harolde was a simple Harold and about as French as Camden High Street. There were net curtains at the windows which were steamed up making it impossible to see inside without entering, so that is what I did.

A lumpy girl at the cash desk looked up lazily from a magazine she was perusing and gave me a non-committal glance. If she were an example of Chez Harolde's expertise with hair, I didn't think much to it. Her barnet wasn't so much styled as ruffled and looked not unlike a mop head which needed a good wash.

She cocked an eye of query at me, speech having obviously been denied her for the moment.

'I'd like to see Mr Crabtree?'

'You mean Harold?' she said without a flicker of interest.

I nodded. 'Yes, the owner.'

'What for? This is a ladies' hairdressers. He don't do men.'

'I have some business with him,' I said tartly. Already the girl was beginning to irritate me.

Without another word she retreated into the shop past two girls busily attending to their customers' hair. One woman had her head over a sink, having her scalp massaged with soapy suds, while the other was having a set of curlers attached to her thinning grey hair.

The French flavour indicated by the sign outside certainly did not make its presence felt inside the shop. It was a very ordinary, and rather down-at-heel hairdressers which had probably seen better days before the war. However, as I caught sight of myself in one of the mirrors, a pale, shabby-looking chap with an eye patch, I reckoned that could apply to me also.

The charming receptionist had disappeared behind a pink

curtain at the far end of the shop and moments later a man emerged. I deduced this must be Harolde/Harold. He was a tall but very chubby fellow who wore a white smock coat at the neck of which a large pink bowtie jiggled unnervingly, rather like a butterfly flapping erratically at his throat.

He walked, or rather glided, down the length of the shop towards me, stopping on the way to speak to the lady with the curlers. 'That's looking lovely, Mrs Barker. Your husband won't recognize you when you're done.' A dubious compliment, I thought. She muttered something in reply. He gave a little satisfied giggle and moved on.

By the time he reached me, the smile had disappeared, but the light sibilant voice remained. 'Can I help you?' he said, in such a tart tone that it reversed the meaning of his query.

I produced my card. Harold scanned it suspiciously and handed it back. 'Well, Mr Hawke, what's it all about?'

'I'm making enquiries about Beryl Garner who used to work here.'

'Well, she did, but that was ages ago. And she's dead. Got killed in a car crash. Terrible accident.'

I nodded to indicate I knew all this. 'I just want some details about her. Was she a good hairdresser?'

Harold pursed his lips and made a squeaking sound. 'Yes,' he said slowly, dragging the word out. 'She was a good worker, but I wouldn't say she was an *artiste*. You see, I like to employ artistes with hair. Hairdressing is an art form, you know. Just like a painter we start with a bare canvas and with care and finesse you create a work of beauty. Beryl did not have the lightness of touch or that inspirational streak. What she did was workmanlike and reliable but no more.'

'Did she get on with her fellow workers?'

'My girls. Oh, yes, she was a pleasant enough soul.'

'Did she talk about her private life at all?'

'Not to me she didn't.'

'Did any men friends call round here to see her?'

'No.' The eyebrows shot up in indignation. 'Chez Harolde is not that kind of establishment.'

'Did she have a particular friend in the salon?'

He paused for a moment. 'Well, yes, yes she did. Sylvia Moore. Now Sylvia *was* an *artiste*. It was a sad day when I lost her, I can tell you. You should see what she could do with a mop of lank hair and a pair of curling tongs.'

'Sylvia and Beryl were friends?'

Harold nodded and his bow tie fluttered again. 'They had a real good natter during the slack periods and they often took lunch together. They acted like sisters really. In fact they looked a lot alike.' Suddenly Harold stopped as though he realized he had said more than he should have. 'Look, what is this all about?'

I sidestepped the question with one of my own. 'Do you know where Sylvia went to after she left you?'

'No, no I don't. Actually, it was all very strange. She seemed perfectly happy here and then one day out of the blue she handed in her notice. She didn't really give a reason. Said she fancied a change and … well, that was it. She left at the end of the day and I never saw her again.'

'Was this around the time of Beryl's death?'

Harold's bright blue, piggy eyes widened. 'Why, now you come to mention it, I reckon it was.'

'Have you got an address for Sylvia? Where she was living when she worked for you.'

'Well, I do, but that's confidential. Why do you want to know these things?'

'I'm making some enquiries on behalf of an insurance company. Nothing for you to get alarmed about, but it would be in your interest to release that information. It will save trouble later on.'

Harold looked aghast and his chin wobbled, setting the bow tie off again. 'Trouble. What do you mean by trouble?'

I looked around suspiciously and then leaned forward to whisper in Harold's ear. As I did so I caught a whiff of eye-wateringly pungent cologne. 'We're trying to keep the police out of it. Your assistance would be a great help.'

At the mention of 'the police' I thought Harold was going to have a seizure. His substantial frame shook with apprehension and his chins juddered like jelly straight from the mould.

'This is a respectable establishment. I don't want any more trouble with the police.'

'Any more?'

Harold cast me a sheepish glance. 'There was an indiscreet episode before the war. It was simply a case of misunderstanding with a soldier. I've not been in trouble since.'

I nodded sympathetically. 'Just let me have that address and I'll make sure you're not bothered by the cops.'

Harold nodded eagerly. 'Just a minute while I get my book.' He waddled back down the length of the shop with some urgency and disappeared once more behind the pink curtain. He reappeared some moments later carrying a large ledger-like tome.

On reaching me, he riffled through the pages of the book, his stubby fingers stabbing at the elaborate scrawling handwriting within. 'I have my customers and my staff in here,' Harold muttered almost to himself. 'Here we are,' he announced at last. 'Sylvia Moore, 27a Cromwell Road, Islington.'

I made a note of the address. 'Is there anything else you can tell me about Sylvia. Any boyfriends? Family?'

'She never mentioned any; boyfriends or family. I thought she was a lonely soul really. Perhaps that's why she was so friendly with Beryl.'

'You said that she and Beryl looked a lot alike. Can you describe Sylvia?'

'Well, she was tall. Nice and slim but with broad shoulders. She kept her hair – a dark auburn colour – cut short, urchin-like. Good bone structure, but her face looked a bit miserable in repose though.'

'A pretty girl?'

'Not really. She was rather plain. That's why she had no boyfriends, I suppose.'

'I suppose. Did she have any distinguishing features?'

'None that I can recall. She was pretty ordinary really. Didn't stand out in the crowd.' He paused and ran a single podgy finger across his moist brow. 'Is that all, then?' He was eager for the interview to be over.

I reckoned it was. It seemed to me that my plump fey hairdresser had revealed all he could about Beryl and her friend, the tall, slim, nondescript Sylvia Moore.

'Thanks for your help, Mr Crabtree. Keep my card and if you think of anything else which may help, please give me a call.'

He picked it up casually and held it gingerly with his plump fingers. I was fairly sure that as soon as I had departed, he would drop it into the nearest wastepaper basket.

He nodded with relief as I headed for the door. It struck me as I emerged into the cold air of a December day, that Harold Crabtree and I were in some ways brothers. We were both outsiders – he because of his sexual proclivities and me because of my orphan status and disfigured face and neither of us was able to fit in easily or completely with the world around us.

S I X

'I thought I'd find you here.' Vic Bernstein leaned over the shoulder of his brother Anthony at the gaming table.

'What do you want?'

'A few words. A few sensible, instructive words.'

'What the hell are you talking about?' He leaned forward and placed five chips on the green baize for number nine.

'I'm talking about Gina.'

'That bitch. She can go to hell.'

'Indeed. She probably will. But we can't allow her to arrange the trip herself.'

Anthony frowned 'Will you stop speaking in riddles.'

Vic placed a hand on his brother's back. 'In simple terms then: we need a plan.'

Anthony frowned again; the roulette ball had landed in the slot marked twelve.

Harold Crabtree was a troubled man. He sat in a hunched posture at the back of his shop, hidden behind the pink curtain, smoking a cigarette in an impulsive fashion and intermittently biting his nails. He knew that he had said too much – told that private detective fellow more than he should. Especially giving him Sylvia's old address. He shouldn't have done that. He had betrayed a confidence. He took another long nervous drag of the cigarette, but it failed to calm his nerves.

It was when the detective had mentioned the police that he had cracked. He certainly didn't want to get mixed up with them again.

He'd had enough last time. They had made his life a misery. He still felt the pain of the shame and humiliation. And all because he had misjudged the situation. If he'd known the soldier wasn't the least bit interested – it just seemed at the time that he was. How could he have been so wrong?

Even now he came out in a cold sweat if he saw a policeman in the street. The uniform brought vivid images of that cold, damp, foul-smelling cell in which he spent the worst months of his life and the jibes, name-calling and surreptitious violence of the other prisoners. He knew in his heart of hearts that he'd rat on his own mother rather than go through that experience again.

Nevertheless, Harold Crabtree felt guilty at being so loose with his tongue to the snooper with the eye patch and, as he stubbed out the cigarette, he came to a decision. Snatching up the telephone from the table, he dialled a number swiftly before he had chance to change his mind.

It rang several times before a voice answered.

'Oh, hello, Sylvia, It's Harold here. I thought I'd better warn you ...'

With slow, deliberate movements, Leo Bernstein took his time slicing the end off his cigar and lighting it with an onyx table lighter. Then he sat back on his chair with a smile of satisfaction and blew a cloud of smoke in the direction of his visitor. It was a little performance to illustrate how at ease he felt and he hoped it would annoy the hell out of the copper sitting across the desk from him.

David Llewellyn contained his impatience and indeed his growing irritation. He had experienced this kind of mannered ceremony before from all kinds of malefactors, but Leo Bernstein was a master. He had met Leo on several previous occasions. He was one of those smooth, small-time villains who had the remarkably facility of wriggling from David's net whenever he thought he had a secure catch. But this was the first case that he'd come to see him regarding a murder.

They were seated in Leo's oak-lined office on the top floor of the Bamboo House. David knew it as the sort of club where the crooked rich came to spend their ill-gotten gains on black-market food and booze and a fritter away a small fortune on a dodgy roulette wheel. There were many such establishments in London now. They had grown in number since 1939 like dark festering cultures in a Petri dish. If he had his way he'd close down the whole damned lot of them, but first of all, of course, he'd need the proof and even if he had that, he feared that he'd be leaned on heavily by certain factions in the establishment to turn a blind eye. It was in the interest of certain exalted personages that such places functioned without constraint. All that was really left for David was the ability to pick off the odd corrupt individual connected with these fun palaces who had grown a little careless.

Seeing Leo Bernstein on his own territory wasn't an arrangement that David Llewellyn liked. He much preferred to question ne'er-do-wells in his own office at Scotland Yard – or better still in a dank cell at the same establishment, but at present he had no official reason to force Leo to make a trip to the Yard.

'I wondered how long it would be before you came a knocking at my door, Inspector,' Bernstein said, puffing contentedly on the cigar. 'I heard the news about Paulo Ricotti. Terrible business.'

'He was shot in the head at point-blank range.'

'And it couldn't have happened to a nicer chap.'

David flipped his trilby to the back of his head. 'Let's cut out the bullshit, Leo. I smell revenge.'

'How dramatic, Inspector. Revenge for what?'

'The guy who got his throat cut down by the river a couple of months ago.'

For a brief moment, Leo Bernstein's face dropped its supercilious mask and Llewellyn could see the pain and misery in his eyes. 'You refer to my brother's death,' he said at length, the mask back in place.

'His murder, yes.'

'And how are your investigations progressing in that direction? Can we expect an arrest any day now?'

David narrowed his eyes with irritation. He knew Bernstein had him there. The detective was pretty sure Ricotti had been the killer but he had no proof. The fellow had covered his tracks with extreme care. David had brought Ricotti in for questioning, but there was no chink in his smooth Italian armour and he'd had to let him go. As a result, it seemed clear to him that one of the Bernsteins had taken the law into their own hands: an eye for an eye.

'Your silence speaks volumes,' Leo Bernstein was saying. 'So, Inspector, what exactly is the reason for this visit? You've not come to arrest me for Paulo Ricotti's murder surely?'

'Maybe. You or one of your boys.'

'Come now, Inspector. You know us. You've taken an interest in our little dealings over the years. You see us as naughty boys. Well, maybe we are naughty boys at times – but murder?' He shook his head and pursed his lips in a reproving fashion.

David knew he had a point. The Bernsteins were villains, greedy and unscrupulous, but murder really wasn't in their line. However he wasn't naïve enough to be aware that sometimes even the mildest of men can become dangerous if provoked enough.

'I assure you, Inspector,' Leo Bernstein continued, 'that I can provide you with a water-tight alibi if required. And that goes for my two boys also.'

Suddenly David Llewellyn's spirits sank as he realized he had to accept that he was reaching yet another dead end. If the Bernsteins, one or all of them, had been responsible for killing Ricotti, it wasn't going to be easy to prove. Not easy? It would be almost impossible unless he had one of those miraculously lucky breaks that cops seem to get in the movies. But this was real life and far more complicated. Neat, happy endings were far less frequent.

With a heavy heart he rose from his chair and moved to the door. 'It's not over yet, Leo. We'll nail the guilty one, have no fear. You are being watched, you and your family. One slip and we'll have you.'

It was an empty threat, but he felt obliged to make it. It helped him feel better and gave him a suitably dramatic exit line.

After David Llewellyn had gone, Gina Bernstein came into the room by another door.

'You heard all that?' said Leo.

Gina nodded and extracted a cigarette from an ebony box on

Leo's desk. 'They haven't a speck of proof that we're involved.' A ghost of her smile touched her lips as she corrected herself. 'That I'm involved.'

Leo clicked the onyx lighter and lit Gina's cigarette. He admired the girl's nerve and her self-assurance. But he also found it a little disconcerting. There was something of Michael's sharpness and swagger, but she lacked his warmth and humanity. Such steel and resilience in a woman so young was not natural. When he considered Vic and Anthony, they seemed like reckless children compared to Gina.

'You need to keep a low profile for some time. If the cops get a whiff that you're a Bernstein ...'

Gina crossed to stare out of the window into the dingy street below. 'I know that. It suits my purposes for the moment to be little Miss Gina Andrews. But that doesn't mean we can't set certain things in motion. Move forward.'

'Move forward?'

'I was serious about taking over, you know. I have plans.'

'Perhaps we should wait until the dust settles over the Ricotti business.'

Gina shook her head. 'No,' she said, her voice blade sharp. She flashed her eyes at Leo defying him to challenge her. He didn't. He was now a different man from the one who had so smoothly dealt with Inspector Llewellyn. That had been a performance, one that he'd been used to giving, but now he was cowed, dominated, and if he was honest with himself, a little fearful.

'I want to move now,' Gina continued. 'I have plans which I intend to get off the ground, *tout suite*. We need a family conference. Can you arrange that? Get the boys here for eight this evening.'

'Well, yes, I could ...'

Gina turned to him, her face hard and emotionless. 'Well, do it. I want to get my show on the road.'

SEVEN

With my overcoat pulled around me for warmth and my hands stuffed deep into my pockets, I trudged my way up Tottenham Court road *en route* to Priory Court and the dubious comforts of home. It was around four in the afternoon and already the streets were dark, ambushed by the shifting fog and the encroaching winter night. Pedestrians loomed up before me like shapeless ghouls before gliding past and disappearing silently into the gloom once more. Muted traffic was heard but barely glimpsed, with the occasional sharp high-pitched croak of a motor horn rending the air like the cry of some strange bird.

As I trudged through the murk, I tried to weigh up how successful I'd been in my investigations that day. After chatting with my hairdresser friend, Harold Crabtree, he of the erratic bow tie, I had taken a trip to the last known address of Sylvia Moore. This endeavour had been blessed with mixed results. It was to a small boarding-house in Islington where the landlady was most reluctant to release any information about her former lodger, or indeed any information at all. The lady in question was the formidable Mrs Bentley, Hermione to her intimates, if she had any. She was a woman of some fifty-odd years, wiry of build with a face like an angry whippet, her features moulded by a thousand disappointments. She appeared at the door draped in a wraparound pinafore and headscarf tied into a turban, arms folded across her skinny chest, ready to repel boarders.

I knew that if I mentioned that I was a detective, I would get no further with the interview. Hermione's whole demeanour oozed suspicion and self-protection which, I suppose, in wartime wasn't a bad thing, although it made my job a lot tougher. 'I don't buy things from tinkers,' she said, before I had been able to take a breath.

'Quite right too,' I smiled, raising my hat in an approximation of a gentlemanly gesture – the way I had seen the toffs do it in the movies. Indeed, I realized that if I was going to make any headway with this wiry dragon, I had to indulge in some play-acting of my own. I wasn't going to get anywhere by plying the truth so I sharpened up my vowels and planted a lively smile on my mush.

'I'm an agent for Bairstow, Waghorn and Brown, the solicitors in the Strand.' I made a little pantomime of trying to find a card in various pockets to verify my statement. Needless to say, I failed, but by the time my hands had stopped searching I had moved on to purvey more false but hopefully enticing information.

'I am attempting to contact Miss Sylvia Moore.'

For a moment she seemed to chew on some inedible titbit that she had excavated from a gap in her teeth before replying. 'Sylvia? She no longer stays here.' The voice was harsh and sour.

I suspected as much. That would have been too easy. However, I was prepared for such an eventuality. I nodded sympathetically. 'That is a pity. You see I have some very good news for her concerning an inheritance.'

The fierce blue eyes sharpened with interest. 'Inheritance,' she repeated the word slowly, as though she had never heard it before and knew nothing of its meaning.

'Yes. She has come into a tidy sum of money.'

'Has she now?'

'I cannot go into details. You will appreciate it is a matter of the strictest confidentiality but' – I leaned forward conspiratorially and lowered my voice – 'it's a very tidy sum indeed, I can tell you.'

Old Hermione was definitely interested now. Her eyes brightened and a pallid tongue licked her lips. 'She never struck me as someone who had wealthy relations. Are you sure you've got the right person?'

'Oh, yes.' I nodded vigorously. 'I've spoken with Mr Crabtree, Miss Moore's previous employer, and the trail has led me here. This is her last known address.'

'A tidy sum, you say?'

I mouthed the words 'A thousand pounds', and Hermione's jaw dropped open.

'Heavens above!' she squawked.

'When did Miss Moore move away? Was it recently?'

'No, no, it wasn't recently. She's been gone about a year, I reckon.'

'Oh dear. How disappointing. Do you happen to know where she is now?'

Once more the features tightened and the eyes narrowed. 'Who do you say you're from?'

'Bairstow, Waghorn and Brown, the solicitors in the Strand,' I said, relieved I'd remembered the names that I'd conjured out of thin air. 'You can give them a ring if you wish to verify my story.'

But please don't – they do not exist.

'We ain't got no telephone here. Who's left her this cash then?'

I shook my head. 'I'm afraid I can't say.'

Hermione did not like this. A deep corrugated frown appeared on her forehead and her hand reached for the door handle. I knew I had to dig out more lies.

I looked around me in an exaggerated fashion as if to ascertain that we were indeed alone with no one within eavesdropping distance, and then I leaned towards the wizened harpy once again uttering my lies *sotto voce*. 'It's an old aunt from Worthing who popped her clogs about two months ago. Apparently Sylvia was her favourite niece. Very favourite. A thousand pounds favourite.'

Hermione nodded, her face alive with envy. 'Wait here,' she said at length.

She returned a few minutes later with a scrap of brown paper torn from a piece of wrapping I assumed. It bore some scribbled writing in pencil.

'This is the address I had off Sylvia. She gave it me when she left in case any post came here for her. Nice girl in her own quiet way.'

I raised my hat again. 'Much obliged,' I said with as much unction as I could muster.

'A thousand quid, eh?'

I nodded.

'Lucky bugger.' With this parting shot, the lady closed the door on me.

The address was Cartwright House, Kensington. Certainly a more salubrious environment that Mrs Bentley's gaff in Islington. It looked like our Sylvia had gone up in the world – come into some money perhaps. But not left to her by a fictitious old aunt from Worthing. It was now heading towards 2.30 and I hadn't had any lunch, so in order to stop my stomach rumbling any louder and annoying my fellow pedestrians, I called in at a snack bar by the tube station and had a mug of hot tea and a paste sandwich. We private detectives know how to live it up.

As I devoured my repast, I decided to put off my visit to Cartwright House until the following day. I was rather tired and already the short wintry day was beginning to fade. Sylvia Moore would have to wait until tomorrow. Besides, I had a date that evening with my girlfriend Max. I still felt odd using that term 'girl-friend'. I'd had a few encounters with girls before I lost my eye at the beginning of the war, but very little since and certainly nothing that could be said to have been on a steady footing. Max had brought a warmth and a kind of serenity to my life and although we had only been 'walking out', as they say, for about three months, I knew I wanted her around for good. Affection had been at a premium in my life so far. And the lack of a mother and father had made me insecure and uncertain regarding personal relation-ships. Having just one eye didn't help much either.

But, I thought, with a smile, that was the old Johnny. Now I had Max and somehow she made me feel whole. Simple pleasures took on an extra dimension sharing them with Max. The thought of our planned trip to the pictures tonight to see Bogart and Bergman in *Casablanca* and, with luck, sharing a bag of chips afterwards sent a tingle of pleasure running through me. This was to be our last date for a while because Max was off to Nottingham to help with the masks and costumes for their pantomime there.

As I approached my hearth and home, the paste sandwich began to fight back and once again my stomach began to rumble. Since the outbreak of the war both me and my stomach had forgotten what it was like to experience decent, wholesome, well-cooked food. I suspected that if, by some miracle, I could get hold of a thick, juicy steak with all the trimmings, the whole experience would be so alien to me, I'd probably explode.

With this whimsical thought running around my head, I let myself into my office and moved beyond into my cramped little sitting room. There I found Peter waiting for me, sitting in the gloom with only the orange glow of the electric fire to provide illumination. This was an unexpected visit and, by the look on his face, something was wrong. He presented a very disconsolate picture, sitting glumly on the sofa, his youthful features wreathed in misery.

'Hello,' I cried cheerily, clicking on the main light and pretending not to notice his dour demeanour. 'I didn't expect to see you today.'

'I had to come,' he said quietly.

'I see. How about putting on the kettle? I'm dying for a cuppa.'

'Johnny, you've got to get me some long trousers!' The words rushed out in a manic torrent.

'Really?'

'Nearly everyone in my class has them. And now they're starting to laugh at me, calling me Peter Knobbly Knees.'

I wasn't quick enough to stop the smile reaching my lips.

'It's not funny,' cried Peter petulantly. He stood up and flapped open his rain coat to reveal his knees, pale, forlorn and slightly grubby. I could see what his classmates meant. 'I'm too tall to go around like a schoolboy any more. I'm nearly as tall as you.'

This was a slight exaggeration, but I could see that the boy had a point. I had not realized how tall he had grown and how incongruous this lanky lad looked in the grey woollen short trousers that exposed his pallid knees in an almost surreal way. I'd known Peter for about three years. As a little ragged orphan boy he had entered my life in 1940 and had somehow stuck to me like a limpet. I had become his unofficial father, brother and pal. I was very fond of him. I suppose I still thought of him as that eleven-year-old ragamuffin and not noticed that he was actually changing into a young man.

'I see what you mean,' I said sympathetically. 'Come round on Saturday morning and we'll pop down Oxford Street and find you a nice pair of flannels, how about that?'

Peter's mournful face uncrumpled itself and he beamed. 'Really? I can get some grown-up pants?'

I nodded, grinning too.

'Gee, Johnny, that's wonderful.'

'Now, how about that cuppa?'

My date with Max that evening was special for all sorts of reasons and I remember it vividly. We caught the early show of *Casablanca* and loved it, but instead of the bag of chips afterwards, I splashed out and we went to The Velvet Cage, my favourite nightspot, for a drink and to listen to some jazz. Max was particularly affectionate that night – and sad. She did not relish leaving for Nottingham the next day, leaving behind her little shop and me.

'I feel a little like Ingrid Bergman having to go when I want to stay,' she said clasping my hand tightly.

'We'll always have Paris,' I said, raising my glass and clinked hers. 'Here's looking at you, kid.'

She grinned and snuggled nearer, her large grey eyes misting slightly. 'Before I go away, there's something I want to tell you, Johnny.'

I tensed slightly. 'Yes…?'

'Don't look so worried. It's nothing to be upset about. At least I hope not. I just wanted to tell you that I love you.'

Her words took my breath away. I literally shook with emotion. I cannot remember in my wretched orphaned, one-eyed life anyone saying that to me before. It was an expression that was alien to me. I was delighted and overwhelmed by Max's declaration, but she could not be fully aware of the greater implications of what she had told me. I was lost for words and so I took her in my arms and kissed her.

'That makes two of us,' I whispered eventually when we pulled back from the embrace. It was an inadequate response but it was the best that I could come up with at the time.

Max leant forward and kissed me again, gently on the cheek this time. 'That's convenient then,' she said, smiling.

EIGHT

Hermione Bentley was just settling down with a mug of cocoa and a glass of rum with the intention of listening to some dance-band music on the radio when there was a loud knocking at her front door.

'What now?' she muttered with annoyance, as she wriggled her feet into her slippers before flip-flopping her way down the hall. She opened the door a crack and stared out. The visitor standing on the threshold was a youngish woman, a little on the stout side with dark hair cut short; her squarish features wore a haunted look. Mrs Bentley recognized the face straight away for it belonged to Sylvia Moore, one of her old lodgers: Sylvia Moore, soon to become the wealthy Sylvia Moore, the inheritor of a thousand pounds.

'Hello, Mrs Bentley, I wonder if I could have a word.'

It was Hermione Bentley's motto, newly minted, that one always did favours for wealthy folk because you never knew when it might benefit you.

''Course, Sylvia, do come in,' she said opening the door wide.

Somewhat nervously, Sylvia entered and Mrs Bentley led her into the shabby but cosy sitting room.

'I was just about to take a little nip of rum. Can I get you a glass?'

Sylvia looked unsure. Rum certainly was not her tipple but she didn't want to upset the old harridan by refusing. 'Just a drop – to keep the cold out. Thanks.'

Mrs Bentley poured the drink and indicated that Sylvia should sit down. 'Now then, what can I do for you?' she said, passing the drink to her guest.

'Well, it's a little bit awkward like.'

'Go on, love, you can trust me.'

'I've had word that a fellow's been asking about me, trying to find me.'

Mrs Bentley narrowed her eyes. 'Oh, and how did you come to hear about that?'

'It's sort of complicated, but I wondered if anyone has come here asking questions, wanting to know where I'm living.'

Mrs Bentley took a swig of rum before answering. 'As a matter of fact, I had a chap here today looking for you, you lucky girl. Said he was representing a firm of solicitors in the Strand.'

Sylvia paled. 'Was he a youngish chap with an eye patch?'

'Yes, that's the feller. How did you know? Has he caught up with you already?'

Sylvia clasped her hands together nervously and shook her head.

'Well, don't look so bloomin' miserable. It's good news, my dear,' continued Mrs Bentley, warming to her task. 'You've come into money. A thousand pounds I reckon. An old aunt of yours has left it to you in her will—'

'An old aunt?' Sylvia seemed very distracted now.

'That's right. He didn't give her name. Said it was confidential. Well, I must say you don't seem very pleased. I wish someone would leave me a tidy sum when they snuff it.'

Sylvia attempted a smile. 'It's all a bit of a surprise. I haven't seen this gentleman yet. Did … did you give him my address?'

'Certainly did, my dear. I didn't want you missing out on your good fortune. A thousand quid, eh? What couldn't you do with that stash.'

'Yes, it's quite exciting,' Sylvia said, attempting to elicit some enthusiasm. She rose awkwardly and placed her untouched drink on a side table. 'So this one-eyed man knows where I live?'

Mrs Bentley nodded. 'Indeed, he does. Don't you worry. I've no doubt he'll be calling around tomorrow with the cheque.'

'Well, that's good to know,' she said, edging towards the door.

'Are you going so soon?'

Sylvia nodded. 'I'd better be getting back. It's rather late. I just wanted to know about this fellow.'

'Did you now? It's a long way to come just to find that out. Is there something wrong? You don't seem too happy. You know you can trust me.'

'No, no, there's nothing wrong; it's just one gets nervous when strangers start asking after you. You hear such stories.'

Sylvia moved into the hall and when Mrs Bentley followed, she hurried for the front door. 'Thanks. It's good to see you again. I'll let myself out.' And with that she stepped out into the night and slammed the door behind her.

Hermione Bentley pulled a face. 'Now that's a funny how do you do,' she muttered to herself as she slithered back into the warmth of her sitting room. 'If I'm not greatly mistaken, that girl's frightened of something. Perhaps it is that geezer with the eye patch. Come to think of it, he did look a bit dodgy....'

Just as she was about to resume her seat by the fire, she noticed Sylvia's untouched glass of rum. With a gentle shrug of the shoulder, she poured the measure into her own glass. 'Waste not, want not,' she said, and switched on the radio.

Across the city, in Leo Bernstein's office, on the top floor of the Bamboo House, Gina Bernstein was holding court. She stood by the window, while Leo, Anthony and Vic sat listening to her in uneasy silence. Leo puffed on his cigar almost absent-mindedly, well aware that he was no longer the patron of the group but just a mere bystander – and in some ways rather relieved to be so. He was too old a dog to be learning dangerous new tricks.

'I assure you it's an easy thing to operate,' Gina was saying with controlled enthusiasm, 'and it brings in wads of cash. I ran a similar operation in Dublin before the war and it was a great success.'

'But we've never done anything like this before,' said Anthony, shifting uneasily in his chair. He was all for the status quo. That suited him. He was against anything that might disrupt the comfortable equilibrium of his life. Newfangled schemes involving danger and effort were not for him, especially when they were to be controlled by this bossy tart.

'All the more reason to go ahead now,' said Gina. 'This business is in danger of going stagnant.'

'What if they refuse to pay?' asked Anthony.

'A little rough stuff usually does the trick. Trust me.'

Anthony glanced at Vic hoping to elicit his support, but he seemed to be studiously examining his fingernails.

Gina ploughed on. She really didn't care too much if she convinced them she was right, they were going to do it anyway. She was boss after all and each one of them in the room knew it.

'I've picked out a few premises for a trial run tomorrow.'

'Tomorrow!' said Vic in surprise.

'Why not? Why wait? The sooner we get started, the sooner we up our profits. I want you to join me in the morning, Vic, for our first sortie. It should be fun.'

Instinctively Anthony leaned forward about to object. Why should Vic be chosen for this new venture? He always seemed the favoured one. But before he was able to open his mouth, common sense held his tongue. If this crazy and somewhat dangerous enterprise succeeded, he'd still profit. If it failed, he was well out of it. Let Vic act the role of guinea pig. Good luck to him.

In the meantime, Vic had said nothing either. He sat impassively, staring at some spot in the idle distance.

'Are you up for it, Vic, or are you going to bottle out?' Gina said softly, but there was no mistaking the taunting tone of her question.

Vic gave her a weary grin. 'A cheap trick to suggest I might not have the guts to frighten a few shopkeepers. Shows how much you don't know me.' He winked hard at Gina. 'Sure I'm up for your little scheme, missy. You are on. Give me the time and the place tomorrow and I'll be with you.'

NINE

That night, we went back to Max's little flat and made love. It wasn't hurried, clumsy and frenzied like it had been the first few times. It was slow and passionate, real desire taking the place of animalistic lust, emotional euphoria blending with physical satisfaction in a cramped little bed in Max's tiny bedroom. It was probably the happiest night of my life. At long last I belonged to someone. And she was mine also.

Afterwards, we lay in the darkness, entwined in each other's bodies, saying nothing. I just listened to her gentle breathing in a state of simple happiness. We parted with a final embrace at the door of her flat, Max promising to keep in touch, to write and telephone me often and begging me to take care of myself. 'It's only about three weeks. They'll pass in a trice,' she said, her eyes moistening.

'Sure,' I said, and gave her hand a squeeze before heading off into the night to my own bed.

I slept the sleep of the just that night, or what was left of it, and rose late the next morning. The euphoria of the previous evening had worn away with the dingy dawn. I had hit the anti-climax. Even in daylight, the world seemed lifeless and bleak. I considered my immediate prospects and realized they were dull: a troublesome case and three weeks without Max. I tried to shake off my malaise with a brisk bath. By the time I was walking the streets and having given myself a little lecture about having to focus on my investigation, I did feel a little more positive and programmed. I had a lady to find – the key to the case of the reappearing wife. I gazed at the scrap of brown paper dear Hermione Bentley had given me: Cartwright House in Kensington. I was not sure where this was, so I treated myself to a cab, knowing the driver would be able to find it without any difficulty. And sure enough he did.

It was around eleven in the morning with the sky, an unrelieved leaden grey, leaning down oppressively on the city, when the taxi drew up outside a large block of flats in the hinterland behind Kensington High Street. Somewhere in that Victorian mausoleum was Sylvia Moore. I paid the cabbie and made my way into the building.

The foyer area was large and cold with a crazed marble floor. The sound of my footsteps echoed and re-echoed around me. It was like a ghost building with no sign of humanity about it. There was a lift of the old-fashioned cage type and two staircases with wrought-iron balustrades winding their way up into the upper regions. Affixed to the pillar by the lift was also a board listing the number of flats and their occupants. There were three levels with ten flats on each level. It did not take me long to discover there was an S. Moore on level two, Flat 11. It's moments like this when a simple piece of detective work pays off that I feel a real tingle of pleasure. It was not to last, however.

I harboured a strong distrust of lifts, having once been trapped in one with a large flatulent man with halitosis, so I took the stairs and made my way to Flat 11. Once there I rang the bell. And rang the bell. And rang the bell. I could hear its brisk tones reverberating inside the flat but it elicited no response. Of course, I told myself eventually, my friend Sylvia could be at work. Come to think of it, that was likely. Making sure I was alone on the corridor, I extracted the length of stiff wire I keep in my top pocket for those occasions when I feel a bout of burglary coming upon me. Inserting it into the lock and with a few deft movements – tricks of the trade, you might say, that I had learned from an old lag I knew when I was in the police force – I soon had the door open. Within a trice I had let myself into Flat 11.

And the cupboard was bare! And I mean *really* bare. In the words of the old expression, whoever had lived here had done a moonlight flit. There was not one personal item left in the flat. The drawers and wardrobes were empty. There were no photographs, trinkets, or jewellery that could give any indication of the nature of the person or persons who had once inhabited this flat. However, there were signs that two people had been living here. I found two cups on the draining board, two cigarette ends in an ashtray, one with bright red lipstick and one without; and in the bedroom the dents in the pillows on the double bed suggested double occupancy.

After twenty minutes, I gave up looking for further clues. I'm sure there were none – or certainly none that I would be able to interpret. All I knew was that whatever prompted the couple to scarper, they had done so in a hurry which suggested that they were frightened. But of what?

I pulled the door to and rang the bell of the flat next door but got no reply. I tried my luck further down the hall and at Flat 15. At last I got a response. A youngish, unshaven fellow who looked as though he had just risen from his pit answered the door.

'I wonder if you could help me,' I asked politely.

'I doubt it, but you can try me,' came the reply through a stifled yawn.

'I've been trying to get a response from Flat 11. A friend of mine, Sylvia Moore, lives there. She seems to be out or away. Being a neighbour, I wondered if you might know where she'd be.'

His face crumpled with irritation. 'Now why the hell should I? I don't even know the woman. What's she like?'

'Medium height, squarish features, short cropped hair. She's a hairdresser.'

'Got a bit of a squat nose…? I think I know the one you mean. Yeah, I've seen her about. Never spoke to her though. They keep themselves to themselves at that flat. Agnes might know.'

'Who's Agnes?'

'Agnes Colthorpe. The eyes and ears of the world. What she doesn't know about what goes on in this building' – he paused to yawn again – 'isn't worth knowing.'

I grinned in a friendly fashion. 'Where will I find her?'

'Down below, Flat 8.'

'Many thanks.'

'S'all right,' he said scratching his head. 'Now if you don't mind I'll get back to bed.' With that he closed the door.

Agnes Colthorpe answered her door after the first ring. She was a tiny woman, bent with age but with a pleasant demeanour and two bright, intelligent blue eyes which gazed at me with enquiry.

'I wonder if you could help me?' I said again.

'Certainly, young man, if I'm able. What is it that you want?'

'I'm trying to trace an old friend of mine, Sylvia Moore. I believe she lives in this building in Flat 11.'

'Flat 11...? Oh yes, I know. Which one is she?'

'Which one.' Now I was puzzled.

'There are two young ladies who live there?'

This was something I had not contemplated. 'Well, Sylvia has short dark hair....'

'Ah, yes, and the other one is a blonde. Artificial, rather a brassy colour.'

I reached into my inside pocket and brought out the photograph that Brian Garner had given me of his wife.

'Is that her, the blonde one?' I asked, passing it to Agnes who held it up to her face and squinted at it.

'I think so,' she said at length. 'I can't see properly without my glasses. Come inside while I get them and I'll be able to tell you.'

I followed the old lady into a neat and tidy sitting room, where everything shone and sparkled from assiduous dusting and polishing. Even the wooden arms of the chair she offered me glowed brightly. She retrieved her spectacles from the mantelpiece and, sliding them gracefully on to her nose, she gazed at the picture again. 'Mmm, well, I think that's her. This was taken a few years ago, I imagine. She's much more glamorous now. Her hair looks quite dull here. Now it's as bright as that film star – that Harlow woman – and her face is always thick with make-up. The other girl, Sylvia, is much more restrained, plainer, dumpier.'

'How long have they lived here?'

'About two years, I should say.' She chuckled gently. 'But I can't be certain. When you get to my age, time doesn't mean as much as it used to. One day is much like the next and yet they fly by.'

I nodded with what I hoped was an understanding and sympathetic smile.

'I'm a little confused,' she said, removing her glasses and peering at me with her clear blue eyes. Which one of these girls are you seeking? You asked me about Sylvia and yet you have a photograph of her friend.'

She had me there.

'Well, I know them both,' I said, with as much conviction as I could muster. 'But Sylvia is a special friend. You see, I'm just briefly in London and I wanted to call in and say hello.'

'That's nice,' she said, but I could tell that the canny old bird didn't believe a word I was saying. She was beginning to see through my paper-thin charade.

'Do you know where she works, or her friend?'

'I'm afraid I don't, my dear. I see them in the foyer from time to time and we pass the time of day but I certainly don't know their intimate details.'

I felt as though I'd had my wrists rapped gently.

'But as far as you know they both work.'

'Well, they leave the building in the morning and return in the evening.'

'You don't know what they're doing now, I suppose? They used to be hairdressers ... but with the war ...'

'I thought you were a friend.'

'It's some time since I've seen her.'

'It would seem so.' The voice had lost its warmth and the features had hardened. I could feel the frost building up inside the room. I knew it was time to depart. I had been too eager to get information from little Agnes and in doing so had underestimated her perspicacity. The shrewd, sharp-witted woman that she was, she had sussed me out.

'Thanks for your help,' I said as I reached door.

'If I should see Sylvia, who should I say was asking after her?'

I uttered the first name that seemed appropriate: 'Brian Garner.'

As I was leaving the building, a burly postman brushed past me with his bag and a little light flickered in my head. I lingered in the foyer until he had departed. And then I retraced my steps to Flat

11, stepping inside once more. There, lying like large pristine snowflakes on the doormat were two letters. I scooped them up. They were both addressed to Miss S. Moore. I opened the first one. It was a bill from a milliners for a 'black pill-box hat'. It told me nothing of consequence for my investigations, only that my Sylvia had a penchant for perky headgear. The second, however, was more fruitful. It was a short letter from someone who signed themselves 'Aunt Ada'. The handwriting was crabbed and spidery suggesting that this aunt was quite old. She hoped that Sylvia was fine and that she had got over the '*sad loss*'. *It seems like only yesterday, but I find it's nearly two years*, she added. What was of particular interest was the sentence, *I hope you are still enjoying your senior position at Madame Rene's Beauty Parlour. I knew you had the skill and talent to obtain a position in a high-class hair salon in such a nice area.* Aunt Ada closed with extra best wishes *for the forthcoming festive season.* There were three tiny kisses following the scribbled signature.

I left Cartwright House with something of a spring in my step. Slowly but surely I was moving forward. No big questions had been answered yet, but at least I wasn't facing a large blank brick wall. I wondered what the considerate Aunt Ada had meant by her reference to Sylvia's 'sad loss'. Perhaps she had a boyfriend or husband killed in action. Unfortunately that was an all too common occurrence these days. As my thoughts petered our regarding the case, I found my mind wandering towards Max again. I wondered if she had reached Nottingham yet. I tried to picture which of her outfits she would be wearing for the journey. It brought a smile to my face.

So, I now had to find this high class salon, the extravagantly named Madame Rene's. Aunt Ada had said it was 'in such a nice area'. Well Kensington was a 'nice area' and that's where Sylvia lived so I reckoned it was worth checking to see whether it was somewhere in the vicinity.

Kensington High Street was busy with shoppers, mainly woman in thick winter coats and neat hats. I popped into the first newsagent I came across. I bought a copy of the *Daily Mirror* and then asked the grizzled fellow behind the counter if he knew where

I could find a ladies hairdressers called Madame Rene's. He gave me an odd look.

'I'm not sure, mate,' came the reply. 'The missus attends to my barnet.' He grinned, rubbing his hand over his balding pate. 'What there is of it. Let me see … Madame Rene's sounds a bit posh, don't it? There is rather a posh place on Scarsdale Road, down the High Street to your left and third road going off to your right.'

He was correct. The 'posh place' was indeed Madame Rene's Beauty Parlour. I'd hit bull's eye with my first throw of the dart. And it was a 'posh place' indeed. Certainly the exterior was several notches up on Chez Harolde. There were two tubs with small conifers either side of the door and a crimson doormat with the name of the establishment emblazoned on it in cream lettering. I wiped my feet and entered.

A tall, elegant, but rather imposing woman moving regally towards middle age was at the appointments desk. She eyed me with barely concealed disdain. I suppose that as a man I was in alien territory and as a man in a shabby overcoat and even shabbier trilby, sporting an eye patch I was out of my sartorial depth also.

'How may I help you, sir?' she said, as though that was the last thing on earth she would wish to do.

'I'd like to see the manageress.'

Now that surprised her. 'May I ask what is the nature of your business?'

'It is a very personal and private matter … of the greatest delicacy.'

She cast an eye at the copy of the *Daily Mirror* I was carrying and her lips quivered with distaste.

I leaned forward and lowered my voice. 'There is a certain amount of urgency involved if we are to prevent the scandal getting out.' I tapped my newspaper apparently in an absentminded fashion.

Her eyes widened with alarm. 'Please wait here,' she announced, in her Kensington-honed clipped tones and disappeared through a door on her left.

I did not have to wait long.

My snooty friend emerged in less than a minute with another woman, shorter, fatter and older, but wearing a vibrant gown that probably cost more than I earned in a year. I took her to be Madame Rene.

'You wish to see me, Mr...?' Her voice and manner were out of the same stable as her tall companion.

'Hawke. John Hawke.'

'Please come through to my office.' She bade me enter.

The room could hardly be regarded as an office. Not in my world anyway. True, there was a desk at one end, but there were also a couple of well-upholstered carved chairs, a *chaise-longue* and bowls of artificial flowers everywhere. The overall colour was powdery pink and the air was thick with the sweet smell of women's perfume. It was like wandering into a giant box of Turkish Delight.

Madame Rene reclined gracefully on the *chaise-longue* and, with a flowing gesture of her hand, indicated that I should avail myself of one of the carved chairs.

'How may I assist you?' asked Madame Rene.

'I am making enquiries regarding one of your employees: Sylvia Moore.'

Her eyebrows rose in surprise. 'Sylvia?'

I nodded. 'She does work for you?'

'Yes,' she replied slowly. I could feel the drawbridge being hauled up so I came out with the old story about representing a firm of solicitors – the remarkable but fictitious Bairstow, Waghorn and Brown – and that Sylvia was in line for a small inheritance. As I completed my tidily presented pack of lies, I saw Madame Rene relax a little, although she still viewed me with some suspicion. I suppose she was wondering what a flashy firm of solicitors was doing employing a scruffy character like me.

'Oh, I see,' she said. 'Well, yes, Sylvia works for me. She is one of my senior consultants, but I'm afraid she is not here today. She rang me this morning to say that she was feeling unwell and would not be in. I must say that is not like Sylvia at all and it is highly inconvenient. I have the Duchess of Bridgestock coming this afternoon and she always insists that Sylvia attends to her hair. It's very dry and difficult.'

I nodded sympathetically while masking my own disappointment. This was getting to be a habit. Little Sylvia seems to have slipped through my grasp again.

'However, she did assure me that she'd be back in the salon on Monday.' With some effort Madame Rene pulled herself up from the *chaise-longue* to indicate that the interview was drawing to a close.

'I'll call back then.' I rose, too, and moved to the door. 'If I could crave your indulgence, however ...'

Madame Rene's eyes widened with apprehension. 'In what way?' she asked warily.

'Please don't tell Miss Moore anything about my visit or enquiries. We at Bairstow, Waghorn and Brown are keen to be the first to impart the good news. We want it to come as a complete surprise to our client. So, if you don't mind, mum's the word.'

'As you wish, Mr Hawke. As you wish,' she replied, ushering me from her richly scented lair.

As I returned to the cold and dreary streets once more, a little cloud of disappointment settled around my shoulders. I realized that despite my various efforts, I was still not significantly further in my pursuit of Beryl Garner. Both she and her cohort, Sylvia Moore, were proving most elusive. In fact they had performed a very effective disappearing act.

TEN

The two figures entered the little tobacconist's shop just after noon. The bell above the door tinkled to announce their presence. There were no other customers on the premises and the owner Ralph Cousins had just brewed himself a cup of tea in the back room. He was about to lift the steaming mug to his lips when the customers entered. With a sigh of resignation, he placed the mug down on his desk and went into the front of the shop hoping he could deal with these customers before his tea went cold. There was a tall, thin, young woman, pretty with bright red lipstick and a well-set-up young man whose expression suggested that he had got out of the wrong side of the bed that morning.

Before he could greet them with his customary, 'Good day, what can I do for you?' they began behaving oddly. The man flicked the Yale lock on the door, snapping it shut, and swivelled round the 'Open' sign so that it read 'Closed' to those outside the shop. He then pulled down the blind.

'Hey, what do you think you're doing?' the old tobacconist said, half in anger, half in apprehension.

'We are just securing some privacy before we conduct a little business,' said the girl pleasantly enough, but her features were hard and cruel.

'What kind of business?'

'Insurance business,' she said, and gave her companion a nod. On cue, he pushed a glass display cabinet, which was perched on the far end of the counter, to the ground. It crashed to the floor, the sound resounding around the tiny shop. The glass smashed immediately, with bright dagger-like shards skittering across the wooden floor, glittering in the dim illumination. The man then kicked the side of the case, splintering the wood. He beamed with satisfaction.

'What a nasty accident,' he said, the sarcasm redolent in his voice.

'That was no accident: you did it deliberately. Are you mad or something?'

'My friend is so careless,' said the girl. 'But then there are so many careless individuals in the world, aren't there? Clumsy folk who have no concern or respect for other people's property. Isn't that right?' The question was addressed to her companion who, in response, stepped behind the counter and knocked a whole row of cigarette packets on to the floor and then proceeded to stamp on them, squashing the contents beneath his heel.

'Stop it! Stop it, you crazy bastard!' cried Ralph Cousins stepping forward towards the vandal who, in an instant, withdrew a pistol from his overcoat pocket. 'I wouldn't come any closer, if I were you, old man. I don't like to be touched. And there's no insurance against one of these.'

Ralph Cousins froze in his tracks.

'All this has been most unfortunate, Mr Cousins,' said the girl in soothing tones. 'And I'm sure you would not want it to happen again.'

The shopkeeper was now shaking with fear, which for the moment robbed him of speech.

'However, we are in the position of being able to guarantee that it will not happen again. That is very fortunate for you, isn't it? All you have to do is take part in a little private insurance policy we have arranged for you. For a mere twenty pounds a month, we will give you the assurance that no further accidents of this nature will take place again.'

'Unless, of course, you miss a payment,' added the tough young man.

'A cheap and secure form of insurance,' continued the girl. 'So, if you'll reach your hand into the till and withdraw twenty pounds, we'll be on our way.'

At the mention of the twenty pounds, the old tobacconist felt his heart constrict. 'But ... but I haven't got twenty pounds in the till. This is a small shop....'

'Oh, dear,' said the man raising his voice. 'Oh dear!' With a vicious sweep of his arm, he dragged another row of cigarette packets from the shelf to the floor and stamped on them heavily. 'This could go on a long time unless you cough up the cash,' he said. 'You don't want to be left without any stock at all, do you?'

Ralph Cousins' face reflected the horror he felt as this nightmare continued. 'I have a little money in the back....'

'That's a good boy. Off you go and get it.'

With an ashen face and shaking hands, Ralph Cousins scurried into his back room and returned some moments later with a wad of notes. Gingerly, he held them out to the man.

'I'll take those,' said the girl, and after a quick count she stowed the money in her handbag. 'It was good to do business with you, Mr Cousins. It is a wise investment indeed. We'll leave you to tidy up.' She moved to the door as did her accomplice who unlocked the Yale, released the blind and swung the 'Open' sign round again.

'Don't forget,' said the man, as a parting shot, 'one of our representatives will call around next month to collect our premium. And just a warning ... complaining to the law will only bring you more trouble. Believe me, Mr Cousins, that is not an idle threat.'

The bell tinkled again as the two intruders left.

Ralph Cousins stood for some time shocked into inaction, staring at the damage that had been done inside his shop. His home had suffered bomb damage in the blitz, but somehow this was worse. These intruders weren't the Nazis. They weren't the enemy. They were British. Bloody British gangsters.

In a slow, mechanical fashion, with eyes moist with emotion, he began to clear up the mess.

Some time later, not far away from Ralph Cousins' shop, in a shady corner of a shabby pub on Henrietta Street, Gina and Vic Bernstein were enjoying a drink. 'You were good, Vic,' said Gina, swilling her gin and tonic around in her glass. 'A natural.'

He grinned. 'Well, I'm not exactly a novice.'

For a moment they sat in silence and then Vic said, 'What interests me is why you chose me rather than Anthony for this caper?'

It was her turn to grin. 'There's no competition. He's a hot head. He hasn't yet realized that in our business self-control and an unemotional approach are essential. I suppose he might learn in time, but, at the moment, he's immature; he could easily become a liability. I suggest you keep your eye on him.'

Vic sipped his beer. 'I do. I've had to pull him out of a few scrapes already.'

'That doesn't surprise me. Anyway, after our successful little experiment this morning with Mr Cousins, I'm turning the whole project over to you. You know how it works. It's simple but effective. You oversee the project now and set Anthony on with a reliable partner to do the calls. Can you find one?'

'I know a chap. We've used him before.'

'Good. Put him on the payroll. I'll provide you with a list of places to target and we'll give it a month's trial. See how it goes. If we get twenty premises on board – small shops too frightened to do anything about it – we should clean up very nicely. In time it will bring us in a tidy sum. Within a year we should be ready to branch out with another club.'

Vic lit a cigarette and scrutinized the girl carefully. 'You are driven, aren't you?'

'Yes. I have a lot of time to catch up. I was kept from the family business against my will for most of my life. What Pops didn't realize is that I may be a girl, but I am also a Bernstein through and through. I've got brains and guts and the determination. And the balls. Don't forget it.' She gave Vic's face a friendly pat. 'I've dreamed of this moment. Believe me, boy, I'm going to take this family somewhere, whatever it takes.'

Max struggled into the buffet bar at Nottingham Station and ordered a coffee and a Bath bun. She sat at the table nearest the stove and warmed her hands. The journey from London had been an uncomfortable one. There had been no heating on the train and the cramped compartment in which she had been sitting had ice on the inside of the window. With the help of the hot coffee and the gentle glow of the stove, she began to thaw out.

She pulled a fountain pen and one of the blank postcards stowed in her bag and began writing. She was surprised how much she was already missing Johnny. It was true that in London she would often not see him for days, but she knew that she could if she wanted to. There was the comfort and reassurance of the close proximity. But now they were truly separated and it was unpleasant. The act of writing the card would help to bring him closer. To be in contact with Johnny, however tenuous, gave her solace, for here she was in an unfamiliar city about to start work with a set of strangers. It was a situation that she had experienced before on several occasions, but she had never left a man she loved behind before to do so. Well, she'd never really been in love before. As this thought came to her, her eyes misted a little.

She sniffed heartily in an attempt to sweep away such maudlin sentiment and finished writing the card. Putting it to one side for a moment, she rummaged in her bag for a stamp. When she picked the card up again, she noticed that the back where she had written her message was smeared in the corner by a small blob of tomato ketchup. In the dim light of the buffet, it looked like a splash of blood.

It was early evening when Vic strolled into the Dog and Duck, a rough and ready pub on Branch Street in Shoreditch.

'Dregsville,' Vic muttered under his breath, as he made his way to the bar. The air was stale and smoky and the sawdust crunched beneath his feet. He attracted quite a bit of attention in his dark-blue overcoat and smart trilby. The rest of the customers, mainly men, could, by contrast, have entered a scarecrow competition. Shabby and worn-out clothes were *de rigueur* at the Dog and Duck. Envy and distrust of this stranger – this toff – radiated from their haggard faces and mean-spirited eyes, but their attention span was brief. Quite quickly they returned to their drinking and desultory conversations. The barman, a Woodbine dangling from his lips, managed to mouth the word, 'Yes' as a form of invitation to buy a drink.

'Half a bitter and have one yourself,' said Vic.

The barman's features softened. 'Right,' he replied, the cigarette only just remaining in place. He pulled the half-pint and plonked on the bar counter, spilling some of the contents in the process. Vic handed over a shilling. 'Keep the change. Is Archie Muldoon in?'

'Who wants to know?'

'I do. He does a little work for me from time to time.'

The barman eyed the stranger carefully. He didn't think he was a copper. He was too well dressed and smooth. Besides coppers don't flash shillings around. What the hell, he thought at length. I'm not Muldoon's keeper. 'He's in the back room,' he said, nodding his head towards a door at the side of the bar.

Vic picked up his drink and sauntered through into the 'back room' where a card school was in progress. Four men were hunched over a small round table in the middle of which was a small pile of copper coins. Each face turned in Vic's direction as he entered. Only one of them registered recognition.

'Hello, Vic. Long time, no see,' said Archie Muldoon with a mixture of surprise and apprehension.

Vic always thought of Archie as The Crumpled Man. Everything about him was in this condition from his crinkly uncombed hair, to his screwed-up bulldog of a face to the creased pinstripe suit that encased his ample body.

'I'd like a word,' he said. 'But finish your hand first, eh?'

The other three men who had eyed Vic up on his entrance had already returned their attention to their cards.

'Sure, won't be a mo,' said Archie.

He was true to his word. The game was over in a trice and Archie lost his money. Vic surmised that he had been losing all night. As usual. Archie was a mug where money was concerned.

'Let me buy you a drink and then we can chat over a proposition I have in mind,' he said.

Archie gave him a crumpled grin. 'Sure.'

They found a quiet corner in the main bar and Vic bought Archie a pint.

'I suspect that you could do with some loot at the moment. Is that right?'

Archie, who had no artifice, nodded eagerly. 'Too true. I'd be down on my uppers if I had any uppers to be down on.' He chuckled at his own conceit. Vic responded with an indulgent smile.

'I'm back with Sarah,' continued Archie, 'at the old spot in Crimea Buildings – so there's two mouths to feed and things have been a bit rough.'

'Well, I'm here to offer you a job, Archie.'

Archie's face brightened. 'Really? That's great. Is it in my usual line?'

'Not quite – but you'll soon pick it up. You still got a shooter?'

Archie glanced around nervously and then nodded. The Bernsteins had never asked him to carry a gun before. This was a turn up for the book.

'Good. You'll need it … just as a frightener you understand.'

'What's it all about?'

Vic left the fug and the noise of the Dog and Duck some twenty minutes later having briefed Archie fully on the protection scheme. Archie was enthusiastic – well, he would be as there was money involved – but Vic knew that he'd be good at it. Despite Archie's rough simplicity he was reliable, as steady as a rock, unlike Anthony. Ah, Anthony! thought Vic. Now I have to tackle him. Bring him aboard. But that should be no problem. He knew how to play Anthony. It should be fairly easy to convince him that for the moment at least he should sail under the same flag as Gina. It really was in their best interest. Vic knew he had to bide his time with her. She was formidable, ruthless and wily. But she would not triumph in the end. He was determined about that.

ELEVEN

It was clear to me that Sylvia Moore's little holiday from work – her period of being 'rather unwell' – was simply an excuse to give her time to re-establish new quarters after she had done a bunk from Cartwright House. It was also apparent that she had been living there with the supposedly dead Beryl Garner. It was now clear that there were more dark twists to this affair than had first appeared. There was a strange conspiracy here that I had still yet to uncover.

I was sure that I was the reason for this hurried move. Sylvia had caught wind that I was on her trail – probably from the fragrant Harold Crabtree. And so the pair of them, determined not to be found, had upped sticks with alacrity and moved elsewhere. Undoubtedly I was on the right track and whether my client Brian Garner believed that he had seen a ghost or not was of no consequence; he had certainly unearthed some kind of mischief. Beryl and mate Sylvia had pulled off an act of deceitful, unlawful chicanery and were now on the run. All I had to do was catch them. However, discovering the whereabouts of two ladies who were desperate not to be found was not going to be easy. While the facts of the case were now somewhat clearer in my mind, my task remained a tough one.

After leaving Madame Rene's, I popped into a call box and rang Brian Garner at his shop to tell him that I was making slow but positive progress. 'You'll have to be patient,' I warned him. 'It is a case of softly, softly catchee monkey, but obviously my enquiries have stirred up the muddy waters.' I was conscious that I was overusing metaphors even as I spoke, but Garner did not seem to mind. He was pleased with my news. 'I've waited two years, I reckon I can wait a bit longer,' he said.

'I'll be in touch early next week,' I said before replacing the receiver.

My stomach told me it was lunchtime, so I called in a café on Kensington High Street for a sandwich and a cuppa before heading back to the office.

The following morning was the big shopping trip. Peter arrived early and refused both tea and toast, so eager was he to be off down Oxford Street to purchase his long trousers. I can't remember how many times he used that phrase 'long trousers' but it almost became like a mantra for a new sartorial sect. We ended up in the menswear department of Bourne & Hollingsworth where a bald-headed Pickwickian gentleman with a long tape measure flapping around his neck took Peter under his wing.

'I think sir would find these charcoal worsted trousers an ideal choice,' he said, with practised charm. Peter swelled with pleasure at being addressed as 'sir'.

Indeed, they were an ideal choice. They fitted him perfectly but what to me was so remarkable, magical even, was the change they brought about in Peter's appearance. He entered the changing cubicle as a lanky schoolboy and emerged as a young man. Even his face, wreathed in smiles, seemed more mature, more defined – the puppy fat of childhood having melted away.

'Can I have these?' he said with admirable restraint.

I nodded.

'Your son looks quite the grown-up now,' said Mr Pickwick.

I was about to correct him but didn't. In so many respects Peter was my son and I was proud to be considered his father.

'How about a lunch at Uncle Benny's? You can show off your new pants to him,' I suggested after we had left the store, with Peter now in his transformed long-trousered guise.

Peter's face lit up at the prospect. 'He might not recognize me,' he chuckled.

As always Benny was delighted to see us. Duly impressed with

Peter's new image, he made a great play of feeling the trousers and praising the cloth, but I was aware that there was something muted, something restrained about his behaviour. Peter didn't notice it, but I'd known Benny for many years and seen all his moods and I could tell when he was upset and attempting to hide it.

We grabbed a table and having made our selection from the menu, Benny scurried off to the kitchen to attend to our order. It was then that I noticed that the glass was missing from the case on the counter where he displayed his cakes and buns.

'Won't be a sec,' I said to Peter, resisting the habit of ruffling his hair as I left my seat. Such an action now to this grown-up long-trousered fellow would have been to him the height of indignity. I had to accept the fact that I no longer had a little boy for a companion but a burgeoning young man. I suppose it had been happening for quite a while but this had been the catalyst which had alerted me to the fact.

However, for now it was Benny who concerned me most. I made my way across the café, behind the counter and slipped into the steamy kitchen. Being Saturday and a quiet day for the café, it was his helpmate Doris's day off, but remarkably the old fellow coped on his own.

'Hey, you're not allowed in here. This is for staff only.'

'What's wrong, Benny?'

'I'll tell you what's wrong: you're in my kitchen.'

'Don't prevaricate.'

Benny raised his eyebrows. 'Prevaricate? I don't even know what that means.'

'Something's upset you. Is it the broken glass of the confectionery case?'

At this, his face darkened and he grew hesitant.

'What is it?' I asked. 'I've known you long enough to know when you're trying to cover something up—'

'Look, you want to eat today? If so, get out of my kitchen so I can prepare your grub.'

I grabbed hold of his shoulders and shook him gently. 'Tell me, Benny.'

His body sagged and he sighed heavily. 'Ten years I've been in this place. Ten years there has been Benny's café. Ten years and there's been no trouble. Until now.'

'Trouble. What kind of trouble?'

Benny sighed again and ran the back of his hand across his mouth. 'Protection. They came first thing this morning, just as soon as I'd opened. There were two of them.' He shrugged. 'If I want a quiet existence with no problems, I pay them twenty quid a month for the privilege. If not there'll be some upset. They smashed the glass to prove their point.'

'Do you know these men?'

Benny shook his head. 'Never seen them before.'

'And you paid…?'

'No, I didn't pay. I don't have that kind of money on me first thing in the morning. But I said I would pay after I'd been to the bank.'

'When?'

'They're coming back this evening at closing time.'

'We can get them then.' The excited voice came from the doorway. Benny and I both turned to see Peter grinning like a clown.

'How long have you been there?' I asked.

'I heard it all. We can rough these fellows up when they come back, can't we, Johnny?'

Before I could reply, Benny responded. 'I don't want to involve you, Johnny. It's not your problem.'

'I am involved, Benny. You're my friend, so it's my problem as well.'

'Mine, too,' piped up the junior Sexton Blake by the door, but we both ignored him.

'What were these fellows like?' I asked.

Benny shrugged. 'One was quite young – in his twenties I should say. Bulky but smartly dressed. The other chap was older, scruffier – mean-looking. He said nothing.'

'Did they have guns?'

'Don't know. They didn't show them if they did.'

'Well, you're not going to pay, Benjamin, my friend. That way madness lies. I'll not see you starting to slide down that slippery slope. What time are they due to call?'

'Around six this evening.'

'I'll be here.'

'*We'll* be here,' said Peter.

Benny and I ignored him again.

'Don't bother to protest, Benny. I've made up my mind.'

I left the matter there and returned to the café area, pushing the reluctant Peter ahead of me. As we waited for Benny to prepare our food, I had a serious word with my young friend.

'Look, Peter, this isn't a game. It's not like the pictures. People can get injured ... shot. These are real criminals who won't think twice about hurting anyone. I am not having you anywhere near this caper. You're too young and too vulnerable, and besides you'll probably get in the way. So any notions that you're nurturing about being promoted to my deputy need to be squashed right now. You are a fourteen-year-old schoolboy, not Dick Tracy. Is that understood?'

Peter, who had been staring diligently at the tablecloth during my diatribe, nodded his head sullenly.

'Good. Now we'll go to the pictures this afternoon as promised and then you're to go back to my flat and wait for me there. I hope that's clear.'

Peter continued to stare at the tablecloth, his lower lip protruding in a disconsolate fashion.

'Is that understood?' I repeated, more harshly this time.

'Perfectly,' he muttered.

What I didn't tell Peter was that another reason I wanted him well away from Benny's when the two thugs came calling, was I didn't want him to think that taking the law into your own hands was the right thing to do. As a private detective this was sometimes necessary, but it was always done with reluctance and in the pursuit of fairness and justice. Nevertheless I wasn't about to provide an example for my easily influenced fourteen-year-old companion.

Peter and I did go to the pictures that afternoon. The main feature was *Who Done It?*, a disappointing Abbott and Costello farrago set in a radio station. To be honest my mind was not really on the film, it kept going back to Benny and his dilemma. If the protection racket had moved into this part of London, there must be a pretty big force behind it. I wasn't sure I was up to the job of saving his bacon. However, with Benny being Jewish, that really is that last thing he would want me to do.

I had eventually persuaded Benny that I should be with him in the café when these two thugs came for their money. What would happen then was anyone's guess, but I was going to give it my best shot.

It was dark when we emerged from the cinema and I sent Peter off with some money to buy himself fish and chips and instructed him to go home to Hawke Towers to wait for me. I would ring him if there were any problems.

When I had watched my young companion disappear into the gloom of a December evening in the direction of Tottenham Court Road like the proverbial schoolboy slowly and reluctantly on his way to school, I made my own way back to Benny's café. I arrived at 5.30. There were just a couple of customers now, a soldier and his girl, huddled over their empty tea cups, gazing into each other's eyes, conversation all spent.

I was reminded of Max. The first time I'd thought about her since this morning, my mind having been filled with thoughts of Benny's dilemma. I wondered how she was getting on in Nottingham and when I would hear from her. I hoped her digs were respectable and comfy. In thinking of her now, I suddenly became aware how much I was missing her.

As I took a seat at the back of the café, in the shadows, Benny emerged from the kitchen and gave me a nod of greeting. I could tell from his jerky movements and pale complexion that he was very much on edge. This was far from the relaxed witty Benny I knew. Here was a man with his stomach in knots. And who could blame him?

'I don't think you should be here, Johnny. Let me pay the devils. I'm all for a quiet life.'

'Do that and you'll go on paying until they bleed you dry. We've got to try and sort this out tonight.'

Benny shook his head in despair but made no more protests.

After ten minutes the soldier and his girl departed and Benny turned the sign in the window round to indicate that the café had closed.

'Douse the lights at the back here,' I said. 'I want to be in shadow.'

Benny did as I asked without comment.

And then we waited. The minute hand of the clock crept to the hour of six with infuriating slowness. With every tick and tock, I felt my nerves tightening.

We sat in silence, Benny and I. After all, there really was nothing to say.

At five minutes to six a dark shape appeared at the door, peering through the finely frosted glass. After a few moments, the figure shook the door hard. Benny and I exchanged glances. The man rattled the door again and then his head turned to the window and saw the Closed sign and with some mumbled comment disappeared into the darkness.

Benny gave a sigh of relief. 'I'd better unlock the door,' he said quietly. 'If they can't walk in, they may smash it down.'

I nodded in agreement.

Then we heard in the far distance the chimes of Ben Ben heralding the hour. Before they had faded away, the door burst open with heart-stopping suddenness. Benny's hand flew to his mouth to stifle a gasp and I clenched my fists in anticipation of trouble. There on the threshold stood a tall, gangly figure.

It was Peter.

He stepped into the café, his eyes scanning the room until they lit upon me in the shadows. As he stepped towards me, his hand wriggled momentarily in his raincoat pocket before it finally emerged holding a gun. I recognized it: it was mine. He held the weapon out towards me on the palm of his hand.

'I thought you'd need this,' he said sheepishly.

'You fool. What are you doing here?' I cried angrily.

'I said ... I thought you'd need your gun.'

I snatched it from him and slipped it into my own pocket.

'Now, get out of here, Peter. Go home this instant.'

He turned hesitantly, but it was too late. There in the doorway were two burly men in dark overcoats. They matched the description that Benny had given me: one chubby, well-dressed, young, in his early twenties; the other scruffy and nearer forty. Indeed, they were nasty pieces of work.

They had come for their insurance money.

TWELVE

Earlier that day, as instructed, Archie Muldoon had turned up at Anthony Bernstein's flat ready to start his new job. When Anthony opened the door, Archie stood to attention and gave a mock salute. 'Muldoon, Archibald, reporting for duty, sir!'

'Come in, you pillock,' growled Anthony, tugging at Muldoon's sleeve. Anthony knew Muldoon of old. He had worked for his dad when Anthony was just a teenager. Archie was not the possessor of the brightest intellect but he was reliable and that made him OK in Anthony's book. He led him down the hall to a small untidy kitchen and poured him a mug of tea which he thrust in his hand.

'Get that down you,' he said, not unkindly.

'Ta,' said Archie.

'I gather you know the drill.'

Well, I know what Vic told me. Seems simple enough.'

'Simple? Yeah, it is to Vic – but he's not doing it.' He pulled a sheet of paper from his inside pocket. 'This is the list of premises we're supposed to target.'

Muldoon glanced at the sheet. There were five addresses there. 'Mmm, they're all small concerns by the look of it – all within a mile radius, I should say. Who chose them? Was it you, or Vic?'

Anthony's plump face twisted into a sneer. 'It was her ladyship.'

'Who?'

'Our new lady boss. Gina.'

Muldoon was puzzled. He knew of no Gina. 'Who's she?'

Anthony hesitated a moment. The thought struck him that perhaps he had said too much and then the reckless devil within him whispered, 'What the hell.' After all Archie Muldoon was one of their cohorts and it would be good to voice his anger and frustration. To get his beef off his chest. Certainly his dad and Vic were not prepared to listen to him. They were all for 'biding time', playing a waiting game. He didn't want to wait. 'She is our cousin,' he said. 'She's crawled out of the woodwork after twenty odd years. She is the bitch who thinks she's going to take over the Bernstein family concern'.

Muldoon shook his head and frowned his crumpled frown. 'I don't understand.'

'She's Uncle Michael's daughter. His bloody secret daughter. He hid her away so that she wouldn't get contaminated by the dirty goings on in the Bernstein family. Didn't want the dainty lady to get her fingers soiled with crime and corruption. She's been living in Ireland all this time. Well, now her dad's dead, she's turned up again on our doorstep ready to queen it over us. Ready to take charge. As Michael's daughter she's claiming the bleedin' throne.'

'Blimey! You're not going to let her.'

'Too damn right....'

'Surely Vic isn't happy about this.'

Anthony gave a derisive laugh. 'Vic thinks he's playing it cool – giving Gina her head for a while. If it were up to me, I'd punch her in the face and tell the cow to get lost, but he reckons that could make more trouble for us. So, for the moment, we play along with her. Do as she says like good little boys. It makes me sick.'

'So, all this ... this protection business is her idea?'

Anthony tapped Muldoon lightly on the shoulder. 'I always said you were a bright boy. Yeah, it's our Gina's idea. Now what I've just told you ... forget it, eh? It's in our interest that no one knows about Gina. That way when she disappears no one will be the wiser. No connection. Get it? So ... mum's the word, right?'

'Certainly,' said Muldoon, slurping his tea.

'Right. Have you got your gun?'

Muldoon tapped his breast pocket and nodded.

'Right, drink up, soldier. Let's be about our business. We've got a few shopkeepers to scare the shit out of.'

THIRTEEN

I grabbed hold of Peter's sleeve and, dragging him to one side, I shoved the lad unceremoniously into a chair in the far recess of the room. Out of harm's way – hopefully. He gave a yelp of surprise, but then he was sensible enough to remain silent. The two men moved into the café, slamming the door behind them.

'I see you've got company, grandad,' said one, leaning on the counter. As soon as he spoke, bells rang in my head. I knew that voice, surely. I gazed at those pale-blue, watery, Peter Lorre eyes, the skin that looked like a wrinkled bed sheet and the faint raspberry-coloured ring of acne round his neck and chin. I knew that face as well.

I stood up and moved into the light. 'Bit out of your league, aren't you, Muldoon? Snatching purses is more your thing.' I thought the phrase *modus operandi* might confuse the ugly brute.

The face twitched and his eyes swivelled in my direction, narrowing as they took me in. Then the mouth gaped in surprise, or was it shock? I hoped that it was the latter. 'Hawke. PC bloody Hawke,' he gasped.

'You know this fellow?' asked Benny.

'Indeed, I do. When I was on the force, I pinched him more times than I've had hot dinners. The term 'petty criminal' might have been coined especially for Mr Archibald Muldoon here. Looks like he's moved on from grabbing old ladies' handbags to threatening old gentlemen in their cafés.'

'Less of the old gentleman, if you don't mind,' said Benny indignantly.

'Now, Archie, my boy, if you know what's good for you, I reckon you and your silent partner should turn on your heel and leave Mr Samuels alone.'

'Oh, do you now. Well, you've got another think comin',' growled Muldoon and his hand reached inside his overcoat pocket, but I was too quick for him. I had my gun trained on him before he could drag his out.

'You've made a mistake coming here,' I said, with what I hoped was quiet menace in my voice. 'A big mistake. Accept the fact and walk away undamaged. You're bound to have one or two failures in your line of work. Mark this down as one of them. I'm sure you can come up with a suitable excuse for your masters. If you try to get tough, I'll shoot you. Simple as that.'

That shook the cowardly Muldoon. And coward he was. He had as much backbone as a flounder. In the past when he was nabbed he spilled out a confession at the mere shake of a truncheon. It flowed from him like a gushing fountain.

I held my gun higher, aiming at his spotty mush. 'Go on, get out. And there must be no repercussions. You get out now and never return, or I'll make sure that you suffer personally. You know that I can find you as easy as pie if I want to. You know I can, Archie Muldoon.'

Muldoon's partner leaned forward. 'We're not about to leave it.' His bombastic stance was false. I could tell that he too was unpleasantly surprised by encountering some serious opposition.

'We have to,' croaked Muldoon, severely rattled by my threat. 'I'll sort it. Vic and Gina need never know.'

'Shut your mouth, you stupid bastard,' cried his companion, his face flushed with anger. Not only was he angry, but nervous as well. I noticed a trickle of sweat emerge from his sideburn and roll gently down his flushed cheek. Not a tough guy either, then.

'I think it's time you were on your way,' I said, still maintaining the quiet edginess in my voice, but thrusting my gun a little closer to Muldoon.

'Come on,' said Muldoon, moving backwards towards the door and pushing his companion in the same direction.

'Goodbye, gentlemen,' I said.

'Watch your back, Hawke,' was Muldoon's parting shot of sneering bravado as he slipped out into the night.

After the two thugs had gone there was a moment's silence and the three of us remained like exhibits in a wax museum. Then Peter broke the spell by rushing forward and slapping me on my back.

'Johnny, you were brilliant. Absolutely brilliant.'

'You got any whisky on the premises, Benny? I could really do with a drink,' I said, sinking into a chair.

'For you, Johnny, anything. I can only echo Peter's words: you were brilliant.' He disappeared into the kitchen in search of the booze.

To be honest, I felt more drained and tense rather than brilliant, but my pale imitation of Humphrey Bogart in *The Big Sleep* seemed to have worked.

'I thought you really were going to shoot him,' grinned Peter, with naïve enthusiasm. I was very sorry that he had to be there to witness what was a big sham. No way would I have shot Muldoon. That would have got me into a whole load of trouble with both the goodies and the baddies. I didn't want the boy growing up thinking that a man with a gun was brave and heroic, but in this instance my mock tough-guy act had worked.

Benny returned from the kitchen clutching a bottle of Johnnie Walker and some glasses. He poured me a large measure, which I downed quickly, and served smaller measures to himself and Peter.

'It is all right if the boy has a little nip, isn't it, Johnny?'

I nodded. In for a penny … I suppose.

Peter grinned. Long trousers, gun play and whisky all in one day. My, I thought, he must be feeling *really* grown up now.

'So you knew that ruffian with the gun, eh?'

'Yes. He's been in trouble with the law since he was a kid. He's not terribly bright and was always getting caught. It's clear this protection racket is not his idea. As I said, he and the other fellow must be just worker ants for some gang.'

'That Muldoon character mentioned someone called Vic. Perhaps he's the boss,' said Peter.

'Yes, I clocked that.'

'Anyway, the main thing is you got rid of the pests,' grinned Benny.

I nodded. 'Yes, I don't think you'll be bothered again; but that doesn't protect the other poor devils on their list. It's obvious that you're not the only place they've targeted for their dirty little scheme.'

With this sobering thought, we all drank up and then Peter and I wended our way back to my place.

The telephone was ringing fit to bust when we got back. It was Max. Diplomatically, Peter made himself scarce while Max and I indulged in a rather soppy exchange. She had made contact with the folk at the theatre and was ensconced in her digs – her home for the next three weeks – and she was excited at the prospect of working on the show, helping to design and make the costumes for both the principals and chorus. However, she admitted that she was feeling rather lonely and missing me. I told her about Peter's new trousers which amused her greatly but edited out the incident at Benny's. We chatted some more and then finally blew kisses down the phone, said our 'I love yous' and wished each other a good night.

Replacing the receiver, I felt a strange mixture of sadness and pleasure. I was missing Max like mad, even though she'd only been gone a day, but it was good to know I had someone like her in my life, someone who cared for me.

I wandered from my office into the little sitting room. Peter had already put the kettle on and set up the draught board for our weekly 'tournament'.

'I am determined to beat you this week,' he grinned.

'We'll see about that,' I said, pulling up a chair. 'Just because you've got long trousers doesn't make you a keener player.'

And so the tough, cold-hearted, gun-toting one-eyed private detective sat down to play a game of draughts with a fourteen-year-old boy.

Sunday morning and we had a lie-in; Peter in the cramped campbed in my living room and me in my cramped single bed in the cramped bedroom. We breakfasted on toast and coffee.

'You know, I reckon I'll be needing to shave soon,' said Peter, while crunching on a crust and rubbing his chin at the same time.

'One thing at a time,' I smirked. 'Get used to the new pants first.'

I was relieved that the lad was wrapped up in thoughts of his new-found maturity and not dwelling on the incident in Benny's café. However, it was very much in the forefront of my mind.

While Peter washed up, I rang my old friend David Llewellyn for a chat.

'Got to be quick,' he said rather breathlessly down the phone, 'I'm on Yorkshire pudding duty this morning and the batter needs my full attention.'

As quickly as I could I told him what had happened at Benny's café the day before.

'That's very interesting,' he said. 'This protection business is new. It's very Yankee. You say someone called Vic was mentioned.'

'Yes, and a woman called Gina.'

'Don't know about her – but I do know a Vic Bernstein. He's a canny sod. He's usually been involved with illegal hooch and crooked gambling – his family run the Bamboo House in Covent Garden. Maybe he's stretching his wings a little – trying out the protection racket. What did the other chap look like, the one with Muldoon?'

'Young – early twenties. Chubby, arrogant features.'

'Red-faced with slightly bulging eyes?'

'Sounds like the fellow,' I said.

'Well that would be Anthony Bernstein, Vic's younger brother. They're the Tweedle Dum and Tweedle Dee of the black-market booze trade.'

'That's a fairly soft option in this naughty world. They're really stepping out with this protection lark.'

'It's all very interesting. I wonder where this Gina woman fits in.'

'So do I. Listen, David, allow me to follow this up myself for a couple of days, will you? With them threatening Benny, they've stepped into my domain. I'd like to have a crack at sorting things out.'

'Ah, ah, this is police business—'

'Only because I told you about it,' I insisted. 'I think I can get to the heart of the matter much quicker than you official bods.'

David chuckled. 'I've never been called an official bod before. Is that rude?'

'As a favour …' I wheedled.

'Oh, very well. I haven't got time to argue. I've got to go now and see to my Yorkshires. But, for God's sake, don't do anything rash. Let's meet up for a pint at the Guardsman on Tuesday lunchtime and you can report any progress.'

'It's a date. I'll wear a carnation in my buttonhole so you'll recognize me.'

The rest of Sunday raced by. I hate Sundays. They are grey, soulless days when the world shuts down. The streets are empty, the shops are abandoned and a strange muffled silence wraps itself around the city. It is as though some great spaceship has hovered over London and sucked most of the people and traffic up into it – only to release them on Monday morning.

Peter and I had a kick about in the park, but it was a more genteel affair than usual as the lad didn't want to spoil his new trousers by getting them muddied up. Then we had lunch with Martha and Edith, the two spinster ladies he lived with during the week and who looked after him as though he was their own. I instructed Peter, on pain of death, not to mention a word about the incident in Benny's café. I didn't want to worry the old dears, or have them thinking that I was irresponsibly exposing their charge to danger.

The sisters always made a fuss of me when I came for Sunday lunch. I'm not sure how they coped on their rations, but somehow they always managed to get me a piece of meat. It was a very simple and civilized occasion, the sort that I'd never known as a youngster in the orphanage. We drank sherry before the meal and toasted the King and said grace at the table. It was good to be in such a civilized atmosphere of caring, affection and normality – or as much normality as the war could afford.

I left as it was growing dark and walked home, calling in one of the pubs *en route* for a half pint of beer and a cigarette while I juggled with my thoughts concerning the Garner case. Tomorrow I needed to visit Madame Rene again in the hope that I'd finally meet up with Sylvia Moore. However, in truth, I was keen to follow up on this protection-racket business and reckoned that a private tête-à-tête with Archie Muldoon would clear things up nicely. But that would have to wait.

FOURTEEN

Monday morning loomed, grey, damp and unforgiving. She lay on her back staring at the ceiling for a long time. She hadn't slept much. The pain, fear and misery had all contributed to her wakefulness. She had survived another terrible weekend. Just. But one of these days … she might not. He might just go too far.

She shuddered under the covers with misery. At least he had gone. The beast had departed. Again she asked herself, as she had done countless times in the last few months, 'How on earth did I get myself into this position?' There was no sensible, no rational, no reasonable answer. It was like she had stepped into quicksand without noticing it and was now sinking slowly but inexorably to the bottom.

Oh, yes, he had gone.

But she knew that he would be back.

With some difficulty, she dragged herself from the cold bed and, pulling back the curtains a few inches, she examined her face in the dressing-room mirror. It was a mess. She looked as though she had done a few rounds with Gene Tunney. Gingerly she ran her fingers over the contours of her puffy, darkened flesh and the cut lip. Once she had been pretty, but now she reckoned she looked like a ghoul from a horror film. At this thought she began to cry. Softly and slowly the tears flowed. Her chest heaved gently as she tried to rein in her emotions, but they were too strong for her, so she relented. It was almost a pleasure to let out some of the anguish.

It wasn't just the physical pain and the facial scars that hurt, it was what he had done to her self-esteem and her spirit. At first he had seemed charming – so considerate to her every wish. But those smiles and courteous gestures disguised the demon that he was. As soon as she had given herself to him, he had changed. The mask was ripped away to reveal the neurotic bully beneath. But then it was too late. He had wormed his way into her life and become part of the fabric of her existence. She knew now that it was planned and carefully plotted.

Once there he had slowly but inexorably picked away at her confidence and self-esteem: a sneer here, an accusation there and an increasing barrage of criticisms. Then there were the bouts of jealousy interspersed with the intervals of smooth charm and remorse. The mental torture was more cruel than the blows. Once she had been a confident, happy woman. Once ... before she had met him.

Now she was trapped.

Tears were her only comfort. In a way, she felt it was a kind of luxury to give vent to her feelings; to wail and moan. She was able to do so unchecked, without any kind of restraint. With an agonized sob she dropped her head into her arms on the dressing-table top, her body shaking gently.

An hour later, she had dressed and tidied up her face as much as she was able. A cigarette and a cup of hot tea had not only helped to calm her down, but filled her with resolve. As she sat at the small kitchen table, she relived the incidents of the previous night. The brutish irrational behaviour, the demands, the jealousies, the blows. Above all, the blows. She flinched at the thought of them. The crazy devil could have killed her. Killed her.

Killed her.

She clutched the edge of the table as tightly as she could, deep, hot anger welling up inside her.

'He could have killed me,' she told herself, out loud this time, in a dry, hoarse voice, the first time she had spoken that morning. She repeated the thought as dark, fierce hatred flared in her heart 'He could have killed me. And maybe next time he will.'

It had been a very ordinary Monday morning until she arrived. He was surprised to see her. She looked a little strange and was behaving oddly.

'What do you want?' he snapped. It was the second time of asking. He would not be afforded a third opportunity, for then the unexpected happened.

The knife flashed briefly in the dim light before beginning its rapid downward descent. However at first the blow seemed to him to be unreal, cutting through the air as if in slow motion. Unable to move from the shock, he let out a gruff yell as the blade scraped his face before entering his chest. The sudden searing pain caused his whole frame to contort as though reacting to a violent electric shock. As he staggered backwards, his legs almost giving way, he saw the knife, now red with his own blood, raised against him once more. This time he made a clumsy effort to avoid the blow but failed. Again searing pain racked his body. His arms flailed wildly as his vision began to blur and he fell to the floor. The third stab caught him in the neck and now he knew he was going to die.

As he lay twitching involuntarily on the ground, his attacker knelt over him and continued to rain blows down upon him, but he was no longer conscious of them. The darkness of death had spread its pall upon his damaged and blood-sodden corpse.

FIFTEEN

'She's gone.' Madame Rene's eyes fluttered nervously. 'She called in the salon this morning. Picked up some of her belongings and said she wouldn't be back. She gave no explanation. It is most inconvenient.'

My heart sank. Inconvenient was not the word. It would seem that Sylvia Moore had slipped through my fingers again – and with her the undead Beryl Garner.

'She gave you no indication where she was going?' I asked, knowing the answer already.

Madame Rene shook her head but averted her eyes from my gaze.

'You didn't say anything to her about my enquiries, did you? That I'd be calling in to see her today?'

'I …' Madame Rene stopped, apparently lost for words. But she didn't have to say any more. Her furtive eyes told me all I needed to know. The stupid woman had blabbed about a man with an eye patch calling to see her about an inheritance. I could hear her silly voice in my head gurgling away, 'How wonderful, dear. A windfall. What a lucky girl. The rather shabby fellow with the one eye will be round today to tell you all about it.' With her gossip, Madame Rene had lit the blue touch paper and as a result Sylvia Moore had retired.

Angry though I was at this loose-tongued woman, I contained myself. It was pointless flying off the handle at her indiscretions. That would get me nowhere. The damage was done. And serious damage, too. I no longer had any lead as to where this Sylvia

Moore would be and she had been alerted to cover her tracks. Not only had she left her flat but also her place of employment.

And now she had vanished without trace.

With a curt good day and a perfunctory raise of my hat, I left Madame Rene's establishment, more in sorrow than in anger.

'What to do now? I asked myself.

After some moments pondering while I mooched along the pavement on my way to the Kensington High Street tube station, I answered my own question. I needed to go back to my client and question him again to see if I could extract any further information from him that might give me a glimmer of a clue where I could start looking for Sylvia or his wife.

I made my way to Harper Street, a small thoroughfare just off Russell Square which houses a whole stretch of small shops including a barber, a newsagent, a greengrocer, an ironmonger and, at the far end, Brian Garner's electrical shop. It was there that I was in for my second unpleasant surprise of the day. As I approached the little shop, I observed a police car parked outside and a constable standing guard by the door. A group of half-a-dozen onlookers had congregated near the shop frontage, shifting their feet and muttering like the supernumeraries in a film crowd scene.

I approached the constable, but before I could say a word, he held up his hand as though directing traffic. 'I'm afraid you can't go in there, sir,' he announced sternly in what he perceived as an authoritarian manner.

'What's happened?' I asked, opening my wallet and extracting my detective licence.

'There's been … an incident, sir.'

I showed him my licence. 'Mr Garner is my client,' I said.

'*Was* your client. I'm afraid the gentleman is dead.'

'Dead.'

Now there was a real turn up for the book.

'Murdered. Stabbed something shocking,' said the constable, leaning forward and lowering his voice so that the small group of onlookers could not hear. 'Inspector Eustace is in there now taking stock of the situation.'

It is strange at times like these when the mind goes into shock at such unexpected news and yet it still allows one to continue to behave normally. On the surface, the pool is placid, but beneath the surface the undercurrents are ferocious. It certainly was the case on this occasion. While the bottom seemed to be falling out of this particular investigation – well, things can't get worse than losing your client – to the outside world I behaved with calm equanimity.

'You'd better let me have a word with the inspector. I may have information useful to him in his investigation.'

The constable's face clouded with consternation. 'I'm not sure …' he began.

'I am a detective, after all,' I added, flashing my licence again.

'Very well,' he said with some reluctance, stepping aside, and allowing me to enter.

The shop was dingy inside, crammed with cardboard boxes and an array of radios and a couple of radiograms. There were three people in the cramped service area. Two men and an elderly lady. On the floor by the counter lay a body covered by a grey sheet. Escaping from the folds was a blood-spattered hand curled in a gruesome fashion like a scarlet claw.

'Who the devil are you?' asked the older man.

'Inspector Eustace?' I said quickly. 'I am John Hawke, a private investigator. Brian Garner was a client of mine.'

'A client. Was he now? What did he want a private 'tec for?'

I kept it simple. I was the one who needed to find things out. The inspector would have to cope with slender rations. 'He'd asked me to find his wife.'

'She'd gone AWOL, eh?'

'Something like that. What happened?' I nodded at the sheeted body.

'Somebody stabbed the poor blighter to death. Rather savagely, too. Certainly a crime of passion. This lady here, Miss Peacock,' – he turned to the white-faced woman sitting nervously on the chair, almost in the foetal position, dabbing her eyes with a lace hand-kerchief – 'she found the body when she came in to see if her radio had been repaired.'

Miss Peacock shuddered. 'It was terrible. Such a shock. Do you think I can go now, Inspector? I'm feeling a little faint.'

'Of course. The sergeant here will see you home and take a statement.'

The youthful sergeant helped the old lady to her feet and escorted her from the premises.

'Brave old girl. Had the presence of mind to ring for the police and wait here until we arrived,' Eustace observed almost to himself, before turning his attention to me. 'Now then, Mr … Hawke, was it?' said Inspector Eustace when we were alone.

I nodded.

'Well, Mr Hawke, what can you tell me? Who done it?'

I gave him a thin smile. 'I've no idea. I knew little about the man save he wanted me to find his wife.'

'Ran off with another bloke, did she?'

'Yes. But that was two years ago.'

'Was it now? Took his time deciding he wanted her found.'

I wasn't keen to go further into the complications of the case, so in order to divert the inspector's attention, I pulled back the sheet. It was a horrible sight indeed. The murderer had not simply wanted to kill this man; they had wanted to damage his body into the bargain. There were numerous knife wounds to the chest and neck area. His face, frozen in horror no doubt at the moment of the first stab wound, was smeared with a fine crust of dried blood.

'A lot of hatred in the attack,' I said, pulling the sheet forward and covering the body again.

'Indeed,' said the inspector thoughtfully. 'It's very much a personal murder. It must have been someone he knew. Someone with a hell of a grudge. There's no sign of robbery. The till was full of cash. You don't think it could be this errant wife of his, do you?'

'It's possible, I suppose.'

'And have you found her yet?'

I shook my head. 'I'm afraid I've drawn a blank. I've had very little to go on.'

'You'd better give me what information you can, Mr Hawke and your own contact details.' He took out his notebook and held his pen poised for my statement.

'Sure,' I said easily, already arranging in my mind what facts I was prepared to release. I told him the circumstances of her

supposed death and how Garner had seen her recently on a plat-
form at South Kensington tube station. I also let him know that she
once worked as a hairdresser in Camden High Street. Poor old
Harold Crabtree, he'd get all a' fluster again receiving a visit from
the police. I thought that was enough for the old professional to go
on. He had as much information as I had when I started out. He
took down what I told him in a neat feminine handwriting.

When I'd finished he said, 'So you've had no luck in finding this
woman then?'

I shook my head. 'Needle in a haystack,' I said miserably.

Inspector Eustace sighed, snapped shut his notebook and slipped
it into his raincoat pocket. 'Well, if you think of anything else, get
in touch.'

I nodded and headed for the door. I turned and gazed at the
sheeted corpse one last time.

Once out on the street, I asked one of the crowd of ghoulish
onlookers where Macklin Gardens was. I got full and detailed
directions. It was told it was but a ten-minute walk away and that
turned out to be the case.

Macklin Gardens was a neat little street, not too far away close
to Kings Cross Station, pleasant enough but anonymous. I sought
out number seven. It was a narrow three-storeyed terraced property probably built sometime in the nineteenth century. It was the
late Brian Garner's house. Making sure I was unobserved, I
performed my magic trick with my trusty strip of stiff wire and let
myself in.

I had to be quick because I reckoned it wouldn't be very long
before Inspector Eustace and friends would descend on the property looking for clues. I needed to be out of there before that
happened.

Brian Garner had been a very tidy fellow indeed. There were no
items left about on surfaces, no letters, bills, items of clothing, and
no pots on the draining board, nothing that was of any use to me.
Until, that is, I went into his bedroom. The bed was unmade and
the dressing table appeared to be a shrine to his supposedly dead
wife. There were several pictures of her stuck to the mirror, one was
like the snap he had given to me. On the glass-topped surface there

were several necklaces and various tubes of lipsticks, along with a hairbrush which still had a few fair hairs caught in the bristles. It was like a miniature *Marie Celeste*. It was as though the woman had just stepped from the room. It was quite creepy. Obviously Brian Garner had never got over the loss of his wife. Opening the drawers I discovered other items belonging to Beryl Garner: jumpers, gloves, underclothes, scarves and lace handkerchiefs. Obviously, when she left him she had taken very little of her old life with her, as though she was intent on wiping that part of her history from her mind.

In the bottom drawer was an old shoebox containing pictures and letters. I took it over to the bed and tipped out the contents. I sifted through the photographs first. They were mainly of Beryl, some taken with Brian on their wedding day. They looked a pretty ordinary happy bride and groom, but in all the pictures Beryl's smile always seemed a little unnatural and tinged with a strange sadness. Then I came upon a fragment of a photograph, a portrait of Beryl showing only the lower half of the face. I searched through the box and eventually found the other half and pieced them together. It was a haunting photograph. The eyes were hollow and frightened and the mouth was turned down in misery. She looked as though she had been crying, but what was most disturbing were the visible bruises to her face, dark, livid and fresh. Obviously the poor woman had been beaten up. Who would want to take a picture of her in that state? The answer to that question was unpalatable.

I shuddered with unease as I gazed at this grim picture. I put it to one side and continued my search. I now turned my attention to the letters. A few were from Brian on headed hotel notepaper, one from Birmingham and one from Leeds. He had obviously been visiting these cities on business. They were innocuous, mundane and passionless missives. What was of more interest were two letters from Beryl's mother.

Brian had told me that Beryl did not get on with her mother and that they were estranged. This correspondence told a different story. They were full of warm sentiments and loving phrases. In the most recent letter, one short paragraph stood out: *I hope that husband of yours is treating you better. You know you'll always have a place with me if life becomes unbearable.*

'Unbearable' was quite a dramatic word. What would make her life 'unbearable'? I glanced again at the torn photograph and Beryl's bruised features. That seemed to provide the answer.

I was getting a completely different picture of the domestic life of my late client, the apparently mild-mannered Brian Garner.

I slipped the letters, which boasted an address in Oxford, along with the torn photograph into my pocket and then returned the shoebox to the bottom drawer of the dressing table. Leaving things as neatly as possible, I went downstairs and had a final look in the spick and span sitting room. There was another picture of Beryl on the sideboard, a studio portrait in a silver frame. As I was about to leave, something drew my eyes back to this picture. I went over to the sideboard to examine it closely. Then I realized that the woman in the photograph *wasn't* Beryl. It was someone who looked very much like her, but it wasn't her. There were subtle differences in the features, but certainly this mystery woman had a striking resemblance to the late Mrs Garner. It could almost have been her younger sister. I flipped open the back of the frame and withdrew the photograph. As I slipped it into my coat I was pleased to observe that stamped on the back was the name of the photographic studio where it had been taken.

I made a quick exit. Just in time, for I had only just reached the end of the street when I saw a police car approaching. I hid behind a tree while it sped by but I caught a glimpse of the grim features of Inspector Eustace in the front passenger seat. They were obviously on their way to Garner's house. As soon as they had passed, I legged it back to the tube station.

I had a late lunch at Benny's. He was in a chirpy mood, relieved that the protection business seemed to have been resolved without further damage or stress. He even gave me extra custard on the apple pie with the cheery announcement, 'On the house today, Johnny.'

He *was* in a good mood.

I now knew that my next move in the Garner case was to visit Oxford. I would go there tomorrow after I had carried out a certain early-morning errand. It was a murder investigation now and nearly everything pointed to Beryl as the killer of her husband. She had rid herself of him once, two years ago, but now that he had discovered she was still alive, she realized that she was not safe any more. He had become a real threat again. I thought of the bruises and of the savage blows that must have caused them. The only way she could be sure that she remained safe and free of him was to kill him. Certainly, that was the scenario suggested by the facts as I saw them. But somehow I wasn't fully convinced. Something niggled at the back of my brain telling me there was more to this business than met my solitary eye.

That night I treated myself to some jazz-induced therapy. I took myself along to my favourite dive, the Velvet Cage, the dark smoky club in Greek Street, where the warm, sepulchral atmosphere wraps itself around you like a protective blanket, helping you to forget the miseries of war and the ragged and damaged panorama of London. I had been a habitué of this bolthole since 1939. The booze and the music helped to soften the rough edges of life.

I grabbed a ringside seat to listen to Tommy Parker and his boys improvise their way through a set of standards. On this occasion the group was supplemented by a Negro trumpet player who squeezed the melodies out of his horn with smooth precision. The fusion of alcohol and syncopation relaxed me and I even found myself smiling.

Inevitably when I slip into this kind of mood, my mind begins to wander and I began to think about things in an unstructured and inventive way. While the group were making their way through a soulful version of 'It Had to Be You', I thought about Brian Garner, violent, manipulative and deceitful Brian Garner. The image came to my mind of his bloody corpse punctured with innumerable stab wounds. Whoever had killed him had wanted to damage him also. A clean blow to the back of the head would not have sufficed for this murderer. Those vicious wounds were cathartic, affording some kind of release. There was real, violent hatred involved – and, I reckoned, a disturbed mind.

I've often thought that detectives would make good novel writers because we too have to construct stories, possible scenarios from a set of basic facts that we have accumulated. We have to create motives, opportunities, possibilities on the slightest of clues. Indeed, actually identifying what is a clue is an art in itself. Miss a significant one at your peril. It is then by applying our imagination to these suggestive scraps that we often reach the truth.

As I sifted through all the small pieces of evidence I had at my disposal regarding the Garner murder, I began to build a plot around them. One had to hope that my fictions were in essence realities.

As the group finished their number, prompting a ripple of applause, I felt fairly certain that I knew who had killed Brian Garner and why. If my theory was right, I should be able to close that case quite soon. Of course, it was a big if. How does that canine cliché go? I could be barking up the wrong tree. However, my instincts told me otherwise.

By now the group were well into an upbeat version of 'S'wonderful' at a tempo that reflected my mood to some extent. I decided for the moment to put all thoughts of work aside and give myself over to the music and one more glass of Johnnie Walker before heading home.

On arriving at Hawke Towers just before midnight, I dialled the Nottingham number Max had given me for her digs. After a long while the phone was answered by a grumpy-sounding woman.

'Who is it?' she barked without ceremony.

'My name is John Hawke. I'd like to speak to Maxine Summers, one of the guests at Hallas Lodge.'

'Would you?' came the curt reply. 'Have you any idea what time it is?'

'I'm sorry if it's rather late.'

'Late. It's bloody midnight.'

'I'm sorry – but it is rather urgent.'

There was a long pause filled with a series of irritated sighs. These were followed by a sharp, 'Wait a minute.'

I waited nearly five minutes before another voice spoke to me. It was Max.

'Hello,' she said tentatively.

'Hello, Max. It's Johnny.'

'Oh, Johnny, how wonderful,' she said, her voice brightening immediately.

'I hope I didn't get you into trouble by ringing so late.'

'Sort of. There is only one telephone here and it's right outside Mrs Miller's room. She's the owner. I think you got her out of bed.'

'Oops.'

'We're not encouraged to arrange for incoming calls. I didn't know that when I gave you the number.'

'Oops again.'

'She told me it was urgent. Is everything all right?'

I bit my lip with chagrin. 'Yes, things are fine. Actually, I just wanted to hear your voice and wish you good night.'

Max giggled. 'Oh, Johnny, you old romantic. That's lovely. I think you are a little drunk.'

'Just a touch, maybe. I've indulged in a little *soupçon* of comfort drinking. How are things going on up there in Nottingham?'

'Oh, very well. They're a nice set of people and have made me very welcome.'

'Not too welcome, I hope. I want you coming back to London.'

'Don't you worry, I can't wait.'

'Sweet dreams, then, my sweet. I'd better get off the line before I land you in more bother with that lady dragon.'

Max giggled again. 'Sweet dreams to you also, Johnny. I love you.'

'I love you, too,' I said, without an ounce of self-consciousness and slowly replaced the receiver.

I went to bed with a beatific smile on my silly face and was soon deep in a dreamless sleep. I woke up as dawn was feeling its way around the edges of my black-out curtain. I sat up and reached for the cigarette packet by the side of the bed. A quick drag, I thought, then I'd better get some kip. I had rather a busy and I hoped a fruitful day ahead.

SIXTEEN

I shaved and had a strip wash in my little kitchen area and made myself tea but no toast – the bread bin was bare. By eight o'clock I was ready to do battle with the day. They do say that the early bird catches the worm; I just hoped I was early enough to catch the particularly unpleasant worm I was after.

Crimea Buildings is a rundown, unhealthy, unwholesome tenement block in Shoreditch. If ever there was a suitable target for the Luftwaffe, Crimea Buildings was it. It would be a compliment to describe it as a slum but it hadn't risen to that level of excellence. As I approached it, along a cobbled street full of litter, broken bottles and dog excrement, the brittle winter daylight illuminated the decaying edifice in a sickly yellow hue, exposing the exterior signs of squalor and neglect. I knew this hell's kitchen well when I was a copper on the beat before the war. It housed a whole range of petty criminals, prostitutes, drunkards and drug addicts. The cream of the scum. They swarmed to Crimea House like flies to a dung heap.

On reaching the narrow entrance leading to the stairs which would take me up to the higher landings, I felt like clamping my handkerchief to my mouth so tangible was the odour of corruption and despair. I passed a group of scruffy children playing with a dead cat. They had pale, gaunt, haunted faces, old before their time and stick-thin, ill-nourished bodies. As I walked by, they gave me a casual glance. One of them called out, 'Give us a copper, mister.'

I dug into my pocket and tossed them a threepenny bit. They fell on it like ravenous carrion crows. One lad, no older than seven I would say, managed to secure it for himself and he held it aloft with a cry of triumph. He gazed at me with weirdly malevolent eyes set in a skull-like face. 'Thanks, mister,' he croaked. 'Now you can bugger off.'

The other brats fell about in a fit of hysterics.

It struck me that Peter could so easily have ended up like one of these feral scraps of humanity. Running away from a mother who ill-treated him, he had been adrift on the streets when I encountered him, but even when he was scruffy and starving there had been a kind of rough nobility about him. And there still was.

I made my way up to the top landing and passed down the walkway. Here again rubbish littered my path, along with the occasional line of washing strung across, hindering one's passage. The clothes were grey, cheap and threadbare.

I approached one doorway where an old man was seated on an ancient wooden stool, smoking a pipe. He viewed me beneath hooded lids with suspicion. As I walked by, he spat vehemently on to the ground. I was aware that shabbily dressed as I was in my old overcoat, to him I still looked like a member of the establishment, an inhabitant of the real and comparatively lawful and prosperous world and as such someone to be despised and wary of.

Eventually, I reached my destination: 333 Crimea Buildings. I knocked.

There was no response. So I knocked again, even louder. This attempt prompted a raucous cry from within. 'Don't bang the bleedin' door down. Hang on, yer bastard.' It was a woman's voice.

I did as I was requested and refrained from banging 'the bleedin' door down'.

About a minute later, it was wrenched open and a plumpish woman somewhere in her mid-thirties appeared before me. She was wrapped in a grubby pink candlewick dressing gown; her face was smeared with last night's make-up and her peroxide blonde hair was standing on end as though, cartoon-like, she had just thrust her fingers into the electric socket and this was the result.

She squinted at me with two mascara smudged eyes. 'Who the hell are you?'

It was the kind of greeting one had to expect in Crimea Buildings.

'A friend of Archie's,' I said.

'He ain't got no friends.'

I didn't know if she was joking or not, but she wasn't smiling. She also began to close the door on me.

I put my arm forward and held it open. She gave me a look that could curdle milk, but I stepped forward causing this blonde charmer to retreat into the entrance area. 'Get him,' I said, sharply. 'Or would you like a slap round that fat face of yours?' This wasn't gentlemanly I admit, but it was the language and attitude she would understand and respond to.

Her eyes flickered with fear momentarily but she quickly rallied and stood her ground. 'You touch me and I'll scratch your other eye out.'

I wasn't about to bandy threats with her so I slipped my revolver out of my pocket and aimed it at her face. 'I'd like to see you try.'

That did the trick. Her bravado vanished. She stepped back from me with a sob, her mouth wide with fear.

'Who the bleedin' hell are you? What do you want?' Her tone was now appealing rather than aggressive.

'I told you. I'm a friend of Archie's. Now fetch him!'

She didn't have to bother. The man in question lumbered out of the room at the end of the corridor. He was dressed in his vest and underpants and had a cigarette in his mouth. He moved like a man suffering from the severe constraints of a very bad hangover. I slipped the gun back in my pocket.

'What's all this fuckin' noise?' he growled, shambling towards us.

'Good morning, Archie. How are you this fine winter's day?' I said smoothly.

He noticed me for the first time and his face radiated surprise. As his mouth gaped, I thought for a moment that he was going to lose the cigarette, but it was a thin roll up and it stuck to his lower lip.

'What are you doin' here?' he asked.

'I've come to have a little chat with you.'

'What about?'

I glanced at the woman. 'In private.'

'You can fuck off,' he said, the old empty arrogance reasserting itself.

'He's got a shooter, Archie.'

'She's right, Archie.' I patted my overcoat pocket. 'Want to see?'

Now Archie was lost for words and this time the cigarette did fall from his mouth and tumbled slowly down his vest before landing on the uncarpeted concrete floor.

'Perhaps we should go into your living room while the lady here makes us a brew, eh? I presume you have got a living room?'

'OK,' he replied reluctantly, realizing that he had no other option.

'Milk, no sugar for me,' I told the blonde before following Archie through into the squalid tip which I had referred to as the living room. The first thing to hit me was the smell, a strange potent mix of sweat, mustiness and a pungent unidentifiable rancid odour which attacked my nostrils, making me want to gag. There wasn't a clear space to be seen: clothes, old newspapers, plates with bits of food on them, empty beer bottles littered the place. I sat gingerly on the arm of a decrepit armchair, not wanting to contaminate myself by actually sitting in it. Muldoon scooped up some pages of *The Sporting Life* and a few items of women's clothing and, avoiding a naked spring poking through the faded moquette made a space for himself on the sofa. He looked very vulnerable sitting there in his greying underwear.

'What's this all about?' he said, sitting forward, his ungainly hands dangling between his knees. 'I told you I ain't going to bother your little Jewish friend no more.'

I nodded. 'That's very kind of you, Archie. But there's going to be a quite a few other helpless souls who won't be so lucky. It's not a nice business you're in.'

'A bloke's got to make a living.'

This plaintive response was almost comic. It was uttered with such genuine seriousness. He saw nothing wrong in threatening folk into parting with their legitimately hard-earned cash in order to line his own pockets and those of his masters. It seemed that he'd lived a corrupt life for so long that he had lost the ability to judge what was right or wrong any more.

I decided to cut to the chase.

'Now, Archie, we both know you aren't bright enough to organize this little business yourself. You're just a hireling. I just want to know who does the hiring.'

'What do you mean I'm not smart enough?' he muttered petulantly, his lower lip drooping with dismay.

'Who's in charge? Who's the boss?'

'Get lost.'

'Oh, my friend, you are walking on very thin ice.' I slipped my gun out of my pocket and rested it on my knee. 'I advise you to co-operate or else I might be forced to use this. A trip to the morgue can easily be arranged. No one is going to miss a low life like you and I've enough friends in the force to cover up the matter for me. You catch my drift?'

Muldoon stared at the gun. He seemed genuinely frightened.

'So talk.'

He ran his hand down his pale, tired face before he spoke. 'It's Vic Bernstein. It's his little caper,' he said quietly, so quietly it was as though he hoped he wouldn't be heard. He paused again praying that this titbit of information would suffice. He could see from my expression that this was not the case.

'And you were working with his brother, right?'

He nodded.

'And who is this Gina that you mentioned? I got the impression that Anthony wasn't too happy with you for mentioning her name.'

'Gina?' He pretended he didn't know what I was talking about. I pointed the gun at his groin. 'Gina,' I said.

'OK, OK,' he gulped. 'I don't know her. Never seen her. I ain't been introduced. But she's in cahoots with Vic and she's a tough tart. They're running the operation for old man Bernstein.'

'Leo.'

'Yeah. He seems to be taking a back seat on this one. I reckon this girl is the brains behind it. I reckon Vic always checks with her before decisions are made.'

'And who is she? Where does she come from?'

'Ain't I told you enough?' There was a kind of desperation in his voice now that told me I getting close to something interesting and he started to squirm a little on the sofa. It wasn't a pretty sight.

'Not yet.' I lowered my gun and aimed it at Archie's crotch. 'Who is she?'

Archie eyes widened with fear. 'She's Michael's daughter,' he said in a rush.

'Michael Bernstein, Leo's brother?'

'Yeah, Vic and Anthony's secret cousin. She's a Bernstein. The boys knew nothing about her until a few weeks ago. No one did 'cept Leo. Apparently when she was born, Michael squirrelled her away, out of the country – Ireland – so she'd be away from ... the business.'

'The business?'

'The dodgy stuff, y'know.'

I knew.

'You mean Michael didn't want his little princess to get herself contaminated by their criminal activities?'

'Something like that.'

I smiled. I couldn't help it. There was something absurdly naïve about the idea that Michael Bernstein hid his daughter away so that her feminine sensibilities would not be infected by the family's unlawful shenanigans, as though immorality was contagious.

'And now she's back.'

'With a vengeance. Vic says she's trying to take over the firm.'

My smile broadened. So she hadn't been spared. The taint was in her soul. The Bernstein genes had won through in the end. Apparently taking a rotten apple from a barrel of rotten apples will not cure it.

'As I say, I've not met her,' continued Muldoon now warming to his task, 'but I reckon she's a real tough bitch. She's certainly knocked the smile off the faces of the Bernstein boys.'

'I'm not surprised if she's usurping their throne,' I said, realizing immediately that Muldoon would not know what I meant.

He just nodded vaguely in response. I probed further.

'How does the protection racket work? Who set it up?'

'Vic and this tart did. Apparently she sussed out potential ... customers, mainly round the Soho area. I cover the territory with

Anthony. He's my back up. I do most of the threatening spiel and such.'

'And the girl stays in the background.'

'Yes. Not seen hide nor hair of her; just heard the boys grumble about her.'

'Where can I find the lovely Gina?'

Muldoon shook his head. 'Don't know. Honest. They reckon she's keeping a low profile for the moment. She doesn't want anyone to know about her yet.'

'I wonder why,' I said, more to myself than my companion.

At that moment the girl entered carrying two grubby, chipped mugs of unsanitary looking tea. It seemed like my cue to leave. I certainly wasn't going to contaminate my mouth with that brew and besides, I thought that I'd squeezed this particular unpleasant lemon dry. There was nothing more to learn from Mr Muldoon and I was itching to get away from the sight of the saggy fellow in his grey drawers. I rose from my perching position and slipped the gun back into my pocket.

'Sorry I can't stay to partake of the refreshment after all,' I said to my hostess, 'but I've business elsewhere.'

The blonde gave me a dismissive sneer.

'You're not going to the cops, are you?' asked Muldoon, jumping from the sofa.

'Not yet, Archie boy,' I tossed over my shoulder as I reached the door, and then I turned and looked him straight in the eye. 'But if you want my advice, I'd resign from current employment and lie low. It won't be long before this whole business blows sky high.'

I left them to their foul tea and squalor.

SEVENTEEN

It was nearly noon when the train steamed into Oxford Station. As I peered through the carriage window, I saw a deep-blue sky with the bright December sun slanting down on the ancient honey-stoned buildings, bathing them in what seemed to be an ethereal light. They glimmered and glowed in the sharp wintry air like mirages in a grimy desert.

Leaving the station, I entered another world. It was like a film set for one of those marvellous MGM movies which attempted to recreate ye olde England on a Hollywood sound stage. At any moment now Ronald Colman or Errol Flynn would appear.

I'd never been to this old university town before – my only brush with academia was at police college in Hendon – and I was immediately captivated by it. Part of the magic was the atmosphere, which was so different from that of London; it was not only the ancient buildings that led me to believe that I had stepped back into a more refined and genteel past. There was a tangible mood about the place – the people, the traffic and the shops all seemed unscathed by the drabness of the war. Indeed there was very little sign here that there was a war on at all. Life seemed almost normal.

It was 1938 again.

I caught the mood and strolled nonchalantly into the centre of the town almost forgetting my reason for visiting this enchanted spot. As I strolled down High Street, an old soldier, a veteran of the First War no doubt, turned an old barrel organ; the cheerful melody floating through the air further enhanced my light-hearted

112

mood. I gave him some coins and received a cheery toothless grin in return.

This, I told myself, is what we're fighting for, each in our own way, a return to this approximation of unruffled normality. Nothing special or extreme but simple and gloriously mundane where food was readily available, blackout curtains could be torn down, children could return home from their far flung outposts, and so could the lads in the forces. We could get on with our lives without fear and sacrifice. There would be Sunday lunch of roast beef and proper Yorkshire puds, holidays on the beach, picnics in the fields and people could laugh again without feeling guilty.

However, my sanguine mood took a knock when I encountered three soldiers chatting outside a tobacconist. They seemed a typical bunch of young men on leave, but, as I approached, I saw that each had a serious injury. One had lost an arm, one was walking with a cane and the third, a short lad who looked no older than twenty had terrible livid scars down one side of his face which contorted his youthful features into a cruel mask.

The sight of these soldiers brought me back to reality with a severe bump and very quickly I shrugged off my sentimental musings. I realized that whatever the veneer Oxford presented to me, it was just that: a veneer. Beneath its shining surface there still lurked the harsh realities of the war. Suitably chastened, I applied myself to the task in hand. After a few minutes I spotted a taxi rank and got myself a ride to an address on the Banbury Road situated a few miles from the city centre.

It was a smart red-brick semi with a bay window and a tidy lawn. It was the home of Gladys Stoker, mother of Beryl Garner.

I rang the bell and waited. Eventually the door was opened by a tall, well-built woman somewhere in her sixties. Her blonde hair was turning white but it was still coiffured in a modern fashion. She had a strong face and bright, determined blue eyes which scrutinized me with suspicion.

'Yes,' she said sharply. It was not the warmest of greetings.

'Mrs Stoker, I've come to talk to you about your daughter Beryl.'

'Have you? Well, Beryl is dead so there is nothing to talk about.'

'I have reason to believe that she is still alive.'

This statement did not seem to faze her at all. 'What nonsense,' she said without a pause, her stern expression still intact.

'I think you know otherwise.'

This got her. For a moment she was lost for words, but then with the flush of anger rising in her face, she said, 'Go away. Go away, damn you.'

'I can go away, but if I do I shall have to go to the police and they certainly will not be turned away. I think it would be wise to talk to me.'

The mention of the police caused her body to stiffen and the eyes flickered with unease. I stepped forward, placing my foot over the threshold, effectively stopping her from closing the door.

She fought hard to keep her emotions under control, but I could see that she was disturbed by my threat of the police and, after a pause, she stepped back and opened the door wider.

'You'd better come in then.'

'Thank you.'

We moved into the front living room which was scrupulously neat and tidy.

'You'd better sit down,' she said coldly, not wanting me to sit at all, not wanting me in the house at all.

I took one of the single chairs of the three-piece suite by the right of the fire, which glowed feebly in the grate. Mrs Stoker sat opposite, on the edge of the other chair, her hands clasped tightly in her lap.

I slipped a packet of cigarettes from my pocket. I needed a fag to see me through this difficult interview.

'No smoking in my house,' said Mrs Stoker in a metallic I-Speak-Your-Weight machine voice. And she meant it. Slowly I replaced the packet. It looked like I had to proceed without the aid of nicotine.

'Your daughter, Beryl, was not very happy in her marriage, was she?'

'What makes you say that?'

'Because Brian used to hit her, didn't he?'

She bit her lip in an attempt not to answer but her emotions got the better of her. Her body shuddered with anger. 'Yes, he hit her, all right. He was a beast,' she snapped. 'He got pleasure out of knocking her about. He never seemed to be happy unless he'd given our Beryl a nasty bruise or a black eye. Or worse. I'm glad he's dead.'

'You know?'

'I read it in the paper. Stabbed in his own shop. The world's better off without him. He brought nothing but misery to my girl.'

'Did she give him cause to be angry with her?'

'What do you mean by that?'

'I just thought perhaps she might have done something to upset him, to cause him to lose his temper with her. I'm not saying that would give him the right to knock Beryl about, but it would explain his hatred of her. And he did hate her, didn't he?'

She hesitated a moment before replying. 'Yes, he hated her. He loathed her … because he loved her. Like so many men with their women, he wanted to possess her and when he found that he couldn't he wanted to hurt her and punish her.'

'And why was that?'

'How should I know?'

I allowed myself a grim smile. 'Oh, but I think you do know. You see I have a pretty good idea what went on in that marriage, but I'd like to hear it from you.'

Gladys Stoker turned away from me and gazed in the direction of the window where the light, softened by the net curtains, bathed her anguished face with a pearl-like hue. She was trying very hard not only to control her emotions but to hold back the truth that I believed she was desperate to share with someone. That someone had to be me.

'It was because … she didn't love him. That's right, isn't it?' I prompted her.

She nodded vigorously. 'No, she didn't love him. How could she?' The voice was now strained and emotional.

'Because it wasn't in her nature, was it?'

'I don't know what you mean.'

'To love a man.'

There was a long pause before she gave a reply and when it came, it was quiet and fierce: 'No.'

'And that offended Brian. Offended his masculine pride. He felt cheated, humiliated and so he took his frustration and hurt out on her. He was a bully in the first place, but this gave just cause in his eyes to punish Beryl.'

Mrs Stoker turned to face me again, her eyes were now moist with tears. 'She was a fool to marry him in the first place, but he did seem a quiet, decent fellow before the marriage.'

'But he didn't know it was … a marriage of convenience. Helping her to create a respectable image.'

'She's not a leper, you know. Just because … Beryl didn't deliberately try to fool him. She was determined to live a normal life and she did try to suppress her feelings at first. But it was a struggle. After all you can't force yourself to love someone by sheer will. She did all she could to be a real … a proper wife to him.'

'Until she met Sylvia Moore. Then she could not deny her inner feelings any longer.'

'She couldn't deny what she was? Is that what you mean? She couldn't deny her love for a woman. It's not her fault she's the way she is. We're all God's creatures and we cannot help what he puts into our hearts and minds. It's just the throw of the dice. Oh, my poor Beryl, it is the terrible secret that she's harboured for most of her life. I know because I have shared that secret with her. Great heavens, I was aware she was different even before she knew herself. I tried to help her with her battle to conform, to bury her true self behind that brittle façade. I put no pressure on her or made any attempt to change her. I was just her mother, her confidant and comfort. Even her father didn't know. I shielded him from the truth. He couldn't have coped with it. He went to his grave in blessed ignorance.'

Mrs Stoker's body had relaxed now and she was addressing me almost in a conversational tone. I suspected she was relieved to talk to someone about her daughter and release some of the anguish and pain.

'Perhaps she was misguided … a fool to marry Brian,' she continued, 'but she paid a harsh price for that mistake. Sylvia became her salvation. Between them there was genuine affection, a real love. Kindness. They belonged together. Is that wrong?

I shook my head. 'I'm not here to judge.'

'What are you here for then, if not to wreck my daughter's life further?'

'I've come to clear up the mystery of her supposed death and the murder of Brian Garner. Now you know as well as I do that Beryl is alive and in hiding with Sylvia. The best thing you can do is tell me where they are.'

As soon as I spoke, I realized that I had just touched a dangerous nerve. Without warning Gladys Stoker jumped to her feet, her body shaking with emotion. 'Never!' she screamed at me, her voice hoarse and violent. The change in her demeanour was rapid, dramatic and shocking. It was though she had suddenly become possessed by some strange violent spirit which had taken hold of both her mind and body. Her face contorted with rage as she spat the words out. 'That girl's suffered enough. You can go to hell.' She rushed forward in quick jerky movements and at first I thought she was going to attack me, but she brushed by my chair and headed for a sideboard behind the sofa.

'I'm only in search of the truth, Mrs Stoker,' I said, trying to maintain a reasonable tone in my voice. 'It will come out sooner or later. Now that Brian has been murdered, it won't be long before the police come knocking at your door.'

'Will they now?' she roared, completely taken over by her anger, her whole frame shaking with emotion, her features suffused and demonic. Frantically she dragged one of the sideboard drawers open and reached inside. Now I sensed danger. She gave a grunt of satisfaction as she withdrew a long, shiny carving knife from the drawer. Before I knew what was happening, like a harpy in a wild nightmare, Gladys Stoker turned and ran towards me, the knife raised high.

Instinctively I stepped to one side, but in a flash she was upon me and, as I turned sharply to avoid the blade, as it flashed with some speed in my direction, I tripped on the hearth rug and fell to my knees. In an instant the crazy woman was on my back. From the corner of my eye, I saw the sharp sliver of shiny metal swing close by the side of my face. With a great effort I rose to my feet and flung the crazed woman from my back, but not before she had sliced a piece of material from the sleeve of my overcoat. She landed with a cry on the sofa. But she was up on her feet again in an instant, powered by her fury and manic desire to kill me. She swung the knife at me again, the blade sweeping within inches of my face.

This time, I managed to grab her arm in mid air and attempted to shake the weapon from her grasp but she hung on to it with a fierce unnatural grip. We moved to and fro, as though locked in some kind of bizarre dance.

In all my time as a detective I'd been in many fights, but never with a demented woman. In her fury she seemed to have inherited the strength of a circus strongman. In this frenzied state, bending an iron bar would be no problem to her. As we struggled, the point of the knife came ever closer to my face. I tried to push her towards the sideboard in order to ram her body against the edge. It was an action which I hoped would wind her and cause her to lose her hold on the knife. But before I could accomplish this manoeuvre, she kneed me in the groin. A fierce pain took hold of my senses for a brief moment and I released her arm. I staggered back, the throbbing ache in my crotch taking precedence over everything else, including the imminent danger I was in. Luckily in stumbling backwards in my pain, I had gone beyond her immediate reach and, as the knife slashed down again, it missed my face, but once again it sliced a piece from my coat. This was getting serious. I really was in danger of losing my life. The ignominy of it, I thought irrelevantly, cut down in my prime by a mad pensioner!

As my would-be assassin advanced on me, I threw a punch at her, hitting her squarely on the chin. Not a particularly chivalrous thing to do, sock an old woman on the jaw, but then this wasn't your average old woman. It was a crazed hell cat with a desire to kill. She lurched backwards, the knife slipping from her grasp at last. Her eyes flickered momentarily, but with remarkable speed she recovered her equilibrium and reached down to snatch up the weapon from the floor.

As she did so, a voice rang out, 'No, Mother! No!'

On hearing these words both Gladys Stoker and I froze in our tracks and turned in the direction of the voice. There standing in the doorway were two women. Despite my somewhat disorientated state, I recognized them both: Beryl Garner and Sylvia Moore.

EIGHTEEN

Vic Bernstein slid into the darkened booth opposite the attractive young woman in the tight-fitting raspberry-coloured dress.

'This restaurant is a bit posh, isn't it – especially for lunchtime?' he said.

Gina smiled and took a puff of her cigarette before replying. 'We're on our way to the big time, Vic. Relax and take the advantages while you can. What's the point of earning money if you can't indulge yourself? Personally, I don't believe in that rainy day you're supposed to save up for. As far as I'm concerned it's raining all the time, so treat yourself to a large luxury umbrella.'

Vic chuckled. It was an uncertain response. He didn't like the girl because she posed a threat, but he couldn't help admiring her panache. Admiring it and jealous of it at the same time. He had never met anyone quite so self-assured, confident and apparently resilient as she was. He couldn't help it but he felt a little like a clumsy teenager in her presence. She was a looker, too. He actually felt a frisson of sexual excitement just being with her. Certainly if she were not his cousin, he'd be all over her. Of course, she really didn't seem like any kind of relative to him. She was a cold, pragmatic stranger who had suddenly forced her way into his comfortable life and brought upset and uncertainty with her.

A waiter materialized out of the sepulchral gloom and handed them each a leather-bound menu. 'Would sir and madam care for an aperitif?'

'Certainly,' replied Gina without hesitation. 'I'll have a martini. The drier the better.'

'And you sir?'

Vic gave a 'why not' raise of the brow. 'Yeah, the same for me.'

'So, what's this all about?' he added, when the waiter had gone. 'Why invite me out to lunch on my own?'

'Choose your food first, Vic, then we'll talk. Pleasure before business always. I think I fancy the chicken.'

After the drinks had arrived and the choices had been made and relayed to the waiter, Gina lit another cigarette and sat back, her cigarette displayed elegantly between two fingers of her right hand. 'It's early days with this protection business but Anthony and his cohort seem to be doing OK,' she said casually.

'Yeah, it's been smooth sailing so far. As far as I know there have been no problems.'

'So I reckon it's time for more action.'

'What does that mean?'

'It means I need your help.' Gina stretched her hand across the table and stroked the sleeve of Vic's jacket. 'I believe I can rely on you,' she purred.

God, thought Vic, tingling with sexual tension, this woman uses her femininity like a fly swatter.

'Rely on me for what?'

'It's time to move forward again.'

Already? he thought. The protection scheme was only just up and running. This lady was certainly in a big hurry and he didn't like it. It was clear that he would have to cut her down to size sooner than he planned. Well, not exactly down to size. Just cut her.

'Oh, yeah?' he said casually. 'What have you got up your sleeve this time?'

Gina took a gentle sip of her martini before replying. 'I intend to be the head of this family business in less than a year. It's time for Uncle Leo to step down, to retire. You know that as well as I do. He's too old and, frankly, he's too timid. Age has brought a dulling of the spirit. He's stuck in old-fashioned ways. Leo and my father allowed things to stagnate. There's been no growth, no development. They just meandered along for years doing the same old thing – no progress and no innovation. And to be frank, you allowed them to.'

She held up her hand to silence his protestation.

'Don't splutter. It's true and you know it. But I'm here now. And all that is going to change. Leo should be on a veranda somewhere with a pipe and slippers.'

Vic contained his anger, masking it with a taut smile. Certainly he knew that his father was past it, was no longer up to playing the fast game, but if anyone was going to replace his old man it should be him not this jumped-up arrogant tart. However, Vic knew that for the moment, however galling it was, he had to keep his thoughts and emotions to himself. He had to play it her way for now. It would be foolish at this stage of the game to make an enemy of the bitch.

'You're not going to bump him off, are you? I'm rather fond of my dad.'

'It's a thought,' she replied rather chillingly, with no hint of humour in her expression. 'But no. I think he can be persuaded to stand down completely.'

'In favour of you?'

She raised an eyebrow. 'Who else? You have talent, Vic, and you're coming along nicely, but you've been too lazy, or maybe complacent. I can't figure out which. Maybe a mixture of both. But you don't have the drive or the ambition to go places. I do.'

She paused and stared him hard in the face. 'You'll forgive me for being brutally honest, but I reckon you're bright enough to know that I speak the truth.'

Vic didn't answer. He didn't know how to. Part of him agreed with her and part of him wanted to reach out and strangle the life out of the arrogant cow there and then on the dining table.

'It is important you see how the land lies, Vic. I want you on my side. We could be useful to each other.'

'Really? Why me? Why not Anthony?'

Gina grimaced. 'Do me a favour. That immature little brat. I wouldn't trust him to run my bath water. I reckon I'm a pretty good judge of character and I'm certain you're the man for me. We could make a good team.'

She flashed her eyes provocatively and stroked his arm. Vic's libido roused itself. That fly swatter was out again, he thought, and heading in my direction.

A good team, he mused. Yes … with you as my boss and me as your dogsbody. Go to hell, lady.

'So, are you with me?' she asked.

'I think I know on which side my bread is buttered,' replied Vic.

Later that afternoon, Vic took a solitary stroll along the Embankment, partly to clear his head from the cocktail, the wine and the post prandial liqueur he'd consumed at lunch and partly to rearrange his plans regarding his newly discovered cousin. It could no longer be as he had first intended it to be, a wait-and-see game. Things were happening too fast for that contingency. She was racing ahead and it was important that he not only catch up with her, but overtake the bitch.

He paused and leaned over the parapet and stared into the shimmering greasy waters of the Thames, the fiery late afternoon sunshine seeming to send bright orange ribbons of fire across its surface. The heaving river was like Gina, deceptively attractive but with a cold and deadly depth which could suck a man to his doom.

This affair could have only one outcome, he determined. It *must* have only one outcome – and he certainly wasn't going to be the one sucked to his doom.

NINETEEN

Despite the house rules, I lit a cigarette and attempted to bring my heart rate down. It wasn't every day that I was attacked by a mad obsessively protective mother wielding a carving knife. There is something much more dangerous in facing a wild irrational opponent than one who has cold, calculated tactics and techniques. Rationality is much easier to deal with than insanity. I was lucky to have escaped unscathed. The same could not be said for my overcoat, which was a sorry sight decorated with rips and a seriously sliced sleeve.

I sat on one of the armchairs opposite Sylvia Moore who was perched on the edge of the sofa staring unseeingly at the fading embers of the fire. Neither of us spoke, each lost in our own world of silent thought. Beryl Garner was upstairs putting her mother to bed. She had calmed her down with remarkable power. All the sound and fury had leaked away from her as quickly as it came. Once the anger had left Mrs Stoker's body, she seemed to shrink in size and reacted to her daughter's ministering like a docile child. Without a word she was led away to rest upstairs. It was like a scenario from a bizarre modern drama. There had been lots of activity but little dialogue and as yet no real interaction between me and the two new characters on stage.

I had just finished the cigarette and flicked the tab end into the fire, causing a small splutter, when Beryl came back into the room.

'She's sleeping now,' she said, matter of factly.

'So, Beryl Garner, you are alive after all,' I said.

'I suppose I am.'

'You realize that I'm going to have to call in the police.'

At first Beryl looked distressed at this news, but then she nodded grimly and glanced over at Sylvia. 'We knew this would happen one day. But please keep my mother out of it.'

'She tried to kill me.'

'Only to protect me. She really acted out of character. The whole thing has been a bigger strain on her than us. Looking after me, keeping a secret. Wanting the best for her little girl.'

I could see that she was right.

'Well, I think you'd better tell me the whole story,' I said, reaching for another cigarette.

Beryl nodded, wiping a strand of hair from across her eyes. 'Can you spare one of your fags?' she asked gently.

'Sure,' I said, passing her the packet. After I lit her cigarette for her, she sat on the sofa, close to Sylvia and sighed.

'Where to begin? Where was the beginning? When I was very young, I suppose. Around thirteen or fourteen. My body was changing and I suppose my mind began to focus. While all the other girls in my class at school were drooling over the boys in the nearby grammar school, I had crushes on girls in my own class. Even at that age, I knew it was wrong or not appropriate to feel attracted to them – but I just couldn't help it. It just seemed natural to me. But I quickly realized it wasn't. Natural that is. Quite the reverse. I soon saw myself as odd, an outsider. I knew then it was best to hide my … inclinations. After leaving school and starting work, I realized that I had to do more than conceal my feelings, I had to squash them altogether – deny they existed. I had to fool myself. I was desperate to be normal. To just be ordinary. In the end I confided in my mother who was sympathetic, but to be honest I reckon she thought it was a phase – something I'd grow out of. So, I started going out with boys … but I felt nothing. There was no real connection between us. There were some disastrous dates, I can tell you.' She allowed herself a brief smile.

'It was different with Brian. He seemed a nice chap and I was easy in his company … at first. He was older than me and I suppose he became a kind of father figure. My own dad died when I was fourteen. Brian and I were just friends to begin with and then gradually he started to chat me up. He said he'd fallen in love with me. What could I do? I either had to ditch him as a friend or … accept him as a lover and a husband in prospect. In some strange and, I suppose, stupid way, I thought he could be my salvation. He could cure me of my terrible disease. And so I allowed myself to be wooed by him and eventually we got married. But I knew well before the wedding day that it was a mistake. You cannot alter what you feel, what you are. Anyway, I walked down the aisle, we said our I dos and that I suppose sealed our fate. I was determined to be a good wife, but underneath I was seriously unhappy. At that time I had never heard the word 'lesbian' and was naïve enough to believe I was unique.'

Sylvia Moore slipped her hand into Beryl's and gave it a gentle squeeze, before withdrawing it again.

'Once we were married, Brian changed. It was quite dramatic. He was no longer the caring, easy-going chap I'd known. It was as though now he had me, now that I was his property, he no longer had any need to keep up his pretences. He became violent. He would find excuses to lose his temper with me … and when he lost his temper he hit me. He seemed to gain some special pleasure in using his fists on a woman, on me. I think it aroused him sexually to … to hit me. So you see, I was not the only freak in this marriage.'

Her eyes were now moist and she ran her sleeve across her face to wipe away the tears. I said nothing and waited for her to collect her emotions and continue.

'Then, I met Sylvia. And everything changed. I realized that I wasn't alone, I wasn't the only one. We knew instinctively that not only did we share the same kind of feelings but also we liked each other very much as well. It was a revelation to me … a salvation. The liking quickly turned to love. For the first time in my adult life I was really happy. And so we became lovers.' She paused and gave me an uncompromising glance. 'Does that shock you?'

I shook my head. 'Not at all,' I said simply. I had no wish to say more. I didn't want to distract the flow of her narration. And indeed, it didn't shock me. Why should it? Brought up as an orphan, I knew how precious love and affection were from wherever they came. I cannot claim to understand the attraction that members of the same sex have for each another, but I am not brainy or narrow-minded enough to condemn it. I knew how difficult it was for people like Harold Crabtree to function in society unscathed.

'My life suddenly became one of vivid contrasts: the harsh, violent home life with a man I had grown to hate and the quiet snatched loving moments with Sylvia. It was decided between us that I should leave Brian and we would set up home together, but I knew that if I just left, he would set out to find me and drag me back. After all he had the law on his side. I was his wife – his legal property. Then Sylvia's mother fell desperately ill. We knew she was dying and so we came up with a plan.'

I now saw what I believed was the outline of this plan, but again I said nothing and waited for Beryl to continue and fill in the details for me and confirm my thoughts.

'We decided to fake my death. That would bring a final closure on my wretched marriage and Brian would have to accept it. Sylvia's mother passed away at home and we covered up her death, not letting any of the neighbours know. She had no close relatives and having been ill for such a long time she had lost touch with any friends she'd had in her younger days. We felt awful about using poor Sylvia's mother in this way, but we know that she would have done anything to help us be together.'

Beryl glanced at Sylvia who gave her a supportive nod of the agreement.

'It was then that I pretended I was leaving Brian for another man. Actually I never used the word "man", he just assumed my lover was male. We arranged to crash the car with Sylvia's mother's body inside dressed in my clothes. We made sure the cab of the motor was a burnt-out shell so that the corpse was unrecognizable. The registration, which was in the Garner name, and some luggage in the boot gave evidence as to the supposed identity of the driver.

'The plan worked remarkably well. Brian – and the authorities – believed that I'd perished in the crash. Well, they had no reason to be suspicious. At last Sylvia and I were free to start a life together, helped by the thousand pounds I had taken from our bank account.

I suppose you might call that stealing, but it was in essence both our savings and I thought I'd earned it through all the beatings I'd suffered at his hand.

'It all seemed to be going well. We rented a flat in Cartwright House and both returned to work as hairdressers – but in different salons. And life was sweet. Then a couple of weeks ago, I saw Brian again. At South Kensington tube station. What was worse, he saw me. He recognized me … called out my name. It was such a shock. I panicked and fled but he chased after me. Thankfully I managed to lose him. However, I knew he wouldn't let the matter rest there and sure enough you came snooping after me, following my trail – and Sylvia's. We felt like trapped animals on the run. We had to leave our lovely flat and run to ground – here at my mother's house. She's always been supportive. She knew everything: my relationship with Sylvia and my faked death. She was with me all the way. I think she hated Brian even more than me.'

'Did your mother kill him?'

Beryl shook her head. I could see from her expression that she considered the idea as being preposterous. 'No. You must believe me about that. I know she went wild with you, but you had cornered her in her own home; she was desperate to protect her little girl. Besides, she hasn't been out of the house, except to the shops down the road, for the last two days. She couldn't do anything like that in cold blood.'

I did believe her but that still left me with a problem. 'Have you any idea who might have murdered Brian?'

She flinched at the word 'murdered'. 'No,' she said decisively. 'But I can't help feeling relieved to know he's dead.'

The three of us sat without speaking for some moments, the ticking of the clock sounding unnaturally loud in the silence.

Sylvia was the first to speak. 'What are you going to do now?'

It was a good question. I wasn't sure I had the right answer. These two women were not evil, merely victims of circumstances and indeed emotional forces beyond their control. Certainly Beryl had suffered more than enough at the hands of her brutish husband. What, I wondered, would be the benefit in reporting them to the law? Beyond faking a death they had not committed any really serious offence. There were no wrongs that could be righted in this case.

I pursed my lips and sighed. 'Nothing. I am going to do nothing.'

I left them shortly after that and took a long walk back into the city of Oxford. I wanted time on my own to think. I had a strange empty feeling inside my stomach. That wretched situation was over for Beryl and Sylvia, I guessed. Very shortly they would be able to pick up the strings of their life where they had left off, but because of the very nature of their relationship things were never going to be easy or relaxed for them. They were still outcasts. And for that I felt sorry for them.

And of course there was one strong niggling question lurking at the back of my mind. Who had killed my wife-beating client Brian Garner?

TWENTY

Max finished the last of her lunchtime sandwiches while chatting to a couple of the chorus girls who were bright and giggly local lasses and 'so excited' at appearing in 'a proper show' and being part of the glamorous world of 'show business'. It was their first professional engagement as dancers and they were over the moon at being engaged to take part in this pantomime. She confided in them that this was her first show working on costumes. Their enthusiasm and happiness was infectious and, as Max made her way back to her little workshop at the very back of the theatre, she couldn't help smiling. Despite being alone in a strange city and parted from Johnny, she had found herself part of a new small family at the theatre – a team of really friendly folk. Certainly the show would not be as lavish as the ones in London, but it would be colourful and fun and she knew it would bring some much wanted cheer and escapism so necessary in these difficult days.

In recent months she had extended her talents beyond that of making theatrical masks into costume making and design. This had been for practical reasons. There was much less demand for masks than there had been before the war and she knew that she had to diversify a little if she were to make enough money to survive. After several ventures, this job at Nottingham Playhouse was her first big challenge and she was enjoying the experience.

Although she missed Johnny, it was wonderfully comforting to know that he felt the same and that he would be waiting for her with open arms when her tasks in Nottingham were complete and she returned to London. In many ways, she thought, she had never been happier.

Caroline was waiting for Peter at the school gates as she said she would be. He recognized her lithe silhouette with her long tumbling hair and tightly belted gaberdine mac and in the gloom he could see the bright white daisy she had painted on her gas-mask box which was slung around her shoulders.

He felt a tingle of excitement as she turned at his approach and smiled.

Gosh, she was pretty. And she was waiting for him.

'Hello,' he said shyly, matching her smile.

'Hello.'

They stood awkwardly facing each other, both not knowing what to say next as the stream of schoolchildren flowed past them.

'Shall we go for a walk then,' Peter said at last. 'Maybe get a cup of tea?'

'Yes, that would be nice.'

They set off down the road together, Peter itching to take hold of her hand but not daring to.

'Did you have old Mother McGovern for maths today?' Caroline asked him casually. To Peter's mind she seemed much more relaxed about this meeting than him.

'No ... but I've got her tomorrow. Worse luck,' he replied.

'She's as mad as a hatter. I'm sure she's a German spy sent here to make our lives miserable.'

Peter giggled. 'In that case she must be in league with Fancypants Fanshaw. He's enough to drive anyone up the wall. I'm sure that monocle of his is some kind of secret weapon.'

They both laughed comfortably and Peter allowed his hand to brush against hers. She did not flinch at the contact. Was this a sign? Taking a deep breath, he slipped his fingers so that they interlocked with hers. She said nothing but gave his hand a little squeeze.

Fifteen minutes later they were sitting in the Elite Café drinking tea and sharing a rather dried up Eccles cake between them. 'It's the last one, I'm afraid,' said the lady who served them. Secretly Peter was relieved. His pocket money was running a little low.

They were now comfortably holding hands across the table like a real girl and boyfriend. Peter thought they were like one of those couples that he had seen in the pictures: he in uniform about to go off to war, she dabbing her eyes with a lace handkerchief and trying to be brave.

In the light of the café Peter could see that Caroline was wearing a little make-up: her cheeks were powdered and she had lipstick on, making her lips all shiny and red. As a result she looked older than her fourteen years. Quite the young miss.

'I think your flannels are brilliant,' she said, brushing the crumbs of the Eccles cake from her chin.

'Thanks. Johnny bought them for me. You know, I've told you all about him.'

Indeed he had.

'I bet you're glad to get out of short pants,' she said, smiling.

'You bet. They were really embarrassing.' In truth he knew that Caroline Weston would not be sitting here in the Elite Café holding hands with him if he were still in those wretched short trousers.

As they finished their tea and the waitress brought the bill, it seemed like it was time for the big moment. His heart began to beat faster and he felt sure his palms were beginning to sweat. Nevertheless, he was not going to funk it.

'Caroline …'

'Yes?'

'I was wondering …' He hesitated, courage beginning to fail him.

'Yes?'

'I was wondering if … if you … I was wondering if you'd like to be my girlfriend.'

He looked away. He couldn't bear to watch her reaction.

She leaned forward and gave him a gentle kiss on the cheek. 'Of course,' she said, a wide grin on her face.

As dusk fell on the city, Gina was luxuriating in the bath, up to her neck in scented foam and deliberating on her lunchtime meeting with Vic. At the thought of his handsome but troubled features, she smiled. She knew that he was not to be trusted and she also knew that he felt the same way about her. But, as long as she kept her wits about her, she felt confident she could make him biddable.

All in all things were going her way. Here she was ensconced in her own smart hideaway, the address known only to Leo and the boys. Better still the police had no knowledge of her and yet she was already pulling various strings and laying the foundations for her own little empire. Growing up away from the warmth and security of a family – however corrupt and immoral the family were – had not only instilled into Gina a cast iron self-sufficiency but had also made her very ruthless. She didn't form attachments and had no time for sentiment. In many ways her early institutionalized years were not too dissimilar to those of Johnny Hawke, but they had affected her differently. Unlike Johnny, she cared for no one but herself and was not prepared to let anyone stand in her way. Anyone who tried would be dealt with speedily and without mercy.

Gina scooped up a handful of foam and gently blew the white bubbles into the air with a satisfied chuckle.

TWENTY-ONE

The train crawled its way back to London, grinding to a halt on several occasions for no apparent reason. At least it gave me time to mull over my various concerns. I believed that I had done the right thing in deciding not to alert the authorities to the fact that Beryl Garner was still alive, although I'm sure David and his police chums would have a different opinion. But for me morally, it was the correct decision. No real good would come from exposing Beryl now and she had suffered enough. Also, bringing her into the open may very well muddy the waters regarding Brian Garner's murder. On reflection I believed that I could clear that up fairly quickly, although it wouldn't bring me great pleasure to do so. Garner had died as he had lived: violently. I am not saying he deserved to die, but at the same time I believed that he had brought it on himself and I had no sympathy for him.

My other thoughts were on the Bernstein business and my concern here was to find out more about the mysterious Gina. She was the key to the Ricotti murder and the protection racket. As the train juddered its way towards Kings Cross, I hatched a little plan which would aid me in this investigation.

The station was heaving when I arrived and, despite my valiant efforts of pushing, shoving and squeezing, it took me nearly five minutes to pass through the crush of passengers to reach the exit. Once outside, I hailed a taxi but the rush-hour traffic clogged the roads. I may well have been quicker walking. Eventually I reached Oxford Street, but Prestige Photographic Studios had already shut up shop for the day. I gave a muted curse and set off on foot for home. I hoped my evening plans would not be so easily scuppered.

On reaching Hawke Towers I found that there was a letter waiting for me from Max. This had a double effect: it cheered me up knowing that she was thinking of me, but also made me miserable realizing it would be ages before I saw her again. I penned a rather plaintive and somewhat soppy reply to post on my way out that evening.

I popped down the hall to the tiny icebox of a bathroom and indulged myself with a fresh shave and a hot bath. By the time I'd donned a clean shirt and my best black suit I felt fresh and eager for a night in fine surroundings. Eyeing my coat with the knife wounds, I realized that I couldn't be taken seriously wearing that thing of shreds and patches. So, reluctantly I donned my other overcoat, the one that I reserved for special occasions, not that I recalled having been to any. I just hoped that no knife-wielding harpy would try taking a piece out of that.

The Bamboo House was situated on Kimble Street, up from the Aldwych on the edge of Covent Garden. Like many dubious establishments in London, it claimed to be a members-only club but that just meant you had to cough up a fair bit of cash to get in. Once inside the drinks were exorbitant, no doubt the gaming table was rigged and there were lovely ladies there eager to lighten your wallet further.

Going through life, as I do, like a Cyclops, one damaged eye socket covered by a black eye patch, has permanent disadvantages. You see the world in a slightly restricted fashion for a start and, as a detective, it is impossible to blend in with the crowd. People will always remember the one-eyed fellow with the patch. Therefore disguises are out. Whatever I wore, whatever accent I used, and whatever facial adornments I adopted to alter my appearance such as beards, moustaches, side whiskers, there would still be the damned patch to identify me. I was convinced that was why Sylvia Moore did a vanishing act. She had been told by two people that a curious cove with one eye had been asking questions about her and that had spooked her sufficiently to make herself scarce. If I'd been a nondescript two-eyed fellow, perhaps no alarms bell would have rung.

So, as I entered the Bamboo House – after paying my evening's membership of a crisp pound note – I knew that I would be noticed and whatever I did it would be remembered by someone. In some instances, of course, this can be useful, but I doubted if that would be the case tonight.

Despite wearing my best suit – the one that causes Benny to observe, 'nice bit of smutter – now you look a real gent' – I still felt a little shabby compared to the well-tailored suits and shiny dinner jackets the other male customers were shimmying around in. No off-the-peg 'smutter' here from the second-hand shop; it was all bespoke stuff. There was an oleaginous air of reckless and shameless wealth pervading the establishment. Despite the war and the deprivations it brought to the ordinary man in the street there were still those who made sure that nothing interfered with their unruffled lives. Here they were, those shady characters who, because of rather than in spite of the conflict, had garnered even more wealth: dishonest types, cheats, crooked businessmen, black-marketeers, gangsters and spivs. They were all in attendance at the Bamboo House in their well-heeled, ill-gotten splendour. Well, they say that scum always rises to the surface.

It's strange that when I find myself in the sort of company that frequents this kind of dubious establishment, instinctively I begin to feel superior and strangely invulnerable. I know that I am better than they are. God knows I am no saint, but my soul remains untarnished and my intentions noble, if sometimes fallible. In that sense, they are beneath me.

I checked in my coat and hat and then passed through the gaming room with its steady hum of voices, the clickety rattle of the roulette wheel and the sea of sweaty, greedy faces with bulging eyes and nervous fingers eager to add more cash to their stash and wandered over to the large semi-circular bar. There were two barmen in attendance. I made signs to the older one of the two, who stared at the world through a pair of owlish tortoiseshell glasses. He looked less arrogant and more world weary. The younger one, with slicked hair and a challenging stare moved with a barely suppressed arrogance as though he owned the establishment. I didn't fancy doing business with him.

'What can I get you, sir?' asked my barman pleasantly enough but without much enthusiasm.

'A whisky and soda and have a drink yourself.'

'That's very kind, sir, but we are not allowed to drink while on duty.'

'Save it for later then.'

That brought a slight smile. 'Well, if you insist.'

I nodded to indicate that I did.

He brought me my drink in quick sticks along with my tab. Glancing at it, I thought I'd bought the whole bottle rather than the simple measure before me. 'This is my first time here,' I said, determined to retain the attention of my new friend.

'I hope you enjoy yourself, sir,' came the programmed reply. He was eager to be about his business. Obviously, he was not paid to chat to the customers.

'I was hoping to see Gina here,' I said, diving in at the deep end.

He frowned. 'Sorry ... who?'

'Gina.'

'Is she one of the waitresses?'

I shook my head. 'Gina Bernstein.'

'Bernstein.' He seemed surprised. 'The Bernsteins own this place but I've never heard of a Gina. Is she one of the family?'

'I guess so.'

'Sorry, I can't help you. You'd better have a word with Mr Leo. That's him, over by the door to the gaming room.'

He pointed. My eyes followed the direction of his finger and lit upon a portly gentleman encased in an expensive dinner suit that sprouted a white carnation at the button hole. He had a kind face with large expressive eyes and was for all the world the ideal image of a benign uncle. But I knew to my cost that appearances can be deceptive and one didn't get to Leo Bernstein's exalted position in the grubby world of crime without an iron will and a ruthless streak.

'Maybe later,' I said, taking a sip of my whisky.

My barman friend floated off to serve another customer.

I sat nursing my expensive Scotch and gazed across at Leo Bernstein. He was in conversation with a small rat-faced man.

Everything seemed very relaxed, but every now and again, Bernstein's eyes narrowed and he turned his gaze from his companion to survey the room as though checking everything was ticking along nicely in his profitable domain.

It was time to put my little plan in action.

I finished my drink and headed for the telephone cubicle and dialled.

'The Bamboo House,' a gruff voice said.

'I need to speak to Leo Bernstein right away. It's urgent. It's about Gina.'

'Who is this?'

I gave a raw chuckle. 'You don't expect me to tell you that, do you? Listen, this is urgent. If you value your skin, tell Leo. It's about Gina.'

There was an uneasy pause and then the gruff voice came again. 'Hang on a minute.'

I looked across the room, my attention focused on Leo. I did not have to wait long. A lanky individual with pale features and a limp moustache hurried up to Leo and whispered urgently in his ear. Obviously, this was Mr Gruff Voice. When he had imparted his information, he stepped back and waited. Leo Bernstein pursed his lips and looked a little uneasy. At length he made his excuses to his rat-faced companion and left the room. So the mountain was coming to Mohammed.

'Leo Bernstein,' said the angry voice in my ear some moments later. 'Who is this?'

'A friend,' I lied. 'I wanted to warn you about Gina.'

'Gina who?'

'Oh, come now, Leo. Gina Bernstein.'

'Who is this?' he said again, the voice rising in pitch. He was rattled now and his anger grew.

'I told you, a friend'

'What do you want?'

'Just tell her to watch her back, Leo. She may be getting an unwelcome visitor any day now. They know where she lives.'

'Who ... who are you talking about?'

I chuckled my menacing chuckle borrowed shamelessly from

The Shadow. 'You don't need me to tell you that, now, do you? *Ciao*, Leo.'

I put the receiver down and smiled. I was quite pleased with my little performance. I stayed put and awaited developments. Before long Leo Bernstein emerged wearing his overcoat and summoned the rat-faced man to join him. They had a brief hurried *tête-à-tête* before the pair headed for the exit. My little ruse seemed to be working very well. I followed post haste. I was only six feet behind them as they reached the door and I managed to catch a snippet of conversation.

'I can't get her on the telephone … I've got to check for myself.'

As quickly as I could I retrieved my hat and coat from the cloakroom and shot out into the street just in time to see Leo and his *compadre* get into some sort of slinky monster motor. I've always been bad on the makes of cars but it was a black monster motor. I hailed one of the waiting taxis lined up in readiness to take drunken punters home.

'Where to, mate?' came a cheery voice from the interior of the cab.

'Follow that big shiny car up ahead. The one that's just pulled out from the kerb.'

'Really? You want me to tail him?'

'Yes.'

'You the police or something?'

'Something, I guess.'

'Right you are, sunshine,' said the cabbie with childlike enthusiasm. 'I'll stick to him like glue.' And with that, he revved his engine loud enough to wake the dead and we shot off into the night close on the tail of Leo Bernstein's monster motor.

TWENTY-TWO

Gina was lying on her sofa listening to music on the radio when the doorbell rang. She gave a sigh of annoyance. Who could it be at this time of night? Whoever it was, they were damned insistent. The bell rang with a constant tone as though the caller was holding the bell push down. By the time she reached the entrance hall, her insistent visitor had resorted to hammering on the door.

Gina looked through the little spy hole and saw the distorted face of her Uncle Leo, staring back at her. He looked far from happy. She undid the bolt and opened the door. There indeed was Leo Bernstein, holding a revolver in his hand. He was accompanied by one of the club's little tough guys.

'Gina, are you all right?' said Leo, pushing his way past her.

'Yes, of course,' replied Gina with some puzzlement, her eyes still staring at the gun. Leo quickly slipped it back in his pocket out of sight.

'Do come in,' she said, with tart irony. She really didn't like being disturbed in this way.

'Thank you,' he said before turning to his companion. 'You stay outside and guard the door.'

The little rat-faced man nodded. 'Yes, boss,' he said.

Gina led Leo through into the sitting room.

'What is this all about?'

'I ... I had a phone call ... at the Bamboo House tonight. Anonymous – but it warned me that you're in danger.'

'From who?'

'Well, the caller didn't say.'

'Whoever it was, how do they know about me?'

He shook his head. 'I don't know. That's what puzzled me.'

'Someone must have blabbed.'

Leo had not thought of that. 'Blabbed! Who? Me and the boys are the only ones who know about you. Who you really are.'

'Well, if it wasn't you, maybe it was them. It must have been. Careless talk and all that. I think Vic is smart enough to keep his trap shut, but Anthony … he has a bit of a loose tongue, especially when he's had a drink.'

It pained Leo a little to accept that this was the truth. 'I'll have words with him.'

'Spilt milk, Uncle.'

'Yes, I suppose you're right. The main thing is that your cover is blown and you need to do a disappearing act pronto.'

To Leo's surprise, Gina seemed unperturbed.

'It was only going to be a matter of time before my cover was blown as you put it,' she said easily. 'It's happened sooner than I wanted but I certainly don't intend to live in the shadows for the rest of my life.'

'But now you'll be their prime target.'

'Whether it's a police nark or some ne'er-do-well who's been on the blower to you, I can look after myself, Uncle. Don't worry about me. I'm on my guard. It seems to me that the purpose of the phone call was to scare us, to get me running scared. Well, I don't do scared. I'm staying put.'

Leo shrugged. He knew it was pointless to argue. 'So be it. But never relax, eh? Now you're here, I don't want to lose you.'

Gina smiled and ran her palm down Leo's face. 'Thank you,' she said. 'Now, seeing as you came all this way to warn me – how about a drink?'

Twenty minutes later Leo Bernstein with his rat-faced cohort left the building and returned to their motor car. Each of them seemed preoccupied, lost in his own thoughts and neither of them observed a man standing in a doorway across the street from the block of flats watching them. He was a tall, young man with a trilby pulled low over his face so that it was difficult to see the black eye patch he wore over his left eye.

141

On returning to the club, Leo went to his office to complete some paperwork before heading home. He was still concerned about the phone call. Gina may think she was invincible, but he could see that despite her chutzpah, she was very vulnerable. But there was nothing he could do about it.

He sighed deeply. He was tired. More tired than he cared to admit. The stresses of the last month had made him realize that he was not the young bravado he used to be. He knew that losing his brother, coping with the return of Gina and Paulo Ricotti's death had put an undue strain on his heart. For the first time, he felt like an old man. Maybe it really is time to retire, he told himself, as he lit a cigar and slumped back in his chair. Time to get out of the circus while I still can and enjoy life. What more is there to achieve? And perhaps my hands are soiled enough....

He gently swept these thoughts way – he'd reserve them for another day – and turned his attention to the paperwork on his desk. Legit bills and invoices. What a bore.

A knock at the door put off the dreaded moment.

The caller was Mike Chadwick, the head barman, an old friend of Leo's, who'd been with the firm in many roles since the early days.

'What can I do for you, Mike?'

'It's something I thought you'd like to know. It may be nothing, but ...'

'Yes, what is it.'

'One of the bar staff, Tom, the fairly new guy with tortoiseshell glasses....'

Leo prided himself on knowing the name of every member of his staff. He nodded. 'I know him. What's up? He been putting his hand in the till?'

'No, nothing like that. It's just something he told me tonight. I thought it's perhaps something you ought to know. It may be something or nothing.'

Leo knew Mike was a shrewd fellow. He was *au fait* with most of the things connected with the Bernstein business and therefore he wouldn't be bothering him if he didn't think it was of some importance.

'Go on then, spit it out.'

'Well, Tom said there was a geezer in this evening asking for a girl called Gina … and when Tom asked, 'Gina who?' he said, 'Gina Bernstein'. Does that make any sense to you?'

Leo averted his gaze and ignored the question. 'Strange. Who was this man?'

'Don't know. Tom said he hadn't seen him in the club before. I gather he was not the usual sort of customer. A bit frayed round the edges. Oh, and he wore a patch over his left eye.'

TWENTY-THREE

I waited until Bernstein's car had disappeared from sight and then I walked casually across the street in to Parkway Mansions, the home of Miss Gina Bernstein. This was certainly a more upmarket block of flats than the one once occupied by Beryl Garner and Sylvia Moore. I checked the names of the residents on the board on the main pillar in the foyer. As I expected there was no Bernstein on the list – well, there wouldn't be, would there? But there was a nameplate that looked relatively new advertising a G. Andrews. G for Gina I wondered. It was worth a try.

G. Andrews resided on the top floor in Flat 16. For a few moments I debated with myself. Should I just make a note of the address and pass it on to David Llewellyn when I saw him in the Guardsman the following lunchtime, or should I simply pay a call on Miss Andrews now?

My curiosity was too great. I headed for the lift. I am a detective after all, I reasoned, and I had been the one to discover where the girl hung out. I told myself, I really ought to check that this really was the little birdie we were after. I didn't want to end up with egg on my face if David turned up at Flat 16 to discover it was inhabited by some fat businessman or a little old lady. I thought that highly unlikely. In truth, I wanted to meet this mysterious woman – get her measure. It was my prerogative.

On this occasion I trusted the lift, which looked sleek and reliable. It hummed efficiently and deposited me on the fourth floor in seconds. I stepped out on to thick luxurious carpet, my feet seeming to sink several inches into the pile. I actually left footprints as I walked. As soon as I reached the door of Flat 16, I rang the bell immediately. Any hesitation now may well have me chickening out of this venture.

I did not have to wait long before the door opened. I don't know what I expected but what I saw took my breath away. Here before me was a tall, dark-haired girl with stunning grey eyes set on a smooth, beautiful face. She wore a long shimmering grey gown which clung alluringly to her slim frame. Both her stance and her expression were coquettish and beguiling.

'Miss Bernstein,' I said, raising my hat.

'Ah, the phantom phone caller?'

She had sussed me out already. She did not seem at least perturbed that I had turned up on her doorstep.

'May I come in?'

She said nothing but gestured me to pass over the threshold.

Sometimes I am the most naïve idiot. Occasionally this can work in my favour. And sometimes not. As I walked into Flat 16, Parkway Mansions, I never contemplated that I might be a very ill-prepared Daniel stepping into this very attractive lion's den. She was, after all, just a young woman. A pretty one at that in possession of a charming way, but nevertheless, not matter how assured and confident she may appear, a lady on her own is always vulnerable. I was a tough guy detective with a pistol in my pocket and she was just a slip of a thing.

As I said, sometimes I am the most naïve idiot.

'You are a busy, I gather,' she said, showing me through to the spacious and beautifully appointed sitting room. It was all white and creams with chocolate-coloured angular furniture.

I smiled. I hadn't been called 'a busy' – the slang term for a copper – for years. 'Not quite,' I said, standing awkwardly in the middle of this Hollywood set. 'I'm in the unofficial sector.'

'Ah, a private tec. Well, do slip off your coat and take a seat. I was about to have a brandy night-cap. Will you join me, Mr...?'

'Hawke. John Hawke,' I said, sitting precariously on a small chrome and leather contraption – built for style but not for comfort.

'John. That's a nice name. Brandy then?'

'Thank you.'

She disappeared briefly into what I guessed was the kitchen, emerging a few moments later with two brandy glasses. She had poured me a generous measure. After she handed it to me, she lounged provocatively on the sofa. Her gown spilt to the knee exposing a long shapely leg.

Was it me, I wondered, or was it rather warm in here.

Suddenly, I thought that this whole scenario was surreal. Where, Johnny, old boy, I asked myself, as I took a sip of the brandy, was this all leading? What is your game plan?

There was no reply.

'So, what is the purpose of your visit, John?' the girl asked, as though she had read my mind.

'To clear up one or two things.'

'Really. Do go on.'

'I assume I am talking to Gina Bernstein, daughter of Michael Bernstein.'

She smiled sweetly. 'Indeed, you are.'

'And you are running a protection racket with the help of your cousins.'

She laughed. It was a delightful, genuine laugh and her eyes twinkled with real merriment. 'You must be thinking of someone else.'

I shook my head.

'Your cousin Anthony has been identified. I was there when he tried to extort money from a café owner in Soho.'

'Really. Well, John, I am not my brother's keeper. I cannot be held responsible for what that rascal Anthony gets up to in his free time. It certainly has nothing to do with me.'

'That's not what Archie Muldoon says.'

This time the laugh did not come. There was a flicker of annoyance in her eyes. I took another sip of brandy while I waited for her response. It was a lame one.

'I'm afraid I don't know anyone of that name.'

'What about Paulo Ricotti?'

She shook her head. 'Him neither.'

'That's strange,' I said tartly. 'It was rumoured that he was responsible for your father's death.'

The face darkened now. I could tell she was trying valiantly to retain her cool exterior but real emotion was crowding in on her.

'He had his throat cut, didn't he?'

She turned her head away and remained quiet for some moments. 'I think you should drink your drink and go now, Mr Hawke.'

She was probably right. There was little else I could do here tonight. I'd satisfied myself that I'd found the right woman. It was now a job for the police. It was time for David to take over.

I drained my glass and extricated myself from the strange chair.

'As you wish,' I said.

She turned to face me again. Her smiling mask back in place. 'What a pity we are seeing each other from different sides of the fence.' She rose from the sofa and, moving close to me, touched my arm. I could smell her perfume: it was heady and sweet. For a brief moment I felt like climbing over that fence.

I turned to go and suddenly I felt unsteady on my feet and very hot. Suffocatingly hot. It came upon me in an instant. It was as though I had been attacked by a virulent fever. I ran my hand around my collar and tried to loosen my tie but failed, my fingers refusing to follow instructions. In some strange transformation they had turned to rubber. Gina stood before me watching with interest, her face shifting in and out of focus. I stumbled forward a few feet and then felt my legs give way. As I sank to the floor, I caught sight of my empty brandy glass on the table where I had left it.

The brandy. Of course, I thought, as waves of sleep rolled towards me. Of course … the brandy …

TWENTY-FOUR

Anthony Bernstein had lost heavily on the roulette wheel that evening and, as a result, he had been drinking to excess. He was at that stage of inebriation where he was not actually drunk, but his mind was failing to function in a completely sober fashion. The losses had put him in a bad mood and this fuelled his incipient anger: the burning petulant resentment he carried around with him all the time. On this occasion it was Gina who was the target of his burgeoning ire. Ever since she had popped up out of nowhere and stirred up the still waters of his calm pond he had felt aggrieved. She consumed his thoughts and dogged his actions. In fact she was probably responsible for him losing at the roulette wheel. He hated her and hated her with a vengeance. Unlike Vic, he did not have the patience or the subtlety to play the long game. Something must be done about her – not in due course, not soon, but now! That was the conclusion the toxic mix of bitterness and alcohol had brought him to.

Why the hell, he brooded, should she swan in and take over the reins of the Bernstein family interests? They belonged to him and Vic. They were the ones who had put in time and effort. And in fact they were still doing it. At least he was – trailing around with Archie Muldoon scaring the hell out of little shopkeepers and squeezing cash out of them. It was a decent enough wrinkle, but he didn't need bloody Gina to oversee it for him. In a matter of days he had been reduced to the role of minion. As he considered this scenario, his anger grew and the veins at the sides of his temple throbbed. Part of his fury was aimed at himself for allowing the girl to take such a grip on the Bernstein business and their lives, but most of it was reserved for Gina. What he didn't know, what lay beyond his mental reach deep in his subconscious was the fact that part of his hatred of Gina was based on the recognition that she had the strong forceful characteristics that he lacked, that he admired and that he envied. Her presence was like a vicious thorn in his flesh. To his simple mind, the elimination of such a creature was the only way to bring him peace and contentment again.

'That bitch has got to go,' he told himself with grim determination as he stepped out of the Crescent Moon Club in Store Street. And if Vic wasn't prepared to do the noble deed, well, he'd have to do it himself. And he'd do it now. Why wait? Strike while the iron was hot.

While the booze gave him courage.

He walked swiftly and with purpose to his car, his mind whirring with thoughts and ideas. It would be best to get rid of Gina before anyone found out about her. At the moment there was no real connection between the family and her. She was living under an assumed name and had kept a low profile. It was an ideal time for her to go, to be disposed of – before connections were made, suspicions aroused and motives constructed. And, bloody hell, he was man enough to do it. He was sure that his dad and Vic would be grateful when it was all over. And he didn't give a fuck if they weren't. He slipped into the driving seat and switched on the ignition. The lights on the dashboard illuminated his face, forming it into the image of a plump skull.

He was grinning.

'Parkway Mansions, here we come,' he said cheerfully.

Gina dragged John Hawke's limp frame into the bedroom and left it by the far side of the bed so that anyone entering the room would not see it. Kneeling down, she frisked him and confiscated his gun. She wasn't sure how long he'd be unconscious. The drug she'd used had variable results so she knew she had to act quickly. Moving back into the sitting room, she made a phone call.

'Sorry to ring you so late. But I've a favour to ask you,' she said smoothly, with no emotion in her voice. She had managed to suppress her panic and approach her dilemma in a calm and stoical manner. 'I've a body I need you to get rid of.'

'A body,' repeated Vic at the other end. 'What the hell do you mean?'

Gina told him of Hawke's visit and how he had sussed what was going on. 'He's a clever little chappie,' she said with a sneer in her voice. 'He knows too much. He's got me in the frame for Ricotti's murder and he's found out about the protection racket. It looks like Anthony's slipped up there. I reckon the idiot blabbed to Muldoon who in turn did the same to my detective chum here.'

Vic cursed silently. He cursed his stupid brother, but more particularly he cursed Gina. All this would not be going on, blowing up in their faces, if it were not for her. And now she wants me to dirty my hands. Get rid of a body! Damn her.

Nevertheless, while these fiery thoughts ignited in his brain and he gripped the receiver with a grim ferocity, he managed to keep his cool when he replied.

'What do you expect me to do with Hawke?'

'Get rid of him,' she repeated, as though she were asking him to pass the condiments at the dinner table.

'How?' Vic had a good idea what she meant but he wanted to hear her say it.

'Bump him off. Drop him in the Thames or something.'

Or something! The cow was crazy. She might have a calm and assured frontage, but the mechanism inside was all buggered up. If anyone was going to be got rid of – dumped in the Thames – it was her. He knew that it would have to happen sometime, but he hadn't reckoned that it would be this soon. But things had got very sticky and now circumstances dictated it. And it would be for the best. She had to go before her identity became known and the Bernstein family were implicated in her misdemeanours.

'I'll come over and try and sort out your mess,' he said pointedly. 'Give me about an hour.'

He put down the receiver and strangely he found himself chuckling.

T W E N T Y - F I V E

Although it was nearly the pantomime season, I certainly hadn't expected to play the role of Sleeping Beauty or, more realistically, Drugged Ugly and when consciousness slowly returned to me, my first thought was to curse my idiot self for being stupid enough to get drugged in the first place. I had reckoned on some funny business, probably involving a knife or a gun, but not the old powder in the drinks routine. What an idiot. I had been seduced by a pretty face and a charming manner. Yes, sir, Johnny Hawke, ace detective had been taken in completely by Gina's apparently civilized demeanour. I hoped I lived long enough for this to be a lesson to me. When consciousness finally and gradually brought me back to groggy life, I tried to raise myself from my undignified recumbent position only to discover that while I'd been out for the count, someone had dipped my body in a very strong solution of starch. As a result my stiffened limbs could hardly move.

I felt rough and disorientated and in other circumstances I would have just turned over and surrendered myself once more to sleep. However, the part of my brain that was working, the portion that deals with self-preservation, told me that I had to get the hell out of here. There was a murderer in the next room and I had as much vim and vigour as a drunken child. It would be disastrous to try and confront her. I would be putty in her hands. Dead putty.

After what seemed an hour, but in the real un-drugged world was less than a minute, I managed to pull my creaky carcass up from the floor and sit on the edge of the bed while I waited for the room to slow down. I checked my coat for my gun. It had gone. So, if she wasn't before, Gina was armed now. Great! A mild panic set in. I wondered what the hell I was going to do. In simple terms I knew that I had to escape. But how? I couldn't exactly leave by the front door.

My eyes were inexorably drawn the window. Like a hundred-year-old man with arthritis, I staggered across the room and pulled back the curtains. A clear blue sky with a rich yellow moon greeted my gaze. I looked down and then I remembered that I was four floors up. The frightening reminder of this ignited a few spark plugs in my brain prompting it into sluggish motion. Like an old jalopy. As I couldn't fly out of the window like a damaged Peter Pan, I was rather stumped. And yet to try and make my way through the flat with gun-toting madam on the loose was not a safe prospect either.

Nevertheless, I had to get out of there quick. Gina could come into the room at any minute. Being shot with my own gun would be the most ignominious of deaths. With that thought in mind, I realized that I just had to go for the crazy option. There was no alternative. Quietly I opened the window wide and gazed out. Sadly the building was too new to have age-old ivy creeping up the wall to provide me with the means of clambering down to safety. Also, I didn't think there would be enough sheets on the bed to tie together reach the bottom. That sort of thing worked in the movies, but this was the real world and I wasn't an Errol Flynn nor a Buster Crabbe.

There was, however, a drainpipe some distance to the left of the window. Maybe … But how the hell could I reach it? I clambered on to the sill and leaned out. The fresh air assailed my nostrils making my head feel even woozier and for a frightening moment I thought I was going to lose my balance. My hand shot out and I managed to snatch hold of the side of the window. With gritted teeth, I remained still in the precarious position for some time, acclimatizing to the cold air and forcing my brain to behave itself.

I realized that the only way I was going to reach the drainpipe was to make a leap for it and hope that I could get a firm enough grip on it to stop me falling. If I failed, I would drop like a stone to the courtyard nearly a hundred feet below. I've taken some risks in my time, but I reckoned this one would take the prize. Edging my way, inch by inch, I positioned myself on the edge of the window sill as near to the pipe as I could get. It was still some six feet away. I gazed at the black cylindrical pipe for some moments and then, taking a deep breath, I jumped.

My hands reached out in wild desperation for the drainpipe. My heart soared as they found purchase on the cold metal. I was able to grip the pipe firmly but my legs flailed in the air beneath me pulling my body from side to side like some bizarre melting pendulum. I could not bring them to order to give me extra purchase by clamping them around the pipe.

As I struggled, dangling wildly in the air, my hands started to slip. The weight of my body began to pull me down. The pipe was smooth and cold and my hands could not grip any harder. I slid down six feet or so, my fingers burning with the friction and knees banging viciously against the wall sending shooting pains up my legs.

For one crazy moment, I thought I could travel in this fashion all the way down to the bottom, but if I did there certainly wouldn't be any flesh left on my hands and I doubted if I'd ever be able to walk again.

I slid another three feet and then at last I managed to arch my back sufficiently so that I could raise my legs up and bring the soles of my shoes flat against the wall to act as a break.

At last I came to a halt. Like a human fly, I was clinging to the drainpipe in a hunched position, some fifty feet above a paved courtyard. I waited a while to catch my breath and then slowly, in this rather undignified and hazardous position, I edged my way downwards. It was difficult and painful but I made progress.

I was about twenty feet from the ground when the drainpipe began to move and shudder. Then I heard a sharp cracking sound. I looked up and, in the moonlight, I could see that one of the brackets that secured the pipe to the wall had come adrift. The weight of my body had pulled it from its moorings.

I could feel the pipe slowly dislodge itself from the wall. Soon it would fall way altogether and me with it. I cursed silently and speeded up my hunched descent. I knew that any moment now the pipe would come crashing down.

About ten feet to go.

Then it happened. With an angry, gurgling crack, the section of the pipe I was clinging to broke free and swung out at right angles to the wall, sending a shower of water splashing on to the court-yard below. I was now hanging on to the pipe like a trained chimp. It started to bend and crack as it no longer could resist my weight. There was only one thing to do now. That was to jump.

Luckily, I had had some parachute training during my brief spell in the army when I had two eyes and had some notion how to fall on a hard surface. There was only about eight feet between me and the ground now. With a deep breath and a brief prayer, I let go and dropped to the floor. My body jarred as it touched down, but I soft-ened the pain with a roll. It was a good job I did for had I stayed where I landed, I would have been clobbered on the head by a length of metal drainpipe which clattered to a halt a few feet away.

I lay still for a moment staring at the pale yellow moon. I was still a little woozy from the drug, but the fall had certainly helped to sharpen the old brain. My body was aching in parts I didn't know I had, but I was thankful I was breathing and still conscious.

Gingerly, I dragged myself to my feet and limped away in the direction of the street. I had escaped. I had survived. It was a bloody miracle.

I soon found a telephone box. I rang David Llewellyn at home. As usual he was irascible at being dragged from his slumbers, but I shut him up and with remarkable brevity I told him my story ending with the words, 'So get here fast, with some men and bring a gun.'

TWENTY-SIX

It was just less than an hour after Gina's phone call to Vic when there was a ring at her doorbell. Snatching up Hawke's pistol, she hurried to the door and gazed through the spy hole. There appeared to be no one there.

Anthony had long ago learned the trick of standing to one side of such contraptions in order not to be seen.

Tentatively Gina opened the door and gazed out into the corridor. Suddenly Anthony appeared before her, a wild manic grimace plastered on his blotchy features. 'Surprise!' he cried, pushing Gina back into the narrow hall and knocking her to the ground. She fell on her back winded and shocked, but with great speed she took in the situation and, sitting up, aimed the gun at her attacker. But before she was able to use it, Anthony knocked it from her grasp with a vicious kick. It skittered down the hallway, out of sight. With a cry of pain Gina scrambled to her feet and ran into the living room. Anthony hared after her and launched himself on to the girl. The pair of them crashed to the floor.

Terror made her quick and drink made him slow. But nonetheless Anthony managed to pin her to the floor, his hands eventually reaching her throat. She struggled desperately and had he been a leaner opponent she would have probably escaped his clutches but his weight and fury were against her.

'You bitch,' he said, his voice hoarse and strained. She saw the drink-fuelled madness in his eyes and suddenly she became very frightened. It became clear to her that she was in great danger of losing her life. She tried with all her might to wriggle free, but to no avail. He had her trapped.

Then his fingers gripped her throat.

And pressed hard against her windpipe.

She began to croak and spittle seeped out of the side of her mouth and dribbled down her chin.

He pressed even harder.

'No,' she mouthed, but no sound emerged.

Her terror only intensified his determination.

She was shocked how quickly she had not only become a victim but a victim who was about lose the battle. God, her mind screamed, I *am* going to die!

She hadn't the energy to struggle any more. She felt her body grow limp. Suddenly Gina knew that she must let her body go limp, must give the appearance of death, but already grey clouds were sailing past her eyes, blanking out Anthony's grotesque visage.

Vic was surprised to find the door to Gina's flat slightly ajar. Cautiously he entered and moved stealthily down the hall towards the sitting room where a bizarre sight met his eyes. There was his brother Anthony down on his knees, looming over Gina's inert body.

Sensing another presence in the room, Anthony turned, his hands held before him as in an act of supplication, and gazed at his brother, a wild, triumphant gleam in his eye.

'She's dead,' he said.

It took Vic a moment to fully appreciate the situation. He stared at the limp body of his cousin Gina Bernstein with a mixture of horror and delight. She was corpse white and her tongue lolled from her open mouth. Well, he'd come with the intention of getting rid of the girl and now it seems that his Neanderthal brother had done the job for him.

'Good riddance,' Vic said at length.

'I knew you'd be pleased,' grinned Anthony, struggling to his feet. 'I couldn't tolerate the situation any longer. I had to do something.' His tone was almost apologetic, confessional, as sobriety began to assert itself.

'That's OK. You did well,' said Vic, his eyes darting around the room.

'What's up?' asked Anthony.

'Gina rang me to say that a private detective had been here this evening. John Hawke was his name. A one-eyed chap. She said he knew all about her.'

'Christ!'

'She told me that she'd drugged him and asked me to dispose of his body. That's why I'm here.'

'Well, where is he then?'

'That's what I'm thinking. You look in the kitchen, I'll check the bedroom.'

Vic spotted the open window as soon as he entered the bedroom. He looked out and saw the broken drainpipe. He grimaced. 'Damn.'

'He's not in the kitchen,' announced Anthony entering the room.

'No, he's gone. Escaped.'

'Escaped!'

'Here, look.'

Anthony stared out of the window. 'You mean he clambered down the pipe?'

Vic shrugged. 'Only explanation. He's not here. Window open, broken pipe. Bloody Houdini, ain't he?'

'What do we do now?'

'We get the hell out of here. Leave our friend Gina for some poor sod to find her. At least she's out of our hair, but now we've got to find this John Hawke chappie and silence him.'

TWENTY-SEVEN

I waited in the telephone box, curled up on the hard concrete floor and tried to get my head together. Whatever drug Gina had given me, it was a persistent blighter. It was still clogging my brain and making thoughts sluggish and my movements uncertain. I was cold, fed up and very tired. I wanted my bed and to sleep for a week but there were more important things to concern me.

Remarkably David turned up with a squad car and two burly coppers in less than an hour. I led them to Parkway Mansions and we went up to Gina's flat. On this occasion I travelled *inside* the building.

David posted the two uniformed men either side of the door and then tried the handle. It opened. Gun in hand he entered the flat with me following close on his heels. The entrance was in darkness but there was a dim light from the sitting room at the end of the hall. We moved slowly towards it. The room was very much as it had been when I'd taken my drugged brandy, apart from one thing: there was the body of a woman slumped on the white rug in front of the fire.

It was Gina.

She was either unconscious.

Or dead.

'She looks like a gonner to me,' David said as we both knelt down by her. I felt for her pulse. Remarkably there was one but it was just about to give up the ghost. The girl was teetering on the brink. Already reddish marks were forming around her neck.

Someone had tried to strangle her and had almost succeeded. Indeed, unless she received urgent medical attention, he may well have done. While David was phoning for an ambulance, I had a quick look around Gina's flat. I made no sensational discoveries, but my search was somewhat enlightening.

Some time later I was sitting by the bedside of the unfortunate Gina in a private room in the Middlesex Hospital in Euston Road. Beside me was Detective Inspector David Llewellyn. Outside the room was one of the burly constables on guard under the strict instructions not to let anyone enter who was not a doctor or a nurse with the appropriate identity card. We had been told that Gina was in a bad way and it was touch and go whether she would survive. This news was no surprise. She had a severely crushed windpipe and the lack of oxygen to the brain could well have affected her mental processes. It seemed to me that whoever had tried to strangle Gina had believed that he had completed his task successfully. She certainly looked pretty dead when we found her.

As we sat by the girl's bedside I explained to David in more detail how I had discovered Gina's whereabouts, my chat with her and how I had ended up shinning down a drainpipe at midnight. After I had finished, he gave a long exasperated sigh and shook his head. His expression was unusually hostile. 'You've done it again, haven't you? Seeing yourself as a one man detective force. Mr Solo out to solve the crime on his own. None of this is really your business, yet you seemed to have been deter-mined to make it so.'

'I found the girl, didn't I?'

'Oh, yes, you found the girl. But in stirring up the waters, you brought out the shark to strike. And this is the result.' He jerked his head towards the prone figure beside us.

'Are you saying I'm responsible for the attack on her? Now you're talking out of your Welsh arse.'

'Just at the moment I'd get more sense out of my Welsh arse than you.' His face was so serious and flushed with such earnest-ness as he said this that I could not help but see the comical side of this interchange. I was tired and still a little drugged and I just laughed.

At first David seemed indignant at my laughter and I saw his hands curl into fists, but then somehow he too saw the farcical nature of our argument – discussing the erudition of his backside – and his features softened and he gave a brief guffaw.

'You're right about the attack,' David said at length, his temper having now evaporated. 'It's not your fault. You just make me mad by not telling me things, not keeping me informed.'

I didn't want to infuriate him again by asserting that I was not employed as a police informer so I just nodded non-committally. David was a true friend and I didn't want to mar that friendship over technicalities. I had to admit to myself that at times I became so wrapped up in my own investigations that I tended to forget David was under as much pressure and stress as I was. He had rules and superiors to obey, rigid procedures to follow and regulations to uphold, where I was a free agent, a maverick, who could follow his own hunches and set his own rules and bend the law if necessary.

He had a point.

And to be honest since the moment we found Gina, I had wondered if in some way my actions had precipitated the attack on her.

Conscience pricking, I took a small object wrapped in a handkerchief from the pocket of my overcoat. 'I think you'd better have this.'

'What is it?'

'A neat little shooter. I found it in Gina's flat just now. She kept it in her drawer by the bed. One bullet missing.'

David took the gun from me and gingerly unwrapped it from the folds of the handkerchief. 'If the bullet matches the one we dug out of Paulo Ricotti's head, we've got our murderer. She'll swing for it.'

'If she survives,' I observed pithily, glancing at the white face barely visible over the white sheets. 'There may be fingerprints on the gun, too, to strengthen the case.'

'Good man.'

'Oh, I'm a good man now. Is that your arse speaking?'

David grinned. 'Anything else you stumbled upon in your search?'

'Not a lot but there were several wigs in her wardrobe which suggests our Gina likes to change her appearance. As you can see, she's dark-haired, but I found blonde, auburn and brown wigs in the flat.'

'Blonde?'

'Indeed; remember the girl who was seen with Paulo on the night he was murdered had blonde hair and her figure – tall, slender – matches Miss Gina here.'

'Another little nail in her coffin.'

'Thank you. And while you're at it, you might as well scoop up Archie Muldoon. With a bit of pressure, I'm sure you'll get all the details of the Bernsteins' protection racket. With his evidence, you'll be able to move in on the family. He hangs out at Crimea Buildings.'

'I know the very spot. I'll see to that tomorrow. I'm going nowhere near Leo or the Bernstein boys for the moment. Not until we've got cast-iron evidence, either from this young lady here if she pulls through or from Muldoon. Now the real question is – who tried to kill this girl?'

'I don't know. Not yet.'

'Not yet,' snapped David, his temper rising once more. 'Well, be sure to tell me if you find out!'

Before I could respond, the door glided open quietly and a doctor in a creased white coat with a stethoscope dangling out of one of the pockets entered. His face was haggard and his eyes weary. 'Good evening, gentlemen,' he said, and then, glancing at his watch, corrected himself, 'or rather good morning.'

Instinctively, I checked the time. It was 2.30 a.m.

Without another word, the doctor checked the girl's progress chart and then proceeded to examine her. Gazing down into her open mouth with a pen torch and shiny instrument with a small mirror on the end, he began clicking his teeth in a meditative way.

'Any change? Any improvement?' asked David.

'Oh, no,' came the dour reply. 'It's far too early for improvement. Her breathing is shallow and her pulse is very weak. The best we can hope for at present is for her condition to stabilize. That could take a while. If you are waiting for her to regain consciousness tonight, you're wasting your time.'

David and I exchanged glances.

'Come back tomorrow around noon maybe. But even then I don't hold out much hope.'

With some reluctance David rose from his chair and I followed suit. 'If you think that's best, Doctor. I certainly could do with a few hours' sleep,' my companion said.

The doctor nodded pointedly. You're not the only one, he seemed to be saying.

'But I will need to know the minute she regains consciousness.'

'I can assure you that it will not be for a while … if at all.'

This was not news we wanted to hear.

'Be sure to let me know if there is any change in the girl's condition.'

The doctor nodded and we left.

It was good to get out into cold, frosty night air, away from the stifling antiseptic atmosphere of the hospital. Those places had unpleasant memories for me, which were always resurrected whenever I found myself within their environs. David and I parted company, each of us wending our way homeward. He had offered to give me a lift back to Hawke Towers, but I declined. I thought I'd knock up Benny and beg a bed for the night. Somehow I didn't think it was safe for me to go home just yet.

As I expected, initially Benny caused a fuss at being dragged from his bed 'at this unearthly time of night' – but he soon settled down and even brought me a hot-water bottle to air the sheets a little.

As I lay in bed I ran through the events of my crowded evening in my mind and came to the conclusion that I was a little wiser but not much happier. Then I thought about Max. Her sweet face and gentle smile. What I wouldn't give for a hug and a kiss from her right now. Then it struck me how horrified she would be if she knew how close to death I had been that night. It suddenly made me realize that I had to be a lot more careful with my life, not be so reckless with my safety from now on. It was not just *my* life that

I could play fast and loose with any more. I was sharing it with someone else. Someone who really cared for me. With this disconcerting thought, I fell asleep.

TWENTY-EIGHT

'Well,' said Anthony chewing the end of his cigarette. 'We've really started something now.'

Vic glanced over at his brother and realized clearly for the first time how much he really disliked him. Disliked? No, he mused, it was stronger than that. It had always puzzled Vic that this man had emerged from the same womb as himself. Not only did they not look alike (thank God for that, thought Vic) but their temperament, intelligence and ability to cope with life were streets apart. As a child Vic had rather prided himself in looking after his young, more stupid brother, getting him out of scrapes, protecting him as one would a naughty puppy, but from adolescence to adulthood, Vic had grown to despise this bond of kinship. They were yoked together in the family business like prisoners on a chain gang and, oh, how he longed to break that chain.

'To be precise, it was you who started this "something",' said Vic quietly. He wasn't going to admit that he had turned up at Gina's flat with exactly the same intentions as Anthony – to kill the girl. But then, of course, that had become essential now that Anthony had blabbed to Muldoon and it would seem Muldoon had done the same to this one-eyed detective bloke called Hawke.

Anthony was not in the mood for arguing. 'Yeah, OK. But now we've got to finish it together.'

It was in the early hours of the morning and they were sitting in the kitchen of Vic's flat with coffee and a whisky each.

Vic nodded. He had to agree to that. With Gina dead, the only threat to their safety now was Archie Muldoon and Hawke. With them out of the way there was no one who could prove a connection between Gina and the Bernsteins. Vic explained the situation and his plans to his brother, slowly and in detail.

'Understand?' he said at last.

Anthony nodded. 'Yeah, I understand. It means we're not going to get much sleep tonight.'

Dawn was always late visiting the inhabitants of Crimea Buildings. The dingy edifice with its tiny, grimy windows was reluctant to let the light of a new day shine in and expose its dirt and decay. Most of the residents were either workshy, unemployed or creatures of the night employed in various nefarious activities and had just crawled under their sheets before the sky lightened. So it was that when someone came knocking on Archie Muldoon's door with the sun already struggling to make its presence felt through a bank of louring grey clouds, there was no immediate response from the inmates. The tenant of Flat 333 was deep in sleep, entwined around his woman, her peroxide hair spilling upwards in a tangle across the grey pillow. It was she who first became aware of the loud knocking. It burrowed gradually into her consciousness. Slowly she raised her head and listened. Now there was no mistaking the sound.

'Archie,' she said, shaking his shoulder. 'There's someone at the door.' She had to shake him again and repeat herself before she got a reaction. 'So what,' he mumbled grumpily, still half asleep.

Before the woman had chance to answer there came a loud thud out in the hallway followed by crashing sound. The noise reverberated around the tiny flat and this finally roused Archie from his slumbers with a start. He had just staggered from his bed to find out 'what the row was all about' when the door of the bedroom burst open and the intruders entered. Archie froze in horror and surprise.

'What the hell are you doing here?' he cried. It was the last thing he ever said. There was a sharp crack of a pistol and an amorphous, crimson wound appeared on the grubby material of his vest. He gazed down in wonderment at the spreading stain of blood which seeped in a star-like shape across his chest. But then his legs gave way and he collapsed on to the floor. He was dead before the dust settled around him.

With an hysterical sob, the woman burrowed into the bedclothes like a child believing that if she was covered she would not be seen. Her actions did not protect her. Two more shots were fired and her quivering body lay still.

Once more unnatural death had visited Crimea Buildings.

Towards noon, Vic and Anthony Bernstein were seated in Uncle Leo's office looking grave as he imparted the news to them.

'Some bastard has tried to kill Gina.'

'Tried?' asked Anthony with some alarm.

'Yes, someone went to her flat last night and tried to strangle her.'

It was the word 'tried' that made Anthony's heart beat and sweat begin to form on his forehead. He shot a wide-eyed glance at Vic who gave a slight shake of the head, warning him to keep his mouth shut.

'Who did it?' asked Anthony, his voice rasping as it emerged from a very dry throat.

Leo spread his fingers widely. 'I don't know. It's very strange and very disturbing. She was left for dead, apparently. She has some spirit, that girl.'

Vic, who had been sitting quietly, examining his finger nails, rose suddenly and began pacing the room. 'Will she live? Where is she?'

'She's in the Middlesex,' said Leo. 'I got that from the commissionaire at Parkway Mansions when I called there this morning. I don't know how she is for certain. The commissionaire reckoned that she was unconscious when they carried her out. But at least she's alive for the moment. But we've got to keep well away from the hospital. All of us. Is that understood? The coppers are buzzing round there like flies. I don't want you getting tangled up with the law. Things are tricky enough as it is.'

'What if she talks?' said Anthony. 'Blabs about our business. We'll all be in the dung then.'

'She won't talk,' said Leo. 'She's tough and resilient. Remember, she's a Bernstein. They'll not crack Gina. I'm just worried that we will lose her.'

'I'd like to get my hands on the bastard who ...' Anthony thumped the desk angrily.

'We'd all like that,' said Leo. 'And we will. All in good time. Meanwhile, we suspend all our operations....'

Anthony raised his hand to protest but Leo waved him down with an angry sweep of his hand.

'We suspend all our operations,' he repeated with emphasis, 'and lie low until we have a clearer picture of events.'

'How do we do that, if we're not to go to the hospital?' asked Vic.

Leo sighed. 'I'll get one of the boys to make discreet enquiries. The porters usually know all there is to know. But you two, stay away. It's bad enough with Gina in trouble. Is that clear?'

Leo stared hard at the two young men. They nodded in reluctant agreement.

'And,' Leo added even more gravely, 'watch your backs. There's a killer about wanting to destroy this family.'

David Llewellyn stepped over the threshold of Flat 333 Crimea Buildings, the remnants of the crippled front door lying askew in the hallway. It had been kicked in with some force.

'They're in the bedroom,' said Sergeant Sunderland, who had arrived ahead of his boss and was standing at the far end of the hall.

Together the two men entered the room. On the floor, flat on his back, his mouth agape and eyes wide open staring at the cracks in the ceiling was Archie Muldoon. Already his flesh was beginning to turn blue. The red wound on his vest clearly indicated the cause of death. He was not a pretty sight in life, thought David, but he was far worse dead.

The covers had been pulled back from the bed to reveal the body of the blonde-haired woman, curled in a foetal position. David could see the two bullet holes, one on her back and one in the neck.

'Who is she?' he asked.

'Her name is Sarah. That's all I could get from the neighbours. She was, to use their phrase, "Archie's woman".' He wrinkled his nose with distaste as he said it.

David gave a heartfelt sigh. 'It's becoming far too familiar an occasion is this, Sunderland. Meeting up with you to view a body – two in this case.'

For some moments David Llewellyn stood in this dingy, stale-smelling bedroom with the two stiffening corpses and photographed the scene in his memory for further reference. He just wished that it wasn't necessary.

'I should have acted faster, but I never thought this would happen,' he said, almost to himself, but the ever alert Sunderland queried him.

'What do you mean, sir?'

'Archie Muldoon's been working a protection racket scam for the Bernsteins. Johnny Hawke advised that I pull him in for questioning but … it seems someone got there before me.'

'The Bernsteins no doubt.'

'No doubt. But prove it. Did the neighbours see anything, anyone? After all, some devil smashed the door in.'

'Sir, this is Crimea Buildings. No one saw or heard a thing. They're all deaf and blind here. Helping the police is tantamount to slitting your grandmother's throat to this lot.'

'I suspected as much.' He sighed. 'OK Sergeant, get these lovelies over to the morgue and have a thorough search of these delightful premises to see if you can come up with anything that has the slightest resemblance to a clue.'

'What are you going to do, sir?'

'Me? I'm going to the hospital.'

'And who might you be?' The bobby on duty outside Gina Bernstein's room rose from his chair and stood in front of the doorway.

David smiled indulgently. 'Good man,' he said, plucking out his warrant card from his inside pocket. The constable immediately stiffened his stance. 'Sorry, sir.'

'Now, don't be sorry. You weren't to know I was from the Yard. I could have been an axe-wielding murderer for all you knew.'

'Yes, sir.'

'Any change in the girl?'

'Don't think so, sir. Doctors haven't said anything to me, but the nurse who brings me a cup of tea said there was nothing new to report.'

David pulled a disappointed face.

'Still, sir, that also means she ain't got worse.'

'That's true,' he agreed, forcing a weak smile. 'Well, seeing as I'm here, I'll just take a quick look at her.'

The constable stood aside to let David enter.

The room was gloomy. The window shades were drawn. The girl looked exactly as she had the night before; her tiny drawn face just peering over the counterpane, expressionless and mask-like. To David's dismay it looked like the face of a dead woman. However, the monitor that recorded her heartbeat indicated there was still feeble life in that vital organ.

'C'mon love,' he whispered, leaning over the bed, 'you can do it. Struggle up towards the light, eh?'

The girl's face remained immobile. Only the gentle bleep of the monitor and the almost imperceptible rise of her chest indicated that she was still alive.

David left the room and went in search of a doctor, although he felt sure that there really would be no news, no progress to report. This was going to be a long wait and in the end it could well be a futile one.

Despite the danger and seriousness of this 'mission' as he thought of it, he was quite excited by the task in hand. It was a new departure for him and he saw it as a way of developing, growing in experience. It wasn't his plan, of course, but he had been happy to be the one to put it into operation.

He had combed his hair a different way and adopted a large pair of dark, horn-rimmed spectacles which he considered made him look older and 'brainier'. Carrying his briefcase with a swagger, he approached the reception desk.

'My sister was admitted here last night,' he said, adopting a nervous urgency in his manner and voice. 'The police brought her in, I gather. The poor girl had been attacked. Strangled. Gina Andrews is the name.'

The young girl at the desk, a pretty little thing hardly out of her teens, did not have to check her register. The hospital had been buzzing with the news.

'She's in a private ward on the second floor. But she's not allowed visitors at the moment. There is a policeman on duty outside her room; perhaps you had better report to him and find out more details.'

'Thank you,' he gushed, wiping his brow as a dramatic gesture.

'It's room 210. You'll find the stairs to your left.'

'Thank you miss,' said the man in the tortoiseshell glasses.

On reaching the second floor, he sought out the gentleman's lavatory. Once ensconced in one the confined cubicles, he removed his overcoat and withdrew a white coat, the sort worn by doctors, from his briefcase, into which he now placed his rolled-up overcoat. He slipped on the white coat, adjusted his glasses and left the cubicle. He checked his appearance in the mirror above the wash basin and was pleased with the result. 'Good Day, Dr Jekyll,' he said, smugly, to his own reflection and gave himself a brief salute before venturing out on to the corridor once more.

Believing now that his simple disguise gave him an invincible immunity, he swaggered through the hospital with great confidence. His next task was to effect a bit of sleight of hand. That should be no trouble to him. He had been an excellent pickpocket before he'd got out of short trousers.

He loitered in the corridor pretending to look at some notes from his briefcase, waiting until a suitable subject came along. He didn't have to wait long. An elderly doctor, with a weary gait and stooped shoulders, came into view. He started to move towards him, and when they were almost abreast, he stumbled and collided with the doctor, knocking him against the wall.

'I'm most awfully sorry,' he said. 'I'm such a careless oaf. Are you all right?'

'No damage done,' said the doctor with some irritation. He pulled himself up straight and dusted himself down.

'Good, good. Well, sorry again.' He moved off at haste, clutching his prize secreted in his hand.

'Now for little Gina,' he muttered.

Following the painted signs on the walls, he soon found his way down a narrow dimly lighted corridor to room 210. There was a uniformed policeman sitting outside reading a copy of the *Daily Mirror*.

'Hello, Constable,' he said cheerily, approaching the officer. 'Any good news in the paper?'

The constable, a young man with wispy hair and a sallow face, glanced up in surprise. He had not heard the fellow in the white coat approach.

'Er, no. Not really. Same old stuff,' he said lamely.

'Just got to see the patient for a moment,' said the man in the white coat, tapping his briefcase. 'Need to administer some drugs.' He made a move towards the door but the young policeman rose from his chair.

'Can I see your pass, please, sir?'

'Certainly,' he replied cheerily, presenting the policeman with the white card which he had taken from the doctor he had collided with some minutes earlier.

The constable barely gave it a glance. 'All in order,' he said, returning the card.

'Thank you, I won't be very long,' the man in the white coat assured the policeman as he opened the door of room 210 and entered.

TWENTY-NINE

Despite my instructions to the contrary, Benny let me sleep late the next morning. I just snored on beyond my usual waking hour. It wasn't just my body that was tired, my brain was weary too. Sleep was the escape from the slings and arrows of my outrageous fortune. Benny brought me a cup of tea and an egg sandwich around nine o'clock. Both were most welcome and I hadn't the heart to complain about him not rousing me earlier. And, bless him, he never enquired about the business that had brought me to his place in the early hours of the morning. He knew I was a detective with an unpredictable and erratic lifestyle – sometimes routines were disrupted and strange measures were needed; he accepted that and didn't pry. I'm sure he felt more comfortable not knowing.

Even when I dragged myself from my crumpled pit, I felt sluggish. Sadly the tea and sandwich followed by a fag did little to revive my spirits. There were too many rough edges in my life at present, too many unresolved conundrums for me to feel at ease and full of vigour. On top of this, I was missing Max. It amazed me how in a few short months she had become such an integral and essential part of my life. I knew her absence would make me a little miserable, but I had not reckoned on the ache that not having her near had generated.

I dressed quickly and hurried home.

I'd had visitors. The lock had been broken and my place had been subject to a gentle ransack. They certainly hadn't got what they wanted because that was me. I had been wise after all not to sleep at home. I rang for a locksmith and carried out my full morning ablutions, hoping a cold wash and a shave, along with a fresh change of clothes would perk me up a little. To be honest, I did feel a little better, more human I suppose, but my spirits still remained on the low side.

While I waited for the locksmith, I tidied up and decided what I ought to do with my day. I knew that really I should visit that photographic studio in Oxford Street in the hope that I would clean up one unpleasant mess, but I knew that particular errand could wait a while. My thoughts were really focused on the girl in the Middlesex – the mysterious Gina. I had a strong desire to see how she was. I really wanted to be around when she regained consciousness. *If* she regained consciousness. If I popped into the hospital first, I could easily make my way up to Oxford Street later. A few hours would not make any real difference. After my lock had been fixed, I ventured out once more.

It was one of those grey winter days which never quite see daylight. Pedestrians hurried along, huddled into their coats, their breath emerging in short puffs of steam into the chill air. I walked as briskly as I could towards the hospital. By the time I got there, I was frozen to the marrow and unusually glad to pass through the swing doors into the warm foyer.

I made my way up to the second floor and along the corridor to Gina's room. There was a new constable on guard outside. The burly fellow from the night before had been replaced by a young chap who, as I approached, seemed to snap himself out of a daydream and rise quickly from his chair. His expression was not welcoming. Before he could say a word, I flashed my pass at him, the one they'd given me the night before.

'I am a colleague of Detective Inspector Llewellyn,' I said.

The constable looked askance at this fellow in a shabby overcoat with slit sleeves and eye-patch, but the pass erased any resistance.

'I've come to see how the girl is,' I added.

'I don't think there's been much change,' said the policeman, eyeing me with suspicion. 'There's a doctor in with her now.'

'Good. I'll get a progress report from the horse's mouth,' I said quickly with a brief smile and, before he could stop me, I swept past him and opened the door.

The room was gloomy. The shade was drawn and the only illumination was a small bedside light. Silhouetted against this was a figure dressed in a white coat bending over the patient in the bed. At my entrance, he jerked upwards and turned in surprise to face me, his features masked by harsh shadows. All I could tell was that he had dark hair and wore a large pair of thick horn-rimmed glasses.

'Doctor,' I said in greeting. 'I'm John Hawke, associated with the police. I was the person—'

I got no further because I had to dodge a water jug that the white-coated figure had hurled at me. It crashed harmlessly against the wall.

So, my brain told me rapidly assessing this odd situation, this fellow is not a doctor, or if so, a very disturbed one. He tried to rush past me, heading for the door, but I stood my ground and prevented him. I grabbed hold of the fellow and we tussled in an ungainly fashion, like two gorillas attempting a waltz, ricocheting around the tiny room. With a concerted effort, I rammed him backwards against the wall. He was bulkier than me but not as agile and I was able to force him on to the ground, where I placed my foot firmly on his chest and pressed down hard to pin him in place.

'Lie still,' I said, 'or I'll crack all your ribs.'

Remarkably he did as I ordered. Then I noticed his shadowy face glance at something over my shoulder. Before I knew what was happening, two arms grasped me from behind.

'Don't try anything funny,' came a voice in my ear. It was the young constable. Doing his mistaken duty. With a sharp tug he pulled me backwards, releasing my assailant.

'Thank you, Officer,' cried the intruder, jumping to his feet. 'He's some sort of madman. He attacked me while I was treating my patient,' he cried hurriedly, making for the door. 'If you can restrain him for a moment, I'll raise the alarm.' He was out of the room in a flash.

'You fool,' I raged. 'He's not a doctor. He was trying to kill the girl.'

'A likely story,' came the reply. There was stupid arrogance in his tone. 'Now you keep still, Mr Bloody One Eye or it will be the worse for you.'

That did it. Real anger overcame all my emotions. I thrust my arms outwards with great force and broke free of his grasp. Swinging round, I planted my fist hard on his stupid face. I heard his nose crack. With a yell of surprise, he fell to the ground, his body slithering across the floor, his head disappearing under the bed. I didn't hang around to examine the state of his injuries, but sped from the room and down the narrow corridor into the main thoroughfare just in time to see Mr Horn-rimmed Glasses at the far end about to descend the curved staircase to the lower floor.

I raced after him.

It was the sound of my feet clattering on the stone floor that alerted my quarry that he was being chased. He speeded up and bounded down the staircase three and sometimes four steps at a time. He had disappeared from sight by the time I began to descend. As I reached midway and the floor below came in view, I spied him slipping down a corridor to the right. It would, I knew, lead him to the main foyer and freedom. Once out through those large revolving doors, I would lose him as sure as dried eggs is dried eggs.

However, luck was with me – or so I thought – for, as I turned into the corridor, it seemed that my violent friend had collided with a visitor, a tall man in a blue overcoat. The two of them were engaged in what appeared to be an animated conversation. This delay was a real bonus. Then Mr Horn-rimmed Glasses threw a glance back in my direction, said something in urgent rasped tones to the other man before legging it down the corridor.

Then something disturbing occurred. The fellow in the blue overcoat began walking towards me with a strange determination. As he did so he reached inside his overcoat. Instinct, experience, a message from the heavens, call it what you will, but I knew in an instant that this man meant me harm; that this man was in league with Mr Horn-rimmed Glasses; that this man was not reaching inside his overcoat to bring out a handkerchief.

He then became my target. I lunged forward, throwing my whole weight against him and, as we both crashed to the floor, I caught sight of the gun in his hand.

I had been right.

As we struggled together on the floor, he brought the butt of the gun down on my head with some force. I went blind for a few seconds, so intense was the pain. I fell back releasing my hold on the man, while a road drill attempted to burrow its way into my brain.

When I regained my sight – it was a bleared double vision really – I saw what appeared to be a couple of doctors hurrying down the corridor towards me, their voices raised in alarm. My assailant had spotted them too and had taken flight. As through a light mist I saw him disappear in the distance down the shimmering corridor. When the white-coated medic reached me, he bent down, his tired face looming like some ghoulish visage from a fairground distorting mirror. He said something to me, but by then the road drill had broken through the wall of my skull and all I could hear was an all-encompassing roaring noise. Shortly after that I lost consciousness.

When I returned to life I was lying on a bed staring up at the face of none other than Detective Inspector David Llewellyn. By his side was a young nurse whose cool hand held my wrist. With groggy logic I realized that she was taking my pulse.

'What you'll do to get some pretty young girl to hold your hand,' David observed wryly.

I would have liked to have replied, but my mouth was sandpaper dry and my brain was torpid, not to mention the thundering headache that consumed me. Little men were wielding pickaxes digging holes all over my medulla oblongata. In the background, by the door, I saw the young constable who had tried to restrain me. He was in possession of an embarrassed, guilty look and a very bloody nose.

'You've been x-rayed and bandaged. No serious damage, just a bad concussion,' explained my policeman friend matter-of-factly. 'An overnight stay and you'll be able to go home tomorrow.'

'I'm going home now,' I croaked, and attempted to slide my legs over the side of the bed, but nothing happened. They stayed where they were.

'Steady, Mr Hawke,' said the nurse. (David was right, she was pretty.) 'You're still in shock. You need to rest. Give it time for your body to return to normal.'

I slumped back on my pillow. With deep chagrin, I had to admit she was right.

'Who were they?' David asked at length. 'Did you recognize either of the two men?'

'I've not seen them before,' I said slowly, moistening my lips with my tongue. The nurse stepped forward with a glass of water from which I took a few sips. 'Thank you,' I said. 'No, I don't know them, but somehow they seemed familiar. I think the chap who pretended he was the doctor—'

'The one with the glasses?' said David.

I nodded and set off a few explosions in my head. I winced. 'I think the glasses were a bit of a disguise,' I observed with groggy irony.

'I've got his description from the constable here. What about the other fellow – the one who gave you the headache.'

'Tall, well-dressed, in his late twenties I should say. Wore a smart blue overcoat, expensive material.'

'Not a lot to go on. I might show you some pictures.'

'Well, one thing is for certain, I'll recognize the bastard again.'

Then a thought came to me through the cobwebs of my mind. 'The girl. What about the girl?'

David shook his head and ran his hand across his mouth. 'We've lost her, I'm afraid. For whatever reason, our bogus doctor wanted her dead and he succeeded in his mission.'

My heart sank. If only I had arrived at the hospital a few minutes earlier....

THIRTY

Max sat in the rear stalls to watch the opening number. She considered this the best vantage point in the theatre to gain the full effect of the scene and in particular the costumes – her costumes. It was a village-green set. A garish painted backdrop portrayed a row of ye olde world houses and shops. There was a maypole at the centre of the stage around which the dancers would perform and near the wings at the right-hand side there was the magic bean stall, a hand cart that would be wheeled forward when Jack appeared after the first number.

On cue from the director, who was sitting on the front row of the stalls, the small orchestra struck up 'Happy Days Are Here Again' and the villagers filed on to the stage in time to the music and began the show's opening dance routine. Given the limited choice of material and time, Max had gone for bright vibrant colours in a variety of hues for the costumes and ensured that none of the villagers was dressed exactly the same. The result was a pleasing kaleidoscope of moving colour across the stage, the fierce footlights gracing the costumes with a glamour they did not possess in the broad light of day. It was the magic of theatre.

It all looked good. Max was pleased with her efforts.

She heard a rustle in the row behind her. She turned and in the gloom she saw Roger Prescott, the show's producer, shuffling along the seats towards her.

'Hello there, darling,' he said cheerily. 'Admiring your work?'

Max grinned and nodded. 'Just checking it out,' she said.

'Well, you should be admiring it. Those costumes work a treat. You've done a grand job.'

'Oh, thank you,' she beamed. Roger was a no nonsense fellow and she knew that he meant it.

He leaned forward and planted a chaste kiss on her cheek. 'I'm so glad you're working on the show.'

'You'll make me blush.'

'Seriously. Those costumes add a real sparkle to the panto. Look, Max, you've worked wonders in such a short time and got so far ahead, how would you like a few days off? I mean it. You've toiled long and hard to finish the costumes and now there are only the dresses for the ballet sequence to sort out and then we're done. Honestly, we can do without you for a couple of days. I know you've been pining for that boyfriend of yours in London. Why not pop down on a train tomorrow and surprise him?'

'Oh, I couldn't.'

'Why not?'

Max thought for a moment and then beamed. 'Actually I can't think of a reason why not. That would be wonderful. Are you sure?'

'Of course I am, sweetie. Have one night of pash in the Smoke and then come back to us refreshed, ready for the final push before we open to those hordes of noisy brats.'

'I will,' said Max, grinning as broadly as she could.

'We are in the mire and no mistake,' said Anthony Bernstein, running his thick fingers through his greasy hair as he paced up and down.

'So you keep saying,' replied his brother Vic stoically.

'What the hell are we going to do now? All our plans, all our efforts, down the pan. And it's all that bleeding interfering one-eyed bastard's fault. I'll swing for him.'

'Well, you'll swing, certainly.'

'What's that supposed to mean?'

'You killed Gina. Remember? I trust you did manage it the second time.'

'Why you ...' But angry words failed him as so often they did.

179

Anthony always had difficulty articulating his feelings and so on these occasions he resorted to violent actions. With a grunt, he flew at his brother and grabbed him by the lapels of his suit and shook him violently.

Vic was unperturbed. 'Go on, hit me,' he said smoothly. 'Beat me up if you like. Where's that going to get you? I'm the only friend you have in the world now.'

Anthony's eyes bulged with fury and frustration. He let go of Vic's lapels and walked away. 'What *are* we going to do?' he muttered again.

'We don't have too many options. The police will already be round to our gaffs looking for us. It won't be long before they try all our hangouts, including here.'

He looked around the cold dusty premises, a shabby lock-up near the river in Wandsworth. It housed a few cases of illegal liquor and packs of black-market cigarettes. There was also a sink, an electric heater, a couple of makeshift beds and a gas cooker, along with some emergency supplies. They had come here after escaping the hospital and had camped out for twenty-four hours. Vic was aware that sooner or later Hawke would regain consciousness and identify them as his attackers and Gina's killer. They couldn't go back to their respective flats, or even show their faces on the street. Vic knew that their father Leo would be no bloody use. Somehow the old man felt more allegiance to Gina than he did to his own sons, despite the bitch only turning up on his doorstep less than a month ago. No doubt this affection-cum-loyalty was due to Leo's bond, or some weird filial link, to his brother coupled with his vague unexpressed disappointment at his own offspring. Vic sneered at the thought. Sod him, then, sod them all, including that creep of a brother of mine.

'We've got to face it. We're on the run,' Vic said at length. 'Before long the papers will have our mugs plastered all over them. We've got to get out of the city and lie low.'

'You mean we have to run away like fucking scared rabbits?'

'We leave as an act of self-preservation, dummy. If we stay we end up in the clink. You end up on the gallows.'

Anthony blanched. 'Then there's no choice.'

'There's no choice.'

Anthony paused for a moment, his podgy features wrapt in thought. 'We'll need some money and a car,' he said at last.

'Two cars. We can't afford to stick together. Two separate needles in a haystack are harder to find than two stuck together.'

Anthony wanted to complain, resist this plan, but he knew he shouldn't. He didn't want to admit it, but he was scared of being on his own, away from the protection and guidance of his older brother. He was well aware that he wasn't as bright or savvy as he was and it would be difficult functioning without his help and wisdom. Anthony had always felt inferior, always in the shadow thrown by Vic who was harder, more self-controlled than he was. At times he hated him for it, but he knew that in a crisis he needed his bright, arrogant brother. Anthony had no notion just how much Vic despised him.

'We'll have to wait until nightfall,' said Vic lighting yet another cigarette. 'Then I'll take a trip to the Bamboo House, get our hands on the contents of Dad's safe – whether he likes it or not. That should set us up nicely. Then we'll grab us a couple of motors and I'll head for the North and you get yourself down to Devon.'

'For how long?'

Vic shrugged. 'Six months at least.'

Anthony's heart sank. What the hell would he do in Devon for six months? 'Are you sure I can't come with you?'

'I'm bloody certain.'

Anthony glanced at his watch and groaned. 'So we wait until it gets dark.'

Vic nodded and gazed at his useless brother, contempt and hatred burgeoning in his heart. Dark would be good. Dark was the time to do it. Well, this was crunch time and desperate measures were needed. He had put up with this mental cripple for too long. For the sake of the family. Filial obligations and all that. But now those obligations were out of the window. The arrival of Gina had seen to all that. She'd not just rocked the boat: she'd sunk it. His father seemed to care more about her than he did his two sons and Anthony had proved once more what a fucking liability he was. With things being as they are, Vic realized that he could no longer afford to be weighed down by such an encumbrance.

THIRTY - ONE

I did as I was told and spent the night in the hospital. It wasn't just that I was obeying medical advice; I knew that I hadn't the energy or clear-headedness to hail a taxi to take me home, let alone cope with the other rigours of normal life. Certainly, chasing criminals was definitely out of the question. Thankfully, I slept soundly and on wakening I felt a little more like my old self. My head still ached and my mouth was dry, but I could see clearly out of my functioning eye and my limbs seemed to be working in unison.

The doctor came early and examined me. 'I know you're desperate to go home so I'll release you – but you are going to have to take it very easy for the next few days. In simple terms your brain is sore and disturbed and needs to recuperate. Any violent action, energetic activity could upset it further. Just rest, eh?'

I nodded in agreement. Well what else could I do? I didn't want to actually verbalize the lie. How could I take it easy when I had several murderers to lay by the heel? I could see by his tight grin and cynical expression that the doctor didn't believe me. He could see the truth in my eye. He gave a gentle eloquent shrug. Well, it seemed to say, I've done my duty and explained the consequences to the chump; if he chooses to ignore my advice that's his look out.

'Take care, Mr Hawke,' he said as a parting shot and swept from the room.

Like an arthritic robot that needs oiling, I pulled back the covers and got out of bed. I slipped off the hospital pyjamas and dressed myself. It was the first time I realized how many fiddly aspects there are to a man's attire from shoe laces to collar studs and fly buttons to braces. It seemed to take an eternity to make myself presentable and decent to the outside world. With every movement my head complained and occasionally I had to pause for the ache to subside. God, I thought, I hope this state of affairs doesn't last for long.

I gazed at myself in the mirror above the little sink in the corner. I was pale and weary-looking with a bandage around my head. I tried to convince myself that I looked interesting rather than damaged but I failed.

I was just about ready to leave and was struggling desperately with the knot on my tie when David Llewellyn entered, followed by his trusty sergeant, the lugubrious Sunderland.

'You going somewhere, boyo?' David grinned, slapping me on the back. My brain rattled in my skull setting off a few minor explosions.

'No rough stuff, eh,' I grimaced. 'I'm delicate cargo for the moment.'

'Oh, sorry.' He sounded genuinely apologetic. 'I've just brought you a bunch of photographs to cast your eye over. See if we can identify those two fellows.'

I nodded and perched on the bed while he opened his briefcase and withdrew a manila file. 'Take a butcher's at these.'

I searched through the pile of dark grainy photographs, most of them featuring men who looked like the prize exhibits from the ugly farm. Then I came upon one face which was of a different aspect: young, smooth, intelligent-looking in an arrogant way. It was the fellow in the smart overcoat, the one who had slugged me.

I passed this information on to David. He seemed both surprised and delighted at the same time.

'Well, then,' he said excitedly, searching through the pile of photographs, '… if that was the chappie with the gun … Ah, here we are… what about this one as the bogus doc?'

He snatched a picture from the file and thrust it in my direction. I gazed at it for some time. The face staring back at me was young and jowly but it had unruly hair and wore no spectacles. However, it did ring some kind of bell.

'Actually, I have seen this fellow before. He was with Archie Muldoon when he came to Benny's trying to extort money from him. He was the quiet one who said nothing. Not sure he was the bogus doctor though. Just a minute.'

I took a pen from my inside pocket and held it over the photograph. 'May I?' I said

David nodded.

I drew a pair of heavy spectacles on the face and inked in the hair so that it appeared combed and flattened back away from the forehead. My artistic transformation worked.

'Yes, that's the man. That's Gina's murderer.'

David and Sunderland exchanged glances.

'Well,' said David at length, 'you've just identified the Bernstein brothers. The chubby fellow you've drawn all over is Anthony and the sleeker model is Vic. Well done.'

David had offered to drive me home before he and Sergeant Sunderland paid a call on Leo Bernstein. Despite still feeling quite groggy, I insisted that I accompanied them on this particular jaunt. There were so many questions that I wanted answering about this affair and I reckoned Leo was the man to answer quite a few.

'Look, I'll be the silent witness,' I said to David. 'Just let me sit in on the meeting.'

'You look like death warmed up, my friend. You should be back in your own bed sleeping off your bloody concussion.'

'I can do that later. Come on, do me a favour. You owe me one.'

David shrugged. 'Be it on your own battered head,' he said, with a sigh of resignation.

'I'm not sure how much the old rascal knows about this business, but I wouldn't trust him as far as I could throw him,' David observed as we pulled up outside the Bamboo House.

Some kind of lackey answered the door. He had a face that looked like it had survived a thousand late nights, and a ragged moustache darkened by a similar number of cigarettes. 'We're closed, mate,' he growled, rolling his rheumy eyes. 'This is a nightclub. We open at night. Not during the bleedin' day.' He was about to shut the door when Sunderland held up his warrant card. 'Police. We have twenty-four hour access, so step aside.'

The lackey did so mutely. He knew when to keep his trap shut. No doubt his previous encounters with the rozzers had been unfortunate ones.

'Now, if you would be so kind as to take us to Mr Bernstein's office, we'd be much obliged,' said David, with only the slightest trace of sarcasm.

Leo Bernstein seemed surprised and somewhat unnerved to see them. He was seated in his office behind a big desk apparently studying some kind of ledger. The ashtray at his elbow was filled with stubbed out cigarettes. He looked tired and drained. He rose awkwardly as Llewellyn and Sunderland entered and his eyes regained some of their fire.

Bernstein cut to the quick. 'What's that one-eyed toe-rag doing here?'

David seemed amused at the description. I was sure that he'd use it himself on future occasions when he wanted to irritate me.

'Let's say he's helping the police with their inquiries,' he said.

'Inquiries about what?'

'Murder,' said David.

Leo Bernstein's face paled but he said nothing.

David continued, 'Your sons, Anthony and Victor Bernstein have been involved in the murder of a young girl.'

'Murder! That's nonsense. Who is this girl?'

'Gina Andrews.'

Leo gave a strange gargling noise in the throat and fell back in his chair, his face white with emotion. 'Gina?'

David nodded, but Bernstein did not notice, he was staring into space, his mind in shock. Suddenly, he looked very old. The face had sagged, the shoulders stooped and his eyes moistened.

'Who was she, Leo? We know you knew her.'

'Knew her,' he replied slowly, all his bravado having dissipated. 'Yes, of course I knew her.' He glanced up at David and gave him a bitter smile. 'Well, I might as well tell you now. You'll find out sooner or later anyway. She was my brother's child. She was a Bernstein. Michael's daughter. She was his secret child, born out of wedlock to a young actress. He paid for her to go to Ireland and bring Gina up there, away from the business. Away from the way we earn a living. But he visited her from time to time. He never lost touch. In the family, I was the only one who knew about her. Even his wife had no idea. He loved Sophie, his wife, and he wouldn't have hurt her for the world. She died never knowing....'

Bernstein fumbled in his pocket for a handkerchief. Clumsily he dabbed the incipient tears that were beginning to roll down his cheeks.

'So why did Gina come back?'

'When Michael was murdered ... she came back ... for ... the funeral. To pay her last respects to her beloved papa.'

'She came back for revenge,' I said. 'Isn't that the truth? She believed that Paulo Ricotti had murdered her father and she came back to exact retribution. She killed Ricotti, didn't she? An eye for an eye.'

Leo's silence spoke volumes.

'So why did Anthony kill her?' I knew I was breaking my promise of being a silent witness, but I just couldn't help myself. I knew we were getting nearer the truth and like a tenacious terrier, I couldn't let go of the bone now.

'That's rubbish. My Anthony wouldn't kill his own cousin.'

'It's true. I saw him do it, Leo. In fact he made two attempts. He tried to strangle her in her flat and when that failed, he went to the hospital where she was recovering and had another go. This time he was successful.'

Tears now flowed down the old man's face. He turned his head away from us and cleared his throat noisily in an attempt to stifle his sobs. We stood silently watching his grief overcome him. I couldn't help feeling sorry for the man. He was an old crook, but murder was not in his blood. He was a proud family man, even though the family were corrupt felons, but now he was presented with a nightmare situation of family killing family.

'Why did Anthony kill Gina? What was his motive, Leo?' It was David's strong, unemotional voice that broke the silence.

Still unable to speak, Leo shook his head in bewilderment.

'Oh, don't give me that, Leo. You must have some idea.'

'Do you think I would be so upset, if I knew? I'm as much in the dark as you are.' He paused and his eyes flickered with curiosity as though a new thought had come to him. 'What about Vic?' he said. 'You mentioned Vic. How could he be involved?'

'Oh, believe me, he's involved,' I said, touching the bandage around my head.

'Well, we need to find these two and fast,' said David. 'And you've got to help us.'

'Help the police, you must be joking.' He dried his eyes vigorously. 'You can go to hell.' The old Leo had, momentarily, reasserted himself.

'It will be all the worse for you if you don't help us now, Leo.'

'You can't expect me to squeal on my own flesh and blood – whatever you do to me.'

David leaned forward placing both hands on Leo's desk. 'Have you not got it into your head yet? They killed their own flesh and blood, as you call it. Anthony murdered Gina, your brother's daughter. He strangled her while she lay helpless in a hospital bed. He showed her no mercy. And he was aided and abetted by Vic. They were both in it together. You cannot protect them any more, Leo. You know where they are likely to be hiding out. You must have a few boltholes around town. Where have they gone to ground? You have got to tell us!'

Leo's resolve weakened and he tried to speak but failed. Instead he just shook his head.

'Stop prevaricating, and tell us where you think they might be.' David was beginning to lose patience now. 'If not I'll slam you in a cell and make sure you stay there for a bloody long time.'

Strong emotion rippled across the old man's face as he struggled with his conscience. He knew what he had to do but it went against all his natural instincts. He was being asked to shop his own sons.

'Come on,' cried David, thumping the desk. 'For Christ's sake tell us…!'

'Well,' said Leo quietly, 'there is one place….'

An hour or so later two police cars drew up outside a ramshackle building on waste ground by the Thames in Wandsworth. After Leo Bernstein had very reluctantly given us the location of this bolthole, David had been on to the Yard to organize a group of armed officers to join him in smoking the two Bernstein boys out. Despite all protestations, I travelled with David and Sunderland. I wasn't going to miss out on the gunfight at the OK Corral.

Dusk was already falling fast and the shadows of night were growing stronger along the riverside. The cars had parked some hundred yards away from the building, which was already blending with the encroaching night sky. There was some ground cover in the form of shrubbery and long grass and David deployed the three officers with rifles to get closer with their weapons trained on the door and two windows.

'What now?' I asked simply.

'Now I put my head into the lion's mouth,' said David. 'And you stay where you are!' He left the car and walked slowly towards the building. He stopped about twenty feet from the door. There was just a gentle breeze bringing with it vague river sounds from the Thames – the rest was silence.

'Hello, there,' he called, addressing the door of the building. 'This is the police. Come on, Anthony and Vic Bernstein, come on out. There's no escape. We are armed. Just give yourselves up. Make it easy on yourselves.'

His voice echoed strangely in the air. There was no response.

David waited almost a minute before speaking again. 'Please don't be foolish. Come out now and you won't be harmed. Open the door and walk out.'

I could see David's shoulders tense as he waited for something to happen. I prayed that it wasn't going to be a bullet fired at him.

However, again there was no response.

'Perhaps we got it wrong,' murmured Sunderland, more to himself than to me.

'I don't think Leo would have given a false lead.'

David waved for the snipers to move closer to the building.

'If you won't come out, I'm coming in,' he cried, pulling a revolver from his pocket.

'And so am I,' I murmured to myself. In an instant I had slipped out of the car and sprinted in a crouching position to join David. Well, I couldn't just sit and watch as my old friend risked his life alone.

David turned slightly and saw me approach carrying my gun. He gave me a grim half grin. 'I told you to stay in the bloody car.'

'I had to be with my old partner at the shoot out.'

You watch too many cowboy films,' he said, with a smile.

'A man's gotta do what a man's gotta do.'

'Well, let's do it then.'

Slowly we approached the door of the building. It looked innocent enough with its faded peeling paint, cracked wood and rusting handle, but we both knew it could fly open at any moment to reveal two desperate men with guns.

Out of the corner of my eye, I saw the snipers moving in even closer. This should have been some comfort, but it wasn't. Their presence was not going to stop any bullets aimed our way.

'We're coming in,' David called, as we reached the door. 'Don't do anything stupid.'

He glanced at me and gave a brief stern nod.

Slowly, he opened the door and let it swing wide on its creaky hinges. A smell of damp and decay assailed our nostrils, but there was no sound or movement from within.

'After all that, I don't think the bastards are here,' David whispered to me, as he stepped over the threshold.

He wasn't quite correct.

We entered the building, which was only illuminated faintly by the fading grey daylight struggling in through the grimy windows. However, we were able to observe an ominous shape lying on the floor not far from the doorway.

It was a body.

Glancing round cautiously, we approached it. The body was lying face down and there was a vicious wound to the back of the head, exposing what was left of its brain. It looked very much like the fellow had been shot at point-blank range. Splatters of blood covered a wide area, glistening darkly in the gloom.

Carefully, David turned the corpse over so that we could see its face. Filtered light fell on the rigid features of the dead man. They belonged to none other than Mr Horn-rimmed Glasses himself.

It was Anthony Bernstein.

THIRTY-TWO

Leo Bernstein had started on the brandy as soon as Detective Inspector Llewellyn and his two cronies, including the one-eyed meddler had left. He felt emotionally ravaged and was having difficulty coming to terms with the news they had imparted. Was it really true that his own sons had actually murdered his niece Gina, his brother's little girl? It must be. The police wouldn't lie about a thing like that. It seemed like the plot from some gruesome fairy-tale.

Sadly the brandy was not softening the edges of reality as it usually did; on the contrary it was sharpening up the horror of the situation. As he poured his fourth large glass, almost draining the bottle, he found himself crying. All he had striven for all his life, helping to build up the Bernstein family business by whatever means were at his disposal, had come to nothing, to grey ashes. He never thought of what he did as being so terrible. It was against the law, yes, but it didn't really hurt anyone. Yes, a few mugs paid more than they should for a few personal pleasures. So what? It was their dough and most of them were ignorant of their foolishness. But now ... now there was killing. His own sons ... Well, he washed his hands of them. They were his, but they were bastards also.

He sighed and rolled the brandy round in the glass, inhaling its potent vapours.

Now he was alone. Very alone. His wife Susan had died many years ago, shortly after Anthony was born and he had lived through his brother and his two sons. In truth, since his boys had hit adolescence he had felt a distancing in their relationship. If he

191

was honest, and now he could afford to be, he didn't like them much. Vic was too smart for his own good and Anthony was dim and aggressive. Their values were not his. Their sensibilities belonged to the new cruder age. He knew they regarded him as a relic, someone who didn't really count any more. That's why he had treasured his relationship with his brother Michael so much. They were like two sides of the same coin. They could tell what the other was thinking and dream what the other was dreaming. Now Michael was gone the world appeared so much greyer. Life it seemed was a dark tragic joke. Leo took another long gulp of brandy, enjoying the discomfort as it burned his throat.

At first he didn't notice the door of his office open and a dark figure enter. He was only aware of its presence as it stood over him at the side of his desk.

'Hello, Dad,' Vic said.

Leo glanced up in shock. 'You!' It took him some moments to take the situation in and when he did, he rose quickly to his feet, dashing the brandy glass to the floor as he did so. 'You!' he roared, his fury overwhelming him.

'Sit down,' said Vic, pushing the drunken old man back into his chair.

'You swine,' muttered Leo, already the fire of anger fading and self-pity taking its place.

Vic responded with a tight smile. He agreed with the assessment. Indeed he was a swine and a bastard and all those other vituperative epithets that could be hurled at him. How else could you survive in the cruel and unfair world? Being decent and honest got you nowhere. He was glad he was a swine and intended to improve upon his past performance in the role.

'What do you want?' asked Leo.

'Now what do you think I want? I want cash. A large amount.'

'You can go to hell.'

'Indeed, I probably will, but not just yet, eh? Now get yourself to the safe and scoop me out some cash.'

'I wouldn't lift a finger to help you. How could you murder that girl...?'

'To be accurate, I didn't. It was Anthony. But I have to admit it, if it hadn't have been him it would have been me with my hands around her arrogant little throat.'

Leo shook his head in horrified disbelief. 'Why?' he croaked.

'Why?' Vic's face muscles tightened and his relaxed insouciance faded. 'I'll tell you why. I wasn't going to let that bitch turn up on our doorstep out of the blue and take over just like that – as though it was her right.'

'It *was* her right. She was Michael's daughter and the eldest.'

'What the fuck's that got to do with anything? We built this business up. We took the risks, did the dirty work, while she was living the life of Riley abroad, cosseted by daddy's money. Then she comes back and thinks she can start dictating what we do. Well, to hell with that. This business, the Bernstein business was *my* legacy not hers.'

'Yours! Don't kid yourself. You're not a big enough man to sit in this chair.' Leo gave a bitter laugh. 'Well, it's nobody's now. You've brought the roof down on your own head.'

'It's a setback, but I'll live to fight another day. I'll crawl back up to the top in time. I have the guts, the determination – and I watch my back. Which is more than I can say for Anthony.'

'What does that mean?'

'You'll find out in due course. Now, I want that money.'

'You know the police are after you. No matter where you run, they'll get you and you'll hang. You've no chance.'

'We'll see about that, old man. Now get your fat backside out of that chair and open the safe.'

'Or what? You'll kill me, too? Your own father?'

'Maybe,' Vic sneered, producing a gun out of his pocket. 'A desperate man can be driven to do anything.'

Leo froze with horror. The crazy bastard meant it. He *would* kill him. 'I don't recognize you as my son any more. You're a stranger to me, Victor. A nothing.'

'That's fine by me, old man. Just get me the money and then I'll leave you to your brandy.'

'Very well,' Leo said softly. There was little point in refusing. What was a couple of thousand compared to his life and to get Vic out of it.

He took the small safe key out of his waistcoat pocket and crossed the room to where a large painting of a pastoral scene hung over the fireplace. Carefully unhooking the painting from the wall, he revealed a grey wall safe concealed behind it. He stood motionless before it for a moment.

'Go on,' prompted Vic. 'Open up.'

Like a man in a trance, Leo Bernstein did as he was told.

The door swung open to reveal several small brown packages. Vic stepped forward and grabbed one and ripped it open to reveal a wad of white notes. 'How much?' he asked, waving the wad at Leo.

'Each one contains fifty.'

Vic smiled and began stuffing the packages into his coat pockets.

'Where is Anthony?'

Vic paused only momentarily in his task before replying. He did so without turning to face Leo. 'He's somewhere safe. There's no need to worry about him,' he said.

Leo returned to his desk and poured himself another brandy. 'Worried? I'm not worried about him or you. I wash my hands of you both. As far as I am concerned you are no longer family. You are both scum and vermin.'

'Suit yourself,' grinned Vic, stuffing the last packet into his coat and moving towards the door. 'I've got what I came for. You've served your purpose, old man. So this is goodbye.'

He left the room as swiftly and as silently as he came. Leo stared at the door for sometime, his body numb and his brain devoid of thought. A fly landed on his hand and he gazed down at it. A fly, he thought. You rarely saw flies in winter. How come it had survived all this time? And, more particularly, why had it bothered?

The train journey had been quite restful. Despite the carriage being full and cramped, most of Max's fellow passengers had taken the opportunity to catch forty winks during the trip from Nottingham to London. So, apart from some gentle heavy breathing and the odd muted snore, it had been a peaceful journey. She had been too excited to sleep herself. The thought of being back in London, in surprising Johnny and enjoying some time with him before returning to her pantomime chores, kept her mind racing.

King's Cross was awash with passengers like hordes of predatory ants, carrying, lugging, trailing or hoisting various assortments of cases, valises, trunks, packages and boxes. It seemed to Max that which ever way she turned, the flow was coming at her rather than with her and she had to resort to angling her body sideways first this way and then that. Gradually, with a determined effort, she managed to squeeze her way forward. The noise was deafening: voices were raised like a discordant choir, while engines groaned, hooted, hissed and clanked in accompaniment.

In the distance she spied daylight – the outside world. This encouraged her to push harder and with less decorum. At one point she stood on a clergyman's foot; he bore his hurt with muted disdain. She also winded a red-faced fat lady with her small suitcase which collided heavily with her large stomach. The woman looked, thought Max, like one of those well built females from the comic seaside postcards, although her language was far from comic.

At last as she stepped beyond the confines of the great railway cathedral into the cold grey murk of a December evening, Maxine gave a sigh of relief. Here she was back in London again – and soon she would see Johnny.

THIRTY-THREE

With Sergeant Sunderland at the wheel of the police car, we sped back towards the West End and I did my best to justify my thoughts to a certain sceptical inspector.

'This is more than a hunch, David,' I said earnestly. 'It is a deduction based on logic.'

David grimaced. 'Crikey, where's your bloody deerstalker? You're starting to sound like Sherlock Holmes now,' my friend exclaimed.

I ignored the remark. 'I think we both agree that it's most likely that Vic Bernstein murdered his own brother ... to unburden himself.'

'It looks like it. "Unburden himself" – now there's a nasty idea. What sort of heartless sod would shoot his own brother in cold blood?'

'A heartless sod like Vic Bernstein, I suppose. Now that the game is up, he was clearing the path of any hindrances in order to help him escape. Men without scruples will do almost anything once hemmed into a corner.'

'So he saw Anthony as a hindrance.'

'That's the way it looks to me. Otherwise why kill him?'

'There may have been a quarrel....'

'But he was shot at close range in the back of the head. That suggests a cool, calculated execution.'

'You could be right.' The tone was grumpy and reluctant but that was always the nearest David got to concurrence with my ideas. Despite our friendship and camaraderie, to his mind, he was the professional and I was just the lucky amateur.

'So, I reckon that his first port of call would be on his father for cash. The Bamboo House is where the big piggy bank will be kept.'

'But surely the old man wouldn't help him? Not now he knows what the blighter's done. He'll not know about Anthony … but Gina.'

'He'll probably not hand over the cash voluntarily, but Vic has very persuasive ways, doesn't he?' I moulded my hand into the shape of a gun and pointed it at David.

'I get your drift. Well, we'll see.' He glanced out of the window. 'We should be at the club in a couple of minutes and all will be revealed.'

Those two minutes dragged on and when we got caught in a small jam caused by roadworks, they were elongated to ten. As fate would have it, when we eventually pulled up outside the club, I noticed a tall man in a dark-blue overcoat slip out of the main entrance. He was in a definite hurry. He had the collar of the coat pulled up high and his trilby slouched low over his face so that his features were hidden and his manner was furtive and suspicious.

'I believe that's our friend now,' I cried, leaping from the car.

I ran forward towards the man who was rushing down the side street at quite a pace.

'Hey, you!' I called.

Automatically, the man faltered and turned. Now I got a very clear view of his face. Without a doubt it was the nice fellow who had tried beat my brains out in the hospital.

It was Vic Bernstein.

On seeing me his eyes flamed with hatred. He hesitated for an instant as though he contemplated tackling me, but then he thought better of it, probably having seen David and Sunderland bringing up my rear, and he turned on his heel and ran. I followed at speed.

I ran as fast as I could but my aching brain and weary limbs impeded my progress. Nevertheless I began to narrow the distance between Bernstein and myself.

Behind me I could hear the clomping feet of David and Sergeant Sunderland.

'Stop!' bellowed my friend. 'Stop in the name of the law.'

Surprisingly, Vic Bernstein slowed down and turned to face us once more. However, this wasn't in any way a gesture of submission. It was merely to allow him time to pull his gun out of his pocket and fire at us. He let off two bullets in sharp succession. To avoid being hit, I dropped to the ground landing with an ungainly bang on the cobbled surface. I was unhurt, but my head wound began to throb viciously and my vision blurred briefly. The thought crossed my mind that really I should be in bed with a nice hot-water bottle resting rather than chasing after a murderous thug with a gun.

He fired again, one bullet pinging noisily close to my face, taking a neat chip out of the cobbles. Too close for comfort. I clambered awkwardly to my feet as he turned to run once more.

I glanced behind me and saw that Sunderland was down on the ground. He had been hit. David was leaning over him inspecting the damage.

It looked like it was up to me now. Brain-damaged unsteady me. If I didn't put a real spurt on now, Vic Bernstein would escape.

With as much power I could muster, I raced down the street after him, each footfall jarring in my head. The thoroughfare narrowed and led into another back street. However, luck was on my side. As he turned the corner, Bernstein slipped on the wet surface and lost his balance. He staggered a few steps before sprawling to the ground.

I was on him in an instant. Before he knew what was happening, I had landed on his back and wrenched the gun from his hand. My immediate thought was to smash it hard against his skull until he lost consciousness to give him a taste of his own medicine. But what you might call my finer feelings intervened and stopped me. Besides, I thought as I flung the gun down the street as far away from reach as I could, I might very well kill the devil in the process and then I'd really be in trouble.

It didn't take Bernstein long to recover his wits however and he rolled over on his back and punched me hard in the face. It was all my childhood bonfire nights rolled into one: sky rockets whizzed, snow mountains whooshed, golden rains fizzed and sparklers sparkled, all parading brightly before my eyes while a group of penny bangers all exploded in unison in my head – my poor old head which had suffered so much recently that I thought it was about to close down altogether. Fireworks over, whirls of what appeared to be silvery smoke began to roll before my eyes and I slumped backwards on to the cobbles. How I would have liked to have fallen asleep there and then to escape all the pain and discomfort, but I was vaguely conscious of Bernstein clambering to his feet once more.

Goddammit, Johnny, a voice cried from somewhere inside me, you're not going to let the bastard get away, are you? I blinked hard in an attempt to clear my vision and with an energy and a speed which manifested itself from I know not where, I jumped to my feet and launched myself on to Vic Bernstein once more. This time he crashed to the ground face downwards. As he landed, he gave a cry of pain. This brought a smile to my weary features. I knelt on his back, thrust my hand on his head, pressing it down on to the slimy cobblestones. He writhed and twisted in a vain effort to unseat me, but like Tom Mix riding an untamed bucking bronco, I remained put.

Behind me I could hear footsteps. A quick glance back told me it was David.

'Good man,' he called breathlessly, pulling out a pair of shiny handcuffs.

I shifted position slightly, allowing David access to Bernstein's hands and with several dextrous movements he had snapped the cuffs on him.

I clambered off the still wriggling captive, staggered to the pavement and sat down. I felt as woozy as if I'd downed half a bottle of Johnnie Walker in one gulp.

'You OK, boyo?'

'I will be. I think.' Instinctively I touched the bandage that was still around my head. It felt like it was the only thing that was holding it together. 'How's Sunderland?' I asked.

'He'll live. Nothing too serious. I reckon it's just a flesh wound … thanks to this bastard,' he snarled, hauling Bernstein to his feet. 'One wrong move, mister, and I'll bloody shoot you dead.' He pulled out a revolver from his pocket and prodded his captive in the back with it.

Bernstein stared into space. He was neither defiant nor cowed. His face was a blank. Whatever feelings he harboured behind his stony mask, it was clear that for the moment the fight had gone out of him.

'Right, let's get you back to the Yard,' said David.

Sergeant Sunderland was still lying on the pavement, pale-faced, nursing his leg. 'At least you got him. I'd hate to think I'd got this for nothing,' he said, wryly.

'Why, Sergeant, you are the hero of the hour,' I said. 'You'll have a neat scar to impress the girls with now.'

He grinned.

With my assistance, Sunderland got to his feet and with his arm around my shoulder I helped him limp back to the car – the unsteady leading the unsteady.

I drove back to the Yard, with Sunderland in the passenger seat and David in the back with his prisoner. He had radioed ahead and told them to expect us and arrange for medical care for Sunderland and a cell for Bernstein.

As we pulled up in the forecourt of the imposing building, David grunted, 'Well, it's been a messy affair, but I reckon we can draw a line under it now.'

THIRTY-FOUR

Max sat back in the cab and stared unseeingly out of the window at the crowds snaking by on the pavements and the familiar edifices of London as the vehicle made slow progress towards its destination. She had decided that she was too tired to use public transport and, indeed, too distracted to cope with the pushing and shoving and sardine-like crush of either the omnibus or tube. She'd had enough of that performance at the station. But most of all, she was eager to reach Johnny's place – and Johnny.

Since arriving in London something had come over her, a realization of what she was doing or more precisely why she was doing it. Why had she grabbed this opportunity to return to London with such heart-thumping enthusiasm? Well, this was not merely a pleasure jaunt back to the city for a couple of days just to see her boyfriend. This was something much more serious. The break in Nottingham had brought a focus to her life and in particular to her relationship with Johnny. She knew now that he was not just 'a boyfriend', a nice chap to spend her time and have fun with; he was a lot more than that.

As Max pressed her brow against the cool glass of the taxi window, she acknowledged the fact fully for the first time that this was not a casual affair, or a youthful crush. This was serious. She knew that she was in love with Johnny Hawke. Deeply in love. And syrupy as it may sound, she wanted to spend the rest of her life with him. It was an instinct deep in her soul that informed of this. It was a realization that had been growing stronger ever since she had caught that train to Nottingham. And now that she was back in the city, only moments away from Johnny's embrace, she was absolutely certain. It was a great feeling. A smile flickered on her lips at the thought. She believed, well, she hoped that he felt the same as she did.

Eventually the cab drew up outside Priory Court and Max made her way up to Johnny's office-cum-flat. There was no light on and no response from the bell. He was not at home. Disappointed, she let herself in with a key Johnny had given her. She had wanted her visit to be a surprise and so she had not told him about it. Now she was beginning to regret it. Who knew where he was, or when he would be back? His job as a detective made his life very unpredictable and dangerous. She dismissed this latter thought from her mind lest it upset her further. It was foolish to construct scenarios out of doubt and worry. She would simply have to wait. He would turn up eventually.

She shrugged, dropped her bag in the tiny sitting room and put the kettle on. While she waited for it to boil, she automatically tidied the room, trying to bring some order the place. As usual there was little more than bread – half a loaf on its way to being stale and mouldy, along with some soft biscuits in the larder. Turning on the gas fire and huddling before it for warmth, Max sipped her tea and nibbled on a soggy digestive and prayed for Johnny's swift return.

As the underground rattled down its dark labyrinthine tube, Peter sat next to Caroline, holding her hand, trying to suppress his excitement. Today he was really entering grown-up territory. He was out on a proper date with his girlfriend. They were headed for the pictures in town. The film was *Frankenstein Meets the Wolfman*, his choice, Caroline was not that enthusiastic, she would have preferred a musical or a romance – and then he intended to take his girl to meet his friend and guardian Johnny. He had told her all about Johnny and how he was a real-life detective who had solved 'hundreds of crimes' and put 'scores of criminals behind bars'. If he was honest, introducing Johnny to Caroline as his girlfriend, would be the most exciting thing that had happened to him in a very long time. He admired and respected Johnny so much and wanted to show off this pretty girl to him. Having Caroline on his arm was further evidence that he was growing up, turning into a mature young man. He knew Johnny would be impressed. The thought thrilled him to the core.

He looked across at their reflection in the carriage window opposite. Caroline smiled and waved at him in the glass. He returned both the smile and the wave, thinking how very lucky he was.

Constable Chapman blew on his hands and rubbed them vigorously. He was cold – 'bleedin' cold', he told himself – and unhappy to be on cell duty at the Yard. At least when he was on the beat, he could pop into a doorway for a quick fag, or into some café for a mug of warming char, but not down here in 'the bleedin' bowels of the Yard'. And they'd only got three prisoners in at the moment. It was hardly a taxing role. The trouble is, he told himself, they think of me as a has-been just because I'm coming up to my fiftieth birthday. But, he assured himself, there's plenty of life in the old dog yet.

He paused and looked through the grille of cell number four, the one that contained the new inmate, a fellow called Victor Bernstein. A murderer and a nasty piece of work by all accounts. Apparently he'd shot one of the plainclothes men in the leg. For that alone he deserved the noose. No bleedin' respect for the law, these days.

Chapman peered into the dimly lit room. To his surprise, he saw that the occupant was lying on the stone floor face down. To the constable he 'looked like a dead 'un' as he told his sergeant later. There appeared to be a small pool of dark liquid by the prisoner's head.

'Don't tell me the bleeder's topped himself,' muttered Chapman reaching for his keys. He called out to the inmate. There was no response. He waited and watched to see if the man showed any signs of breathing. But there was no sign of life, no gentle rise and fall of the torso. He called out once again. Again: nothing. 'It had to happen on my bleedin' watch,' he muttered to himself, as, with a shaking hand, he unlocked the cell door and entered. To his horror he discovered that the body had gone – disappeared as though by magic – but the small pool of dark liquid remained. Instinctively he knelt down to dip his fingers into the liquid. It certainly looked like blood.

He never saw the blow coming.

On hearing the key in the lock, Vic Bernstein had quickly jumped to his feet and taken a position flat against the wall behind the door where he could not be seen. As Constable Chapman bent down to inspect the blood – Bernstein's own blood scratched from his thumb – he smashed a wooden stool over his head. With a muted groan, the policeman slumped to the floor, unconscious.

Bernstein slammed the cell door shut and began the process of stripping Chapman of his clothes. Within minutes he had transformed himself into a British bobby. The uniform was ill-fitting – most of them were – but he felt sure he could get away with the deception long enough to make his way out of this place at least. If he was able to get to his flat before his escape was discovered, he had a change of clothes, a gun and a little money there.

He wasn't down and out yet.

With a grin, he kicked Chapman in the ribs and left him locked up in the cell.

Less than ten minutes later, Vic Bernstein was out on the streets of London once more. Now he was a man with a mission.

THIRTY-FIVE

I was given a steaming cup of reviving tea in David's office at the Yard while he left me to supervise Vic Bernstein's incarceration in a cell in what he referred to as 'the dungeon' lodged in the basement of the building, and to arrange for Sergeant Sunderland to be whipped off to hospital to have his leg attended to. Despite my damaged bonce, all the action and rough stuff had in some strange way energized me and, while my head still ached, I no longer felt like the arthritic weakling I had been in my hospital bed.

On his return, David also seemed more relaxed. 'Poor old Sunderland's with the medics now. Thankfully there appears to be no serious damage,' he said, slipping into a chair behind his desk. He grinned. 'He's a bit of an odd fish, but a good man. I like having him at my side. He always seems to take everything in his stride.'

'That might be a little difficult for the next few weeks,' I observed wryly.

David ran his fingers through his hair and nodded, too tired it seemed to appreciate my little joke. I couldn't blame him.

'Would you like a car to take you home? I can arrange that,' he said at length, his hand hovering over the telephone.

'No, that's all right.'

I had other plans.

'I think a walk will do me good.'

'Are you sure?' he said with surprise. 'You look as rough as a sheep's arse.'

'You have such a way with words. No, honestly, I'm OK. It's just

205

that I'm in need of some fresh air. I think my brain is starved of oxygen.'

'Fresh air? When did we have any of that in London?'

'I'll be in touch tomorrow,' I said, ignoring his banter. I rose purposefully from the chair, slipping my trilby gently on to to my tender scalp and made for the door.

'You do. I intend to leave Bernstein to stew a bit on his own today. I'll give him the third degree in the morning. The main thing is that we've got our man and mopped up the mess. All we need now are some answers.' He paused and gave me a shy smile. 'Oh, and by the way, thanks for your help.'

I nodded, patted my old friend on the shoulder and left.

It was dark and misty with it as I emerged from Scotland Yard. London had been taken over by a race of phantoms who hustled and bustled past me silently as I made my way towards Trafalgar Square and up the Haymarket. The air certainly was not fresh but it was pleasingly cool and somehow invigorating. I walked slowly partly because as yet my energy levels were low and partly because I was savouring the experience of being alone and free in the city that I knew and loved. In the last few hours so many burdens and problems had been lifted from my shoulders. I began to feel a sense of ease. Also I harboured the thought of food. While waiting in David's office I suddenly realized how hungry I was. I'd forgotten how long ago it was that I had eaten what I could refer to as a decent meal. That's what I needed to get me back on track: a good fry up. And where better to indulge in this gourmet delight but at Benny's café.

The muted light emanating from the steamy windows of Benny's domain were like a golden beacon in a harsh murky world and I hurried towards it. The clock, I knew was heading for six and the old fellow would be getting ready to close, but I knew he'd bend his opening hours for me.

His greeting was typically sarcastic. 'Look what the cat's dragged in. Johnny the wanderer. Not seeking a bed for the night again are you?' However his old features could not disguise the pleasure in seeing me. To him I was like a part-time son and I was happy in that role. And if I was honest, Benny was the nearest I'd got to a father figure. However, we never discussed our close relationship – that would have exposed it to examination and made us both uneasy – and we covered up sentiment with mild insults and back chat.

When I removed my hat to reveal my by now rather grubby bandage, Benny's face dropped and his joshing insouciance evaporated.

'My God, Johnny, what happened to you?'

'I had a difference of opinion with the butt of a gun.'

'Sit down. You look terrible. Oi vay! Should you be walking around? Shouldn't you be in bed tended by a pretty nurse?'

'If you can conjure one up, that would be dandy – but really I'm fine. It's not as bad as it seems.'

'Thank goodness for that because it looks terrible. *You* look terrible!'

'Now, now, don't fuss. I'm fine. I've had hospital treatment....'

'Hospital! Great heavens.'

'They gave me a prescription for my speedy recovery.'

'Oh, yes?'

'Tea and the best fry up you can muster,' I announced grandly.

It took a while for Benny to get the joke and then he grinned. Making a big show of examining his watch, he said, 'Oh, a big breakfast is it? Is it morning already?'

'Look, old boy, I've had a trying day and I'm short of victuals. I could have gone to the Ritz but I favoured real home-cooked grub so I came here.'

'You made the right decision. Grab a seat, you son of a gun, and I'll sort you out.'

He hesitated for a moment, gazing with disdain at my bandage and then scooted off to the kitchen. I sat back in the chair and relaxed. I was tempted to close my eyes, but I resisted. I felt sure that I'd quickly fall asleep if I did.

I gazed around the room. The café was empty apart from one solitary soul hunched over a table by the window, engrossed in a library book. He had not taken any notice of my arrival.

Benny returned a few minutes later with a mug of tea and a couple of biscuits.

'Just to keep you going,' he said, before disappearing again.

The meal when it arrived lived up to my expectations. Certainly it was greasy and the egg was small as was the portion of bacon, swamped by fried tomatoes, but just then it was ambrosia to me and I wolfed it down with alacrity. Benny sat beside me like a mother hen beaming as I consumed his offering.

'I suppose you are not going to tell me about it,' he said a length, indicating the bandage around my head.

'That's right. I'm not.' I couldn't have felt less like picking over the bones of the Bernstein case. I needed to distance myself from the whole sorry business and place things in perspective before I could get a clear picture myself of what had happened. Benny knew better than to press me on the matter, but he did raise another topic.

'Johnny, when are you going to get a respectable job? One where you don't get bashed about the head and that allows you to go home at night at a respectable time. You carry on with this dangerous detective work and someday soon I'll have to put on my old black suit to go to your funeral.'

It was an old refrain and I hated it when Benny began to warble it. As I've told him before, being a detective is what I know and, on the whole, is what I like, despite the wear and tear. I was about to say all this but as it happened I was saved by the bell. The telephone on the counter rang out shrilly. Benny pulled a face and went to answer it.

He had his back to me so I couldn't catch what he was saying but he suddenly seemed excited, his little body swaying from side to side, his shoulders shooting up and down. He placed the receiver on the counter and hurried to my side.

'It's for you,' he said beaming. 'It's the lovely Maxine.'

'Max!' I said both surprised and delighted.

I leapt up and rushed to the phone.

'Max,' I said breathlessly, 'how wonderful.'

'Hello, darling. How are you?'

I hesitated for only a second before trotting out the lie. 'I'm absolutely fine, but I'm missing you. What I wouldn't give to have a hug and a kiss from you right now.'

'Well, they are on offer.'

'If only ...'

'I mean it, Mr Hawke. All you have to do is come home.'

I frowned. She was losing me. 'Come home...?' I echoed lamely.

'I'm at Hawke Towers right now waiting for you. The panto people gave me some time off. I came up to town for a couple of days to surprise you. I've been waiting here all afternoon for you. That's why I gave Benny a ring to see if he knew where you were. He told me you were stuffing your face.'

'If only you'd let me know.'

'Where's the surprise in that?'

'Look, I'll be with you in less than fifteen minutes.'

'That's great—' She broke off suddenly and made a quiet inarticulate sound.

'Max?'

'Johnny ... Johnny.' The tone of her voice at changed completely. It was tense and frightened. 'I've just heard a noise. Oh, my God, Johnny ... there's someone in the flat.'

And then the phone went dead.

THIRTY-SIX

For Peter, *Frankenstein Meets the Wolfman* had been a great success. Nearly all the way through the horror film, Caroline had clung to him in the cinema, murmuring, 'It's horrible, it's horrible', while nestling her head on his chest. For him this was a very pleasant experience. But better was to come, for during the cartoon and the supporting picture they had spent most of the time kissing. It was a wonderful evening out and it was now going to be enhanced even more when he introduced Caroline to Johnny.

Secretly Caroline was amused at Peter's hero worship of Johnny. Peter had told her all about his past and the part this enigmatic man had played in it. She knew that Peter was trying to impress her with tales of detective work and his exciting friend. But really he had no need to do that. She liked him for himself. He was a very nice boy, good-looking, kind and bright and that's all that mattered to her. But she was happy to indulge him. After all he was her boyfriend.

'Come on then,' he said, as they left the cinema, clutching each other's hands. 'Off we go to Hawke Towers.'

Vic Bernstein's mind was now diseased and unstable. The violent incidents of the last few days had affected his sanity, tilted it rather than destroyed it, for he still had the ability to stand outside himself and make judgements which he perceived as rational and essential. But now the dark alter ego that had been lying, curled up somewhere inside him for many years, had grown in stature and taken over. This, he thought, was the Vic Bernstein as he was meant to be but had never had the courage to realize before. Killing his stupid brother had proved that. He felt no remorse, no sentiment at all over Anthony's death. In simple terms, to the new Vic, it was what the cretin deserved. He grinned broadly at the thought. In shooting his brother, he was now complete ... and fearless. He could face his inevitable destiny with equanimity.

As he hurried through the darkened streets, he viewed London with its damaged buildings, acres of rubble, shored-up edifices and dispiriting black-out gloom as reflecting his own life and situation. Things had gone too far for him ever to return to his comfortable normality. His plan to rule the Bernstein roost seemed almost laughable now. It had been bombed and shattered like so many of the capital's landmarks. All that he was left with was rubble.

He was realistic and clear-sighted enough to be aware that his hours of freedom were limited so he had to put them to good use. There was only one thing that would bring any kind of satisfaction to him now: the destruction of the man he believed had been responsible for his downfall. With his blood on my hands, he mused quite calmly, I can go to the gallows with a smile. The thought of the noose around his neck caused him no consternation, no anguish. Not the new Vic Bernstein.

So far his life on the run had gone reasonably smoothly. On escaping from Scotland Yard he had returned to his flat. Here he had found a policeman on guard outside. A young flat-footed fellow with a yokel face and, it turned out, a yokel intelligence as well. Dressed as he was in PC Chapman's uniform, Vic approached the policeman delivering the news that he was his replacement and the young fellow was to get back to the Yard in quick sticks. The constable, delighted to be relieved of his boring chore, saw only the baggy uniform, not the face of its owner. He asked no questions or expressed any surprise at his new instructions. He was too pleased with his release to be concerned. With a big grin and a few mumbled words of gratitude, he hurried away.

With a practised dexterity, Vic broke into his own flat. He did not dawdle. He knew there was no time to take things easy. He grabbed a dark suit, a white shirt and a tie from his wardrobe and changed into civvies. He extracted fifty pounds from the secret drawer in his desk and, pulling back the carpet by his bed, his lifted up the loose floorboard there to retrieve a box containing a pistol and a pack of cartridges.

As he slipped on his overcoat, he gazed at himself in the hall mirror. A rather pale and gaunt version of the old Vic stared back at him. The once smooth and well-nourished features had faded. He had circles under his eyes and a few days' stubble on his chin. The stubble offended him and he was tempted to shave it off but he knew there just wasn't enough time.

He riffled through the telephone directory until he found the name, number and, more particularly, the address he needed. He made a mental note of it and then with a last glance round his flat – and he knew it would be the very last – he set out for Priory Court.

As he approached the office of John Hawke Private Investigations, Vic Bernstein pulled the loaded pistol from his pocket. He tried the door and to his pleasure and surprise discovered that it wasn't locked. He stepped inside and found himself in an office area – desk, telephone files – the usual stuff. The only source of illumination was a desk lamp, but to his left there was an open door which led to a fully lighted room beyond. As he approached it, he could hear a voice. It was a woman's voice talking with some animation. He crept closer and peered around the corner of the door. He saw a shabby sort of sitting room, with hand-me-down furniture and drab decorations. With his back to him near the fireplace was a woman chatting on the telephone. Although he couldn't as yet see her face, he could tell that she was young, petite with dark elfin hair.

'Where's the surprise in that?' she was saying lightly, a giggle in her voice.

The caller at the other end replied and she added 'That's great....'

Vic opened the door further and the hinges creaked noisily.

The girl's stance stiffened as she sensed Vic's presence. 'Johnny … Johnny, I've just heard a noise.' The tone of her voice at changed completely. It was tense and frightened. She turned sharply and saw

Vic. 'Oh my God, Johnny … there's someone in the flat,' she cried, her eyes wide with terror.

In an instant Vic stepped forward and, grabbing the receiver from her limp grasp, ended the call.

THIRTY-SEVEN

Just when I thought I'd crawled out of the dark and dangerous forest and I was seeing daylight, it seemed some insidious threat had dragged me back into the impenetrable undergrowth once more. Max's last words 'There's someone in the flat' rang repeatedly in my ears as I raced from Benny's café without a word of explanation to the owner and went in search of a taxi. All the while my stomach tightened and the egg, bacon and tomato sloshed around inside me until I felt sick. Who the hell was there? How much danger was Max in? What on earth would I find when I got back home? These questions ricocheted around my brain and the only answers I could come up with were ones that chilled my blood.

It was not until I reached Cambridge Circus that I spied a taxi. Like a madman, I ran in the road waving my arms in front of him.

'Blimey, mate, I've seen yer,' he cried indignantly, leaning out of his window.

'Sorry, but this is an emergency,' I explained, clambering inside.

'You're not having a baby, are yer?'

Play the game, Johnny, I thought.

'You've hit the nail on the head. The missus is about to at any moment.'

'Righto. Where to then?'

I gave him the address and he sped off as though he was competing at Silverstone – God bless him.

Within ten minutes I was racing up the stairs to my rooms. Once on the landing, I stopped, caught my breath and tried to unscramble my thoughts, praying that everything was all right or would be all right. I realized that it was no use bursting in like the bull in that proverbial crockery establishment. That could do more harm than good. I moved slowly and quietly to my door and listened. There was no noise from inside. I peered through the keyhole but that afforded me no further intelligence.

Gently, I opened the door. My office was empty. The table lamp was lit on my desk but apart from that there was nothing to indicate that the premises were inhabited. However, I could see a strip of light emanating from below the door leading to what I referred to as my living room. I was tempted to call out Max's name but I resisted. She had said there was someone in the flat. No doubt that someone was still here. Again I shuddered to think what that meant.

Clasping my revolver tightly, gently I pushed the door ajar. I opened it wide enough to gain a full view of the room. Immediately I saw Max. She was lying on the sofa, her body twisted in an awkward and unnatural posture, an expression of terror seared on to her features. Standing behind her with a gun pointed at her head was Vic Bernstein. His pale haunted face twisted into an expression of demented pleasure. He grinned ghoulishly as he saw me in the doorway.

'Ah, at last. Do come in, Johnny, and join us,' he said smoothly. 'Come on, don't be shy.' He moved the gun nearer to Max's head.

My heart constricted and my mouth went dry.

'Don't hurt her. Please,' said a voice. With some surprise I realized it was mine.

Maxine gave a little sob but remained absolutely still, terrified out of her mind.

Like a man walking on eggshells I moved slowly into the room. I didn't want to make any awkward movement which could prompt Bernstein into a reckless and fatal action. My eyes flickered desperately between Max's terrified features and the sadistic countenance of her captor while desperately trying to think what to do. In truth, I knew there was nothing I *could* do. It was clear to me that if I made one false move, this maniac would shoot Max. My heart felt leaden in my breast.

'That's far enough,' Bernstein said, the smile switched off. 'Now throw your gun down on the floor.'

I did as he commanded. I knew to resist would be a mistake.

'I'm so glad you could join the party, Johnny.' The mocking tone returned. 'It was good of you to come. After all it is a farewell party.'

'Let the girl go,' I said quietly. 'Don't hurt her. Your quarrel is with me. She's got nothing to do with all this.'

'Oh, that's where you are wrong, my friend. She is very much involved. She tells me that she is your girlfriend. Someone close to you. Someone who means a lot to you. Therefore it seems to me that by hurting her, I will be hurting you. And, by God, Johnny, I want to hurt you.'

There was nothing I could say. I had no argument. No response. My brain was numb. What the hell could I do? If I made any sudden move, he would pull the trigger. I knew it. I could see the mad determination in his eyes. All sense of reason and rationality had gone from that gaze. I felt utterly helpless.

'It's because of you,' he continued, 'it's because of you that I've lost everything. Because of your interference … You've messed up my life, Johnny. And so now I'm going to mess up yours.'

And he did.

In one single moment he did.

It is a moment that lives with me and haunts me and propels me into tears in the silent unguarded moments of the day and night. A moment that I hope is a horrible dream from which I will wake. But the nightmare was real. The nightmare *is* real.

One single moment.

Vic Bernstein held the pistol close to Max's head, pressing the barrel against her skin. I could see the pressure on her smooth white temple. He gave a little sigh and then pulled the trigger.

The gunshot exploded in my brain like a thunderclap, but it was the searing silence that followed which was the most shocking and painful. It froze my blood and my limbs. I was held rigid by the horror of what I witnessed. All I could do was just stand there, like some wretched statue staring at Max, her wide lifeless eyes, her

THE DARKNESS OF DEATH

open mouth and the terrible crimson rupture at the side of her head. Beads of blood shivered down her face.

Her dead face.

Bernstein also seemed shocked at the sight of his own gruesome handiwork. He gazed at Max, it seemed to me in retrospect, with a mixture of amazement and fascination. Childlike, he ran his finger across her brow, smearing the blood along her forehead. Before grief and disbelief had time to completely overwhelm my senses, the fierce flame of red-hot anger erupted within my breast. It roared in my ears, it electrified my body, it galvanized me into action. With a demented roar of fury, I launched myself at the beast, my hands instinctively reaching for his throat. I threw all my weight at him, snarling, gnashing my teeth. My attack caught him completely by surprise and he toppled back, hitting his head on the hearth. He gave a muffled croak of pain. I shifted my stance and dropping down I straddled his body. Taking his head in my hands and pressing my palms hard against his temple, I jerked it forward before slamming it back down on the hearth with a pleasing crack. I heard myself gurgle with glee at the noise. Bernstein's eyes rolled about in their sockets, spittle trickled from his mouth and his tongue began to loll. Desperately he lifted his arm and attempted to point the gun in my direction. I banged his head down again. Harder this time. The gun went off, the bullet, wide of the mark, smashing an ornament on the sideboard.

Bernstein's body sagged, the eyes closed and unconsciousness overwhelmed him. I lifted his head in readiness to smash it down on the tiled hearth for the third time. I was sure that one more blow would smash his skull and kill the bastard. Kill the bastard, destroy the man who had shot my beloved Max. But something stayed my hand. Something held me back. Call it conscience, common sense or some moral rectitude within my soul, I'm still not sure what it was. I only know I realized that I didn't want to kill this bag of scum.

I wanted him to hang.

To hang by the neck until he was dead.

I let his head fall back gently and got to my feet.

Slowly I turned to my love, lying on the sofa.

And then grief came. It rolled in great waves over me crushing me.

How can this be? How can a vibrant beautiful human being become a bloody lifeless shell in just a matter of seconds? In one moment, a life erased. The awful truth that I had lost her, lost her forever, came like a knife stabbing me in the heart. I'd never hear her voice again, or her laugh; I'd never feel her kiss on my cheek, her hand in mine; I'd never feel her arms around me and her fingers stroke the back of my neck. I'd never ...

My legs weakened and I slumped into the chair opposite wanting to cry, wanting to sob my heart out – but failing to do so. I was too empty even for tears. I stared at the dead body of my love and the inert form of her murderer on the rug by the fire, unable to think or move. All I could do was stare.

I don't know how long I sat there. It could have been minutes, it could have been hours. I was in some kind of numb cocoon, protected for a time from reality and the pain that went with it. All I could hear was the steady tick of the clock on the mantelpiece and then I became conscious of another sound: a movement in the other room. And then voices. Like an automaton I rose from my chair and walked slowly and stiffly into the office.

Standing just inside the outer door was Peter and a young girl, with long tumbling hair and a pretty face.

They looked a little sheepish as I entered.

'Hello, Johnny,' said Peter chirpily, overcoming his embarrassment. 'This is Caroline. She's my girlfriend.'

EPILOGUE

The church was decorated for Christmas. In the nave there was a nativity scene created by children from a local school with small dolls representing Mary and Joseph and the baby Jesus. Papier mâché shepherds and farmyard animals, garishly coloured, were in attendance at the cardboard stable, along with the Three Wise Men. A spindly fir tree stood at the side of the altar adorned with tinsel, paper chains and a series of tired coloured baubles while on the ledges of the windows there were sprigs of holly and ivy. It was strange dressing for a funeral, but it was somehow comforting and I knew that Max would have smiled at the children's work and been touched by it.

It was a small turn out. She had no family living and so the mourners consisted of people we knew together. There was Benny, the sisters Martha and Edith, Peter and David Llewellyn. The production company in Nottingham had sent a very nice wreath and the producer had written me a touching and sympathetic letter about my lovely Max. I cried for the first time while reading that letter. There is something very moving about the kindness of a stranger.

We sang a few hymns. The vicar made a suitable address, one I suspect he had used many times before. And I said a few words. Just a few words. What good are words? They don't have the power to bring people back. Do they?

A couple of days before Max's funeral, I had accompanied Inspector Eustace and his sergeant, a fellow called Jones, to an

219

address in Bermondsey. To the home of June Forsyth. I had obtained the name and address from the photographic studio in Oxford Street. It was June Forsyth's photograph that I had taken from Brian Garner's house the day he had been murdered. The photograph revealed that she had a remarkable resemblance to his wife Beryl. It seemed clear to me that she was Garner's new girl-friend and had been receiving the same treatment as his wife. He was a bully and once a bully ... I suspected that she may well have been the savage killer of Garner. You can push a woman so far. I did not verbalize this theory to Eustace. I just said I thought that this woman could help with the police enquiries into Garner's death. I avoided explaining how I had come into possession of the photograph in the first place and he was a wily enough old profes-sional not to question me on this point.

The house was in a row of tidy terrace houses in a warren of streets each possessing a similar row of tidy terrace houses. We knocked loudly on the front door but received no reply. Eustace was about to begin another round of staccato thumping when the door of the house next door opened and an elderly lady in curling pins shot her head out into the street. She had nosy parker written all over her peaky mush.

'I think she must be away,' she said. 'It's June Forsyth you want, isn't it?'

We told her it was.

She nodded sagely. 'Well, I haven't seen her in well over a week, so I reckon she must be away.'

'Thank you, madam,' replied Eustace.

The woman waited a while to see what we would do next.

Eustace raised his hat. 'Good day,' he snapped, indicating this was then end of the exchange. He stared at her until reluctantly she retreated inside, slamming her door shut.

'I bet she knows what size shoes this Forsyth woman takes,' he said wryly.

'I think we go in, don't you?' I said.

Eustace nodded.

Some shoulder work by Eustace and Sergeant Jones soon got the door open. I saw the net curtains twitch at the window of the neighbour's house as our informant peeked around the edge. I gave her a wave and she vanished at speed.

There was some mail piled up behind the door and a strange unpleasant smell in the place.

We found June Forsyth in the living room in an armchair. She had been dead for quite some time. The flies had already gathered to carry out their gruesome business. The smell of death was strong in the air. There was a half empty gin bottle on a table by her side along with several empty bottles of pills.

'She's topped herself,' observed Jones.

'Very astute of you, Sergeant,' said Eustace, with a roll of the eyes.

I picked a sheet of paper from the floor by her chair.

'What you got there?' asked the Inspector.

'What you'd expect. It's the note.' I scanned it quickly. It was tragic and trite. She couldn't stand the beatings 'no more'. 'He treats me like an animal'. He didn't love her anyway. He was still obsessed with his wife. She couldn't get away from the bastard so she killed him and she was glad. Now she could escape.

I passed the note to Eustace. He grimaced as he read it.

I looked at the poor woman. The ravages of death were already taking their toll on her. The body stank. The face was puffy and blue and the features were ghoulish.

Here was an encounter with yet another corpse.

'Well,' said Eustace, clapping his handkerchief to his mouth, 'that tidies this little matter up. Let's get out of here before I deposit my breakfast on the carpet. I'll get the path boys to clear this mess away.'

We walked out back into the fresh air, although somehow to me it wasn't that fresh any more.

Victor Robert Bernstein was executed at nine o'clock in the morning of the first of February 1944. I did not attend the hanging. I was at home in the room where he had killed Max, sitting with a cup of coffee and cigarette hunched over the fire while I watched the hands of the clock on the mantelpiece creep their way inexorably to nine o'clock. As they reached the appointed hour, my body shuddered as though a ghost had passed through me. I imagined the sound of the mechanism, the snap of the trap door and the creak of the rope as it stretched and twisted with the weight of his body.

It was over.

Did I feel better?

No.

It wasn't over. How could it be over? How could it be better? Max was still lost to me. In the end Vic Bernstein's execution meant nothing. I was still adrift. Still mourning a lost dream. My life would be forever blighted by the darkness of her death.